HELL

Jarret Manning was attractive, successful, experienced—and from the moment they met Helen Chase felt mingled antagonism and fear every time she was in his company—which was far too often for her peace of mind. But after all, she was happily engaged to Charles, wasn't she, and soon to be married. Why should this virtual stranger disturb her so?

*Books you will enjoy*
*by ANNE MATHER*

### APOLLO'S SEED

After five years apart, Martha had been virtually forced to return to Greece to live with her husband Dion. She soon realised that her feelings for Dion were as strong as ever—but what about him? Wasn't it only too clear that his only reason for wanting her was to get their child back? And could she be sure he wouldn't take her daughter away from her altogether?

### LURE OF EAGLES

Not surprisingly, Domine and her brother had expected to inherit their family business, so it was disconcerting when instead it was left to their unknown cousin Lisel in Peru. However, Domine found herself agreeing to the masterful Luis Aguilar's suggestion that she should go with him to South America to meet Lisel. But then she realised that her cousin represented an even greater threat to her peace of mind...

### THE JUDAS TRAP

When her 'friend' Diane Tregower tricked her into going to Cornwall and confronting Michael Tregower, Sara Fortune could have found herself in a very unpleasant and dangerous situation indeed—but instead she and Michael fell in love and all could have ended happily. Had it not been for the secret that Sara dared not tell him...

### MELTING FIRE

Olivia owed her stepbrother Richard a lot—no doubt about that. But did that give him the right to declare that he owned her, that what she did with her life was for him to decide? Olivia had to admit that she was becoming more and more reluctant to tear herself away from him—yet if she didn't, how was she ever going to have any life or experience of her own?

# HELL OR HIGH WATER

BY
ANNE MATHER

MILLS & BOON LIMITED
17–19 FOLEY STREET
LONDON W1A 1DR

*All the characters in this book have no existence outside the imagination of the Author, and have no relation whatsoever to anyone bearing the same name or names. They are not even distantly inspired by any individual known or unknown to the Author, and all the incidents are pure invention.*

*The text of this publication or any part thereof may not be reproduced or transmitted in any form or by any means, electronic or mechanical, including photocopying, recording, storage in an information retrieval system, or otherwise, without the written permission of the publisher.*

*This book is sold subject to the condition that it shall not, by way of trade or otherwise, be lent, resold, hired out or otherwise circulated without the prior consent of the publisher in any form of binding or cover other than that in which it is published and without a similar condition including this condition being imposed on the subsequent purchaser.*

*First published 1979*
*Australian copyright 1980*
*Philippine copyright 1980*
*This edition 1980*

© Anne Mather 1979

ISBN 0 263 73173 1

*Set in Linotype Plantin 10 pt.*

*Made and printed in Great Britain by*
*Richard Clay (The Chaucer Press), Ltd., Bungay, Suffolk*

# CHAPTER ONE

THE apartment was silent except for the clatter of the typewriter, when the doorbell rang. It was a frustrating intrusion into the mood of the narrative, and the man seated at the machine stopped typing abruptly to rest his balled fists on the desk. Then, stilling the impulse to tear up the ruined page of the manuscript, he rose to go and answer it, a second peal grating in his ears as he crossed the floor. He was not in the mood for casual callers, and friends of long acquaintance knew better than to interrupt him at a time like this, but his suspicions as to who it might be were realised when he opened the door.

'Jarret!' The reluctantly-ageing blonde who crossed the threshold without waiting for his invitation caressed his cheek with an elegantly-gloved hand. 'Mmmm, you haven't shaved this morning, darling. But I love you anyway, rough or smooth!'

The sensuous tones of the woman's voice had little effect on their recipient. With the grimness of impatience tightening his lean features, he leaned against the door frame, making no move to close it, and his feminine visitor allowed a slightly nervous trill of laughter to escape from her lips.

'Darling, don't stand there looking at me as if I wasn't welcome ...'

'You're not!' he retorted.

'... particularly when I came here with some rather exciting news for you.'

There was a controlled expellation of breath, and then he said flatly: 'I'm not ready for this, Margot. As you can see, I'm working ...' he waved a careless hand towards the desk, 'and I'd like you to go as soon as possible.'

'Oh, we are a sourpuss today, aren't we?' she teased, showing no immediate inclination to obey him. Instead, she descended the two steps that separated the body of the apartment from the entrance on perilously high heels, and did a deliberate pirouette beside his desk. 'What's the matter?' she asked, puckering her lips, gloved fingers flicking the pages beside the typewriter without interest. 'Did we have a heavy night last night, or did we just get out of bed the wrong side this morning?'

'Get out of here, Margot!'

The demand was made almost mildly, a narrow-eyed mask guarding his expression, and she chose not to respond to it.

'Don't be so grumpy, Jarret,' she pouted. 'Aren't you even going to offer me a drink? The traffic in Knightsbridge was terrible, and I'm simply dying for something long and cool and satisfying. Just like you, darling.'

'I warn you, Margot . . .'

The quietly threatening tone at last got through to her, and with a gesture of offence she tilted her chin. With the lines of her throat ironed out by the attitude, it was one of her best poses, and she knew it, but Jarret felt the tightness of repulsion in his stomach as he surveyed the deliberate come-on.

'Can't you at least have the courtesy to close the door for a moment?' she demanded at last, when her ploy produced no reaction. Her mouth compressed. 'You really are the most selfish bastard, Jarret. I don't know why I care about you.'

'Don't you?' Jarret's expression was resigned, but after a slight hesitation he closed the door and came down the shallow stairs to where she was standing. 'So?' he said, brows arching enquiringly. 'To what do I owe the pleasure?'

Lady Margot Urquart's lips twitched frustratedly. She did not like the forbearing tone of his voice, nor trust the superficiality of his words. In spite of their different social backgrounds, he was still able to make her feel like a gauche ingénue, and despite the fact that she was more than ten years his senior, the cool blue-eyed stare reduced her to an open-mouthed sycophant.

'You're a brute, Jarret!' she protested, running a deliberate hand into the unbuttoned neckline of her silk shirt. 'Here I am, making a special journey just to do you a good turn, and you treat me like a—like a leper! I know you're working, I know you want to get on with your book.

But that's why I'm here—to help you.'

'I didn't know you'd taken a course in typewriting, Margot,' Jarret commented dryly, brushing past her to tug the offending sheet out of the machine and roll it into a ball between his palms. 'But I'm sorry to disappoint you, I prefer to work alone, and with fewer interruptions the better.'

'Oh, Jarret!' Margot's lips pursed. 'You know I didn't mean that. And why are you destroying that page? Surely I didn't spoil your train of thought.'

'I've screwed it up,' remarked Jarret unpleasantly, and her chin tilted once more. 'And that's not the only thing that's screwed up around here. I'd be grateful if you'd get to the point and go!'

Margot sniffed. 'If you're going to be like that ...'

'What? Like what?' Jarret rested his denim-clad hips against the desk and folded his arms across his chest. 'How am I expected to behave? I didn't invite you here, Margot.'

'It's that Sinclair girl, isn't it?' she exclaimed suddenly, switching tactics completely. 'Jo told me you'd been seeing her. That's why you're being so utterly beastly—because of her!'

Jarret's expression did not change. 'Why don't you tell me why you've come here, Margot?' he suggested, ignoring her outburst, and with a sound of deep frustration she flounced across the room.

'Well, if you won't offer me a drink, I'll help myself,' she declared, glancing at him over her shoulder as she halted by a tray of bottles and glasses. 'Can I get you one, the hair of the dog, and all that, or will that disturb your creative impulses too?'

'I don't want a drink, Margot,' he refused, levering his lean body into the leather chair beside the desk and draping one leg casually over the arm. 'I don't need that kind of stimulation this early in the morning.'

'It is half past eleven, darling,' Margot defended herself sulkily, pouring a generous measure of Scotch into a tumbler chinking with ice and adding the merest touch of American dry. 'Hmm, that's better,' she affirmed, licking the traces of alcohol from her full lips and viewing him mistily. 'The first drink of the day is always the best.'

'And that's the first?' mocked Jarret sceptically, and then regretting the impulse to arouse further recriminations, added: 'Are you going to tell me why you've come here now, Margot? Or must I assume that was just an excuse to pacify the beast in me?'

'No, it wasn't.' Margot was indignant, flicking her pleated skirt with a careless finger, drawing attention to the slenderness of leg and ankle. 'I really do have some news for you, Jarret, but I'm half inclined not to tell you, you've been so uncivil to me.'

Jarret's mouth thinned. 'Then don't.'

Margot's face crumpled. 'Oh, darling, don't be like that, just because I choose to tease you. You know I could never deny you anything. I don't know why you persist in treating me like a fool!'

Jarret swung his leg to the floor. 'Look, Margot, I don't have the time to sit here and discuss my shortcomings. Okay, I'm a brute and a bastard and I treat you abominably. So what's the attraction? I've never given you any reason to think you could run my life for me.'

Margot sighed, swinging round on her heels and pacing restlessly to the windows. From this height, the whole panorama of London and its greater outskirts were spread out below in sprawling detail, a grey plume of smoke rising from the chimneys of the power station across the river. It was a grey day, dull and uninspiring, when the metropolis looked somewhat less than its best.

Turning, she surveyed the room behind her with more satisfaction. It was austere, of course, recognisably masculine, but attractive in spite of that. She would have liked to have thought that she had been instrumental in his leasing this apartment, but the truth was its owner had been more than willing to acquire a tenant of Jarret's increasing popularity, and consequently he had been given the pick of the block. That had been more than eighteen months ago now, and his reputation still continued its meteor-like rise.

Jarret, watching the emotions that governed her expression, wondered exactly what Jo Stanford had told her. That lady had her own reasons for feeling aggrieved with him, and he felt the increasingly familiar pangs of dissatisfaction in him, that came from a surfeit of social adulation.

Margot finished her drink, and then, surveying the ice cubes still slipping around in the bottom of her glass, said: 'You know how you've been saying that London is too—hectic for you, that this apartment is too accessible to really provide ideal working conditions? Well ...' she paused to give her next words their full impact, 'I've found just the place for you.'

'Really?' Irritation flicked along Jarret's nerves. '*You've* found just the place for me? How considerate of you!'

'No, really, Jarret, I mean it.' Margot was aggravated by his sardonic tone. 'I'm not joking. I know exactly the sort of place you need, and it just so happens that the owner is a friend of mine.'

'You know, I thought perhaps he might be,' remarked Jarret dryly, getting to his feet. 'Well, thanks, Margot, but no thanks. If and when I do decide to leave London I'll do so of my own volition, not to take up some offer you've contrived to arrange——'

'Oh, you're deliberately misunderstanding me!' Margot almost stamped her small foot in impatience, reaching for the bottle of Scotch again and splashing its contents into her glass. '*I* haven't arranged anything, nor do I intend to. Except perhaps—well, you are the one who has to make the decision.'

'Yes, I am, and if you don't mind——'

'Jarret! Jarret, listen to me!' She swallowed a mouthful of Scotch for sustenance, and approached him severely, holding herself erect. 'I know what I'm talking about. It's not just an idea—King's Green is exactly the place for you.'

Jarret faced her wearily, irritation giving way to endurance as he regarded her appealing features. 'When will you learn that I prefer to do my own hunting, house or otherwise,' he told her steadily, and she plucked wretchedly at his sleeve, unwillingly inciting his sympathy.

'Won't you at least consider the suggestion?' she ventured, encouraged to transfer her hand from his sleeve to his cheek, gazing up at him limpidly. 'It really is a gem of a place, and Alice wouldn't be selling at all, if the upkeep of it wasn't so prohibitive.'

Jarret's mouth twisted. 'So what makes you think I need

such an extravagance?'

'Darling...' She reached up to touch his unshaven jaw with her lips. 'You can afford it, you know you can. And King's Green is the ideal spot for you to work.'

Jarret put her firmly away from him, and ignoring the wounded look she gave him, walked half resignedly across the room. 'Where is this place?' he demanded, massaging the back of his neck with impatient fingers. 'Is King's Green a village or a house or what?'

'It's a house,' Margot offered, at once forgoing her pride in her eagerness. 'Queen Anne, I think. Oh——' this as he started to protest, '—it's in excellent condition. A little damp in places perhaps, but that can easily be rectified, and it's in an absolute dream of a setting.'

'Where?' Jarret distrusted Margot's enthusiasm, but her next words allayed his suspicions.

'A place called Thrushfold in Wiltshire. On the Wiltshire-Dorset borders, actually. Near enough to London to drive up in a matter of hours, but not near enough to attract casual visitors.'

Jarret acknowledged this with a faint inclination of his head. 'Wiltshire,' he murmured reflectively. 'I see.'

'You'd *love* it!' Margot pressed her advantage. 'It's got everything—half a dozen bedrooms, two or three reception rooms, and a library! You could work in there. It overlooks the paddock. And the grounds themselves are just big enough to ensure privacy.'

'How big?' enquired Jarret dryly, and Margot moved her shoulders in a little offhand gesture.

'I don't know exactly,' she prevaricated. 'Does it matter? Forty—maybe fifty, I'm not sure. What's really important——'

'Forty or fifty what?' Jarret interrupted her. '*Acres?* Margot, you must be out of your tiny mind! I'm no landowner!'

Margot pouted. 'That doesn't mean you couldn't be, darling. I think you'd make a marvellous squire! And King's Green hasn't had one of them for—oh, ten years or so.'

'Let me get this straight.' Jarret pushed his thumbs into the low belt of his denims. 'You're suggesting I buy this—this King's Green from some—friend of yours?'

'A school friend, yes. Alice Chase.'

'And she's a widow?'

'Hardly your taste, darling,' retorted Margot spitefully. 'She's twelve stone if she's an ounce!'

Jarret ignored her. 'That's the proposition you came to put to me,' he continued. 'That I buy—King's Green.'

'Why not?' Margot was forced to put her maliciousness aside. 'It is what you've been looking for, isn't it? A place in the country. Somewhere you can work—in peace.'

'Mmmm.' Jarret sounded as though he was extremely doubtful.

'Well, at least come and see it,' she urged him. 'There's no harm in that, is there? I mean, you're not committed to anything, are you? And I'm sure you'll be—enchanted, when you see it.'

'Enchanted?' Jarret stifled his rather wry humour. 'Oh, Margot, you don't know me very well, do you?'

'Well enough,' she murmured huskily. 'But not as well as I'd like.'

Jarret sighed. 'Look, I guess you thought you were doing me a favour, coming here and letting me know about this place, but—well, I can't make a decision just like that. I—need to think about it.'

'Of course.' She sounded as if she had never doubted it. 'But you will make up your mind soon, won't you, darling? I mean, I told Alice I'd let her know within a couple of days.'

'A couple of days,' echoed Jarret irritably. 'Hell, I can't make that kind of decision in forty-eight hours!'

Margot hesitated. 'Come and see it,' she suggested again. 'It's only an hour or two's drive. We could go tonight, and come back tomorrow.'

'*We?*'

'Of course, darling. I promised Alice I'd introduce her to you. She's one of your fans, you know. She has all the books you've written.'

'All three of them?' mocked Jarret cuttingly.

Margot flushed. 'Will you come?'

'I can't,' he stated flatly. 'Not today. It's out of the question.'

'Tomorrow, then,' she persisted, only the tightening of her lips indicating her reaction to the inevitable reasons for his refusal. 'Jarret, you owe it to yourself——'

Jarret cut her off without preamble. 'Tomorrow morning,' he specified abruptly. 'It's Friday. We can drive down before lunch and be back in town in time for dinner.'

'Are you making me an offer?' Margot probed, but Jarret's expression was not encouraging.

'I have work to do,' he reminded her, and she made a sulky gesture of acceptance.

'What time tomorrow?'

'Nine o'clock.'

'So early!' Margot was horrified.

'If I can make it, surely you can,' he averred dryly. 'Is it a date?'

'How could I refuse such a gallant proposition?' she retorted, showing a little of the humour which had attracted his attention in the first place. 'All right, darling, nine o'clock it is. Will you pick me up?'

'Promptly,' he affirmed, with a bow of his head, and forced to the conclusion that for the present this was all she could expect of him, she put down her glass and moved towards the door.

'Until tomorrow,' she murmured, lingering long enough for him to respond if he chose, but Jarret remained where he was.

'Tomorrow,' he agreed shortly, and the door closed rather heavily behind her.

With her departure, Jarret breathed a sigh of relief. Then, raking back his hair with aggressive fingers, he went to take one of the narrow cigars he favoured from the carved box on the bookshelves. He was already regretting the impulse he had had to give in to her, and impatience carved its identity across his dark features. Why the hell had he agreed to such a wasted outing? It was only her way of getting him to spend the day with her. Why on earth hadn't he told her to go to hell, and shut her out of his life once and for all? He shook his head. A country estate was not for him, and she knew it. A house, maybe. That had possibilities. But forty or fifty acres of arable land ...

He slumped down into the chair beside the typewriter and propped his head on his hand. What had he done that morning? Two, maybe three pages! He wasn't even satisfied with what he had written. It was vacuously amateurish, he thought, with savage criticism, ignoring completely the incisive prose which had made a best-seller of his first novel and subsequent successes of his second and third. Nevertheless, the meaningless words and phrases were not Jarret Manning at his best, and the horrible suspicion that he had nothing more to say stirred in his stomach like a corpse in its tomb.

It was useless to pretend he was working at the moment. He was finding it increasingly difficult to concentrate, and where once these minor distractions would not have troubled him, lately he was inventing reasons for not sitting down at the typewriter.

Would a change of surroundings help? He suspected it might. Margot had been right when she had said he was too accessible in London, too open to distraction, and maybe for his own good he needed a change. Too many parties, too many drinks, too many late nights ... The indictment was endless, and he had no one to blame but himself. He had let the fruits of his success dictate his style of living, and for a writer that was professional suicide. Maybe if he got away from town for a while, he would have time to think. In the clean, unpolluted air of the countryside his brain would reassert itself, and recover from the crippling effects of too little stimulation and too much apathy.

Realising he was not about to write anything of significance today, he determinedly put his self-doubts aside and went to wash and shave. Then, adding a navy corded jacket to his denims, he left the apartment. Downstairs in the underground car park, one of the fruits of his success he did appreciate awaited him, and he lowered his lean body behind the wheel, and started the powerful twelve-cylinder engine. It responded without effort, and he reversed out of the space and then accelerated smoothly up the ramp to the street.

It took him less than half an hour to reach his destination, a narrow terraced house in a row of the same, situated in a less salubrious area across the river. The sun was endeavouring to break through the clouds as he parked his car at the kerb, and levered himself out on to the pavement, and he paused to grin at an elderly matron peering through the lace curtains of the house opposite before walking up the path to the house.

It could do with painting, he reflected, letting himself in with his key and slamming the door behind him. 'It's only me, Dad!' he called by means of a warning, and then strolled down the narrow passage to the back of the house.

The old man was not in the living room or the kitchen, but the open back door indicated his whereabouts. He was in the long narrow garden, pottering about in the greenhouse, and Jarret pulled a wry face as he went to show himself.

'What are you doing here?' the old man demanded peevishly, not entirely able to hide his pleasure nevertheless. 'I don't normally see you Thursdays, do I? You got some trouble or something, or is this just a social call?'

Jarret grimaced. 'That's some line in welcomes you've got there, Paddy,' he remarked without rancour leading the way back to the house. 'I make a special effort to come and see you, and what do you say?'

'Don't call me Paddy,' the old man grunted, coming into the kitchen after him and reaching for the kettle. 'Do you want a cup of tea or are you needing something stronger? I've a bottle of stout in the cupboard, if it's not too strong for your taste.'

Jarret grinned. 'The stout would be fine,' he agreed, propping himself against the table. 'And how have you been since the last time I saw you?'

The old man busied himself getting out two bottles of stout and levering off the caps. Jarret saw, with some concern, that his hands were getting shaky, and there wasn't the strength in them there had been a year ago. That stroke he had had, had taken more out of him than he cared to admit, and Jarret wished he would let him do something for him.

But Patrick Horton was intensely independent, he always had been, and since Jarret's mother died he had resisted all efforts to share in his stepson's success. It was ironic really, Jarret thought now, that his mother should have died only weeks after his first book was published, and the subsequent success it had enjoyed had never made her life any easier.

Now he accepted the stout the old man handed him, declined the offer of a glass, and raised the bottle to his lips. It was rich and black, and only slightly warm despite the heat of the day, and he drank it thirstily, acknowledging the old man's pleasure in his enjoyment as he wiped the back of his hand across his mouth.

'So?' he urged. 'You're keeping well? No more of those dizzy turns you were having a month or two ago?'

'Psshaw, dizzy turns!' His stepfather was impatient. 'I'm getting too old, that's all that's wrong with me. And you didn't come here to discuss my aches and pains.'

Jarret sighed. 'I wish you'd let me find you somewhere —pleasanter, somewhere smaller. Somewhere you could look after your garden, and not have to bother about taking care of a house. A bungalow, for——'

'I was born in this house, Jarret, and I intend to die here,' his stepfather interrupted him firmly. 'It may seem scruffy and old-fashioned to you, after that place of yours up West, but it suits me down to the ground.'

Jarret shook his head. 'You're an obstinate old fool, do you know that?'

'Why? 'Cause I won't let you squander your money on me. Humph!' He chuckled. 'You save it for those skinny bits of skirt I see you going about with. Don't know what you see in them, I don't honestly.'

'Don't you?' queried Jarret lazily, and his stepfather chuckled once again.

'Well, yes, I guess I do at that,' he agreed wickedly. 'But that's not to say I approve. You'll be getting yourself into trouble one of these days, and then all that money of yours won't be enough to get you out of it.'

'Mmm.' Jarret took another mouthful of his stout as if considering the point, and the old man continued:

'Like that Honourable what's-her-name you used to see sometimes. Margaret something or other.'

'Lady *Margot* Urquart,' amended Jarret dryly. 'As a matter of fact, I saw her this morning.'

'Did you?' His stepfather made a sound of contempt. 'So

she's still hanging around, is she? What the hell do you want with an old bird like her?'

'I have to remind you that it was Margot who persuaded James Stanford to publish *Devil's Kitchen*!' he retorted, shrugging. 'Besides, she's not that old, Paddy. I doubt if she's even forty.'

'And you're thirty-one,' his stepfather pointed out shortly.

Jarret sighed. 'Well, as a matter of fact, Margot did have a reason for visiting me . . .'

'I can believe it!'

'No, really.' Jarret had finished the contents of the bottle and now he took mock-aim at the old man. 'She's suggested I buy some place out in the country.'

Patrick Horton absorbed this in silence for several minutes while he examined the contents of his small pantry. Then, realising his stepson expected an opinion from him, he turned and glanced at him over his shoulder.

'What kind of a place?'

Jarret shrugged. 'A house—and some land. It belongs to an old school friend of hers.'

'And who's going to live there? You and Lady Margot?'

'Of course not.' Jarret was impatient now. 'Me! Just me!' He pushed back his hair with a weary hand. 'I'm getting stale, Dad. The words just aren't coming any more. I need to get away—I'm stifling in London.'

'What you mean is you're bored, don't you?' his stepfather remarked shrewdly. 'Too many late nights and too much alcohol. And too many women!'

'All right!' Jarret heaved a deep breath. 'What you say is true. I'm too easily diverted. Maybe out at Thrushfold I'll be able to breathe again.'

'Thrushfold?' His stepfather frowned. 'Where's that?'

'I'm not precisely sure. Somewhere in Wiltshire. The house is called King's Green. A genuine old property!' he added, with mock transatlantic reverence.

'So you've made up your mind then?'

'No.' Jarret put the bottle on the table behind him and shoved his hands into his jacket pockets. 'No, I haven't decided yet. I haven't even seen it. That's one of the reasons why I wanted to see you—to ask you what you thought. To find out whether you think it's a good idea or not.'

'Hmm.' The old man grimaced. 'You had anything to eat?'

'Some toast, at breakfast time,' replied Jarret patiently. 'What's that got to do with anything?'

'I think I'll open a tin of soup,' declared Mr Horton consideringly. 'Which would you prefer? Chicken or oxtail? It's all the same to me.'

'I'll take you out for lunch, Dad,' protested Jarret, shaking his head, but his stepfather declined.

'If my soup's not good enough for you——' he began, and with a gesture of acquiescence Jarret shed his coat and reached goodhumouredly for the can-opener.

Later, seated at the kitchen table ladling spoonfuls of oxtail soup into his mouth, Jarret returned to the object of his visit. 'About this house, Dad,' he began uncertainly, 'what do you think? Ought I to go out of town for a while?'

Mr Horton considered for a few moments, and then he nodded his balding head. 'I'd say it was the best idea you'd had in a long time,' he asserted, frowning. 'But not if you take anyone along with you.'

'If you mean Margot, I've no intention of doing so.'

'I didn't mean her, actually. I meant that other one I read you'd been seeing. Some model girl, isn't she? Comes from America. They gave you quite a write-up in the *Gazette*.'

'Vivien Sinclair,' remarked Jarret flatly. 'Don't tell me you didn't notice her name. Yes, she's a model. And I've been seeing her for over six months. But there's no likelihood of her joining me in my country retreat. She likes the bright lights far too much for that.'

He didn't sound heartbroken, and his stepfather gave him a disapproving stare. 'You don't care, do you?' he exclaimed, permitting a brief word of criticism. 'Jarret, when are you going to give up this artificial existence and settle down? You know your mother would have wanted you to.'

'Oh, Dad!' The younger man lay back in his chair and surveyed his stepfather humorously. 'Don't give me that old line. What Ma would or would not have wanted is immaterial, isn't it? I mean—well, she's dead, and my idiosyncrasies aren't going to hurt her, are they?'

Patrick Horton sighed. 'You'll find your own way to the devil, I suppose,' he muttered.

Jarret shook his head and sat up again. 'So how about you coming with me instead? Then you could keep an eye on me, ensure that I ate the right food and got to bed at a reasonable time, and didn't sleep with any strange women!'

His stepfather's lips twitched in spite of himself. 'Oh, no!' he denied at once. 'I'm not your keeper, nor would I want to be. And as for removing myself to the wilds of Wiltshire at my time of life—no, thanks!' He paused. 'But you go, Jarret, son, you go. I'm all in favour of that. I'm in favour of anything that will make you happy.'

'Thanks, Dad.' Jarret leant across to squeeze the old man's arm, and they finished the meal in a companionable silence.

It was after four when Jarret arrived back at his apartment. Despite the unsatisfactory beginning to his day he felt reasonably content, and half inclined to anticipate the journey to Thrushfold with some enthusiasm. If the house was any good, the sale might be completed before the end of May, with the long lazy days of summer to look forward to. In previous years he had gone to Bermuda and to Cannes, and last year he had spent some time on the west coast of the United States, but the prospect of spending the summer in a home of his own was appealing, and he wondered how he would react to so much isolation.

Vivien Sinclair's reactions were characteristically opposed to his leaving London.

'Jarret, you can't!' she wailed, when he casually mentioned the idea at dinner that evening. 'Honey, you'd die in a place like that! Come to Barbados with me next week. You know I've got that modelling assignment, and you could work at the hotel while I was at the studios.'

Jarret grimaced. 'No, thanks,' he declined gently. 'I need to work, not to play baby-sitter while you take off your clothes for someone else.'

'But Jarret,' she protested, clasping one of his hands in both of hers, regardless of the interested eyes of their waiter, 'when will I see you, stuck out in this Godforsaken hole——'

'Hardly a hole,' he corrected her dryly, removing her fingers. 'Now, do you want yoghurt or ice-cream to finish, or shall I just order coffee for two?'

'I couldn't eat another thing,' she protested sulkily, pulling a handkerchief out of her handbag and sniffing miserably into it. 'You can get me a brandy with my coffee instead. I need something to sustain me after what you've just told me.'

Jarret shrugged and summoned the waiter, and ordered the drinks with the minimum amount of fuss. Then he relaxed in his seat while Vivien recovered her humour, apparently immune to her tearful performance.

'And when do you leave?' she ventured at last, when it occurred to her that she was doing herself no favours by causing a scene, and Jarret looked up from lighting a cheroot through the narrowed fringe of his lashes.

'It's not even definite yet, Vivien,' he told her flatly, putting his lighter away. 'I'm going down to see the place tomorrow. I'll know more about it after that.'

'But how did you learn of its whereabouts anyway?' she exclaimed, putting her handkerchief away. 'Thrushfold! In Wilshire? I've never even heard of it.'

'The county is *Wilt*shire,' Jarret amended, realising he might as well tell her the whole tale. 'Margot Urquart told me about it. It belongs to an old school friend of hers.'

Vivien evidently suppressed the retort that sprang to her lips, and asked about the house with as much detachment as she could muster. But later that night, when they were alone in her apartment, she could not deny the need for reassurance that only he could give.

'You—er—you wouldn't consider marrying Margot Urquart, would you, Jarret?' she probed, caressing his ear with mildly anxious lips, and Jarret's laughter came from deep down in his throat.

'No,' he agreed, turning his mouth into her nape, and she breathed a sigh of relief as he kissed her.

## CHAPTER TWO

'WHEN did you decide all this?' Helen Chase rounded on her mother in uncharacteristic aggravation. 'Couldn't you at least have discussed it with me first?'

Mrs Chase expelled her breath on a long sigh, and then replied carefully: 'We have discussed it, Helen. You know that as well as I do. And there is no other solution.'

'How can you say that?' Helen made a gesture of frustration. 'After Charles and I are married——'

'Yes? After you and Charles are married—what?' Mrs Chase viewed her daughter with fond affection. 'My dear, Charles won't want to live at King's Green, and as far as keeping two homes going is concerned ...' she shook her head, 'It's simply not feasable.'

'But there must be something we can do.' Helen paced restlessly across the room, the silky dark hair that resisted all efforts to curl curving under her chin as she moved. She wore it in a simple but effective style, parting it centrally, and allowing the two sides to hang loosely to her shoulders; but now she pushed it carelessly behind her ears, too disturbed by what she had learned to pay any attention to her appearance.

'There's not,' her mother assured her now, resuming the sewing which Helen had interrupted. 'Since your father died things have gone from bad to worse, and it's a relief to me to know that you at least aren't going to suffer by it.'

'Am I not?' Helen sounded less than convinced, and her mother looked up once again.

'Darling, you're getting married in August. And naturally I'm hoping we can stay here until then. Your father would have wanted it that way. But after the wedding ...'

Helen hunched her slim shoulders. 'I still think you're acting hastily. I mean, anything can happen between now and August.'

'Nothing that's likely to make the slightest improvement in our financial position,' replied her mother dryly, used to her daughter's attempts to dissuade her from even considering the idea of selling. 'And quite frankly, my dear, I'm tired of living this hand-to-mouth existence.'

'But why involve Margot Urquart?' demanded Helen, clinging to straws now. 'I mean—oh, you know what she's like! And this man, whoever he is, is just the latest in a long line of hangers-on——'

'Jarret Manning is hardly a hanger-on, darling,' Mrs Chase remarked evenly, returning to her sewing.

'Jarret Manning!' Helen pursed her lips. 'Imagine selling King's Green to someone like him!'

Her mother showed a little impatience now. 'I enjoy Jarret Manning's work, Helen, and I see no reason for you to criticise the man when you don't even know him.'

'Nor do you,' retorted Helen shortly, and her mother subjected her to a pitying appraisal.

'It seems to me, Helen, that whoever eventually buys King's Green, you won't be satisfied. At least, with Margot's intervention, we may be spared the humiliation of having to advertise the house and show crowds of curious sightseers over the grounds.'

'What makes you think Jarret Manning isn't just a curious sightseer?' demanded her daughter crossly, and Mrs Chase uttered a sound of irritation. 'Well,' continued Helen defensively, 'he was born in Stepney or Tooting or some such place, wasn't he? Hardly the background of someone who might find the peace and beauty of King's Green to their taste!'

'You little snob!' Mrs Chase stared at her daughter as if she had never seen her before. 'Is that what you really think? Is that how you feel? Have I brought you up all these years to regard other people with such contempt?'

'No, I——' Helen had the grace to flush now, and the colour deepened becomingly beneath the honey-gold skin of her cheeks. 'That is—oh, Mummy! Is there nothing else we can do?'

'What do you suggest?' Her mother was not inclined to be generous. 'Turn the Flynns out of the home farm? They could never afford to buy it, but I suppose someone else might.'

'No! No!' Helen pushed her fingers through her hair

in a revealing gesture. 'But—Margot Urquart's latest boy-friend!'

Mrs Chase's features softened slightly. 'Look, I know you don't like Margot,' she said quietly, 'but remember, Margot is not involved in the sale.'

Helen shrugged. 'Perhaps she is. Perhaps she's serious this time. She's always coveted King's Green. Maybe she intends to share it with him.'

Mrs Chase shook her head. 'My dear Helen, if Margot had wanted to buy King's Green, why didn't she just say so?'

Helen shrugged. 'I doubt if she could stand being so far from London,' she admitted, and then sighed. 'Anyway, I wish you'd told me sooner. I'd have arranged to be out or something.'

'That's precisely why I didn't tell you,' retorted her mother firmly. 'I had no intention of having to give Margot excuses as to why my daughter had absented herself. And besides, I want your opinion.'

'Really?' Helen sounded sceptical. 'And if I don't approve?'

Mrs Chase put her sewing aside and rose to her feet. 'I must go and speak to Mrs Hetherington. Margot said they expected to arrive about midday. If we have lunch at one-thirty, that should give us time to show Mr Manning the house first.'

After her mother had left the room Helen walked disconsolately over to the windows, staring out with fierce possessiveness over the lawns and flower-beds that bordered the house. This was her home, it was the place where she had been born, and she knew every inch of it with the familiarity of long use. She could see the daffodils, growing in wild profusion between the old larch and fir trees, and she knew, without even looking, that the wooded slopes beyond would be starred with crocuses and pansies, the paths thick with a carpet of pine needles. How could she contemplate handing King's Green over to some stranger without feeling this pang of helplessness and resentment? Particularly when the person involved was one of Margot Urquart's young men!

Of course, she really knew nothing about Jarret Manning, except what she had read on the flyleaf of one of the books her mother collected so avidly. The kind of political thriller he wrote, where the reader was never absolutely sure that what he was reading was fiction or fact, had never appealed to her. She preferred history, in all its various forms, but her mother found them fascinating and was obviously looking forward to meeting the author. There had been a picture of him, too, and it was this as much as anything which aroused Helen's contempt now. He was young—twenty-five or thirty at most, while Margot had been in her mother's year at school, and Mrs Chase was forty-two.

Of course, Margot had been married, three times actually, but those associations had not lasted. She was much too susceptible to masculine flattery and attention, and her wealth and carefully preserved looks often attracted younger men. In her position as the daughter of the late Lord Conroy, himself a patron of the arts, Margot would be a very useful ally for a young author to have, decided Helen cynically, and she wondered how they had met.

Her mother coming back into the drawing room at that moment interrupted her cogitation, and she tried to apply herself to what Mrs Chase was saying.

'You'll be happy to know that Mrs Hetherington agrees with you,' the older woman declared tersely, helping herself to a cigarette from the box on the mantelshelf. 'Really, I just happened to mention that Lady Margot was bringing a prospective buyer down to see the house, and she immediately jumped to the conclusion that she'll automatically lose her job!'

'Can you blame her?' Helen turned from the window to spread her hands expressively. 'Honestly, Mummy, can you see either of the Hetheringtons working for some— some artist, in whatever category?'

'Mr Manning is a writer, not an artist.'

'Writers, artists, they're all the same,' declared Helen airily, dismissing the fact that she had never actually met a writer before. 'Besides, the Hetheringtons are old, Mummy. And you know what they say about old retainers!'

Mrs Chase smoked her cigarette with more aggression than enjoyment. 'Oh, but I wouldn't like to think the Hetheringtons were in danger of being dismissed. I mean,

Hetherington has looked after the grounds for years! The trees and flowers—they're his domain. I never interfere, you know that. The greenhouses ...' She paced nervously across to the window and looked her daughter squarely in the face. 'I shall have to make it a condition of the sale, that the Hetheringtons retain their jobs.'

'I don't think you can do that, Mummy,' retorted Helen bluntly, sustaining her mother's piercing scrutiny. 'After all, this isn't a small business you're selling, it's a house. An estate. And for all we know, Jarret Manning may have his own staff of servants.'

'You don't really believe that, do you, dear?'

Her mother looked really worried now, and with a sigh Helen moved away from her. There were times when Mrs Chase was just a little too intense, and this was one of them. How could she be expected to know what Jarret Manning's reactions to the Hetherington's might be, and in any case, he hadn't definitely decided to buy the house yet, had he?

'Oughtn't we to wait and see what he thinks first?' she asked now, and to her relief her mother accepted the reprieve.

'Of course, of course.' Mrs Chase's face cleared. 'He may not like the house at all, and Margot did say he was doubtful about the amount of land ...'

'There you are, then.' Helen forced a smile and crossed the room to pour two glasses of sherry from the decanter standing on a table near the door. 'Here, drink this. I think we can both use it.'

'Mmmm, thank you.' But Mrs Chase took the glass her daughter offered rather absently, before focussing doubtfully on Helen's jean-clad figure. 'Aren't you going to change, darling? I do think we should represent a certain standard of—breeding, and those jeans are practically indecent.'

'Now who's being snobbish?' enquired Helen dryly, tasting her sherry. Then she looked down at her cotton shirt and matching pants. 'What's wrong with what I'm wearing? You look elegant enough for both of us.'

Her mother accepted the back-handed compliment with a wry smile, but she did permit herself a moment's self-appraisal before acknowledging that it was true. Her pleated dress of soft blue wool disguised the fuller lines of her figure, and the pearls that circled her throat were a gift from her grandmother, and consequently valuable. She looked at home in her surroundings, she thought, fashionable, but not flashy, refined, but not understated.

Helen, for her part, hid her own anxiety, the long lashes drooping over eyes that might reveal her uncertainty. Perhaps she ought to change, she thought, but she rebelled against doing anything which implied an acceptance of Margot's protégé as the prospective owner of King's Green.

The sound of a powerful engine approaching the house stilled all other activity, and Mrs Chase looked at her daughter with something resembling panic. 'It must be them!' she almost whispered the words, and with a feeling of irritation overcoming her apprehension Helen set down her glass.

'Who else?' she agreed tautly. 'Unless Charles has chosen this moment to put in an appearance.'

'Do you think he might?'

Her mother looked almost hopeful, but Helen shook her head. 'Charles is in Cheltenham, as you very well know,' she retorted, looping her hair behind her ears in a businesslike way. 'Do you want me to let them in? Then you can greet them here like the gracious hostess you are.'

Mrs Chase looked doubtful, but Helen was already leaving the room, casting a reassuring glance over her shoulder, trying to feel as confident as she looked.

The doorbell pealed as she started across the hall, echoing around the mellow panelling and bringing an increasing awareness of their own vulnerability. She glanced up at the trembling prisms of a chandelier, at the polished carving of the staircase, and realised how much she would miss all this if she had to leave. Marrying Charles somehow had always seemed such a distant thing, and if she had thought of King's Green at all, it was in terms of her coming here, with her children, bringing them to see their grandmother, and showing them the places where she had played when she was young. She had never pictured the house belonging to anyone else, and even the home Charles was buying for them, beautiful though it was, could never mean as much to her as King's Green.

With these thoughts for company she opened the doors to the porch, her unusually pale features remote and uncompromising. To the man and woman awaiting her reception she appeared cold and indifferent, her casual appearance belying the cold hauteur in her face.

In contrast, Margot Urquart seemed warm and animated, her green silk suit complementing the sunflower brightness of her scarf. Careful make-up had taken years from her finely-drawn features, and Helen could quite see that in the right light she might be taken for thirty-five or younger. The stark sunlight of morning was less sympathetic, but nevertheless Margot had a certain feminine appeal that was ageless.

However, it was the man standing slightly behind her who drew Helen's eyes. She had known what to expect, of course, she had seen his picture on the back of her mother's book, but even so, she was totally unprepared for the man himself. A photograph was flat, two-dimensional, limited by the demands of black and white, whereas the man who was accompanying Margot was flesh and blood, and infinitely more disturbing than any clever likeness. The picture, for instance, had shown him to have fair hair, but not that silvery fairness that lay smoothly against his scalp, without requiring any unsightly hairdressing. Also, he was darker-skinned than she had expected, absurdly so, considering the lightness of his hair, with blue eyes shaded by long gold-tipped lashes. He was not handsome, his appeal was much more subtle than that, and the faintly mocking twist to his mouth convinced her that he knew that as well as she did. In consequence, Helen stiffened still further, and it was left to Margot to say, rather doubtfully:

'Mrs Chase is expecting us. Will you tell her we're here, Miss—er——'

Helen's reserve broke into unwilling explanation. 'I'm Helen,' she said, half believing Margot knew that already, but the other woman's astonishment seemed genuine enough.

'*Helen!*' she exclaimed. 'Good heavens!' A certain trace of waspishness entered her tones now. 'But you were only a schoolgirl the last time I saw you.'

'That was three years ago, Aunt Margot,' Helen replied politely, steeling herself not to respond with the implied immaturity. 'I'm twenty-one.'

*Aunt* Margot clearly didn't like the designation, but she was forced to ignore it for the time being. 'I thought you must be an *au pair* Alice had employed,' she explained, glancing half apologetically at her escort. 'Darling, this is Alice's daughter Helen. Helen, I'd like you to met Mr Jarret Manning.'

'How do you do?' Jarret Manning held out his hand, and Helen was forced to take it. It was a firm hand, hard and masculine, but she had noticed the endearment, and withdrew her own after the briefest of clasps, murmuring her acknowledgement as she invited them inside.

'Oh, this hall!' cried Margot dramatically, as the doors were closed, and the sunlight shafted from the windows on either side. 'Isn't it beautiful, Jarret? Don't you think so? The panelling is so warm—so mellow! It's walnut, you know, and the carving on the stairs is by Grinling Gibbons.'

'Really?'

Jarret Manning arched his brows, and Helen, catching his eye at that moment, felt a sense of irritation. What was Margot trying to do? Was she attempting to sell the house to him? Did she think they needed her assistance? It was humiliating!

'Mummy is in the drawing room,' Helen said now, leading the way across the hall, wishing for the first time she had taken her mother's advice and changed. She was very conscious of Jarret Manning behind her, of his eyes on her, appraising her, assessing her, looking at her tight jeans and imagining she had worn them deliberately.

Mrs Chase came to the drawing room door as she heard their voices, and Margot rushed to embrace her. 'Alice, my dear!' she exclaimed, with her usual effusiveness. 'It's wonderful to see you again. Telephones are simply not an adequate substitute. I declare, you look younger every time we meet.'

'It's good to see you again, Margot,' Mrs Chase assured her, meaning it, her eyes moving to the man who followed the two women into the room. 'Hello, Mr Manning. I feel

I know you already. I expect Margot's told you I'm a great fan of yours.'

Helen drew back against the wall beside the door, wishing she could melt into the panelling. Her mother's first words had convinced her that she had dismissed her earlier anxieties about the Hetheringtons from her mind, and the excitement of meeting Jarret Manning had apparently erased her reservations. Watching the two woman as they fawned around him made Helen feel physically sick, and with a feeling of desperation she edged through the doorway.

'Where are you going, Helen?'

Her mother's sharpened tones arrested her, and with a look of resignation marring her solemn features, she halted. 'I thought I'd go and change, Mummy,' she said, realising it was as good an excuse as any. 'I—er—I'm sure you and Mr Manning have things to talk about, and I shan't be long.'

'Don't be,' her mother advised her shortly, her expression mirroring her disapproval. 'After we've had a drink, I want you to show Mr Manning over the house. You're so much more knowledgeable about its history than I am.'

Helen accepted this without a word, aware that Margot liked that idea no more than she did. But there was nothing either of them could say. Jarret Manning seemed indifferent to all of them, standing on the hearth, gazing up at the painting above the fireplace with an ease of familiarity that Helen found infuriating. It was as if he already owned King's Green, she thought bitterly, wishing the house was hers so that she could refuse to sell it. Tall and lean, and aggressively masculine beside the delicate tracery of the marble, she could almost imagine him dressed in close-fitting breeches and riding boots, instead of the expensive suede suit he was wearing, a riding crop in his hand, one arm resting on the mantel, very much the master of the house.

He turned at that moment and caught her eyes upon him, and immediately a trace of amusement lifted the corners of his mouth. It was as if he knew exactly what she was thinking, and that he also knew how angry it made her. He was everything she disliked most in a man, self-assured and over-confident, convinced that he knew everything there was to know about women, and supremely egotistical about his own appeal to them. Well, he didn't appeal to her, she thought contemptuously. And if he thought he could make silent passes at her, he was mistaken! With a scathing sweep of her lashes she turned on her heel and walked across the hall to the stairs with all the hauteur she was capable of.

In her own room, however, a little of her confidence left her. Sitting down on the side of her bed, she stared moodily down at the engagement ring on her finger. It was infuriating, feeling so helpless in the face of her mother's determination, particularly when it seemed likely that Jarret Manning might agree to buy. She didn't want someone like him living at King's Green, she thought impotently. He was not right for Thrushfold, and he was not right for the house.

Realising she was wasting time, and that if she did not hurry her mother might well come looking for her, Helen got up from the bed and stripped off her shirt and jeans. Then, raiding her wardrobe, she pulled out a shirtwaister dress of polyester fibre, with a bloused bodice and a swinging skirt, and added high-heeled sandals to complete the ensemble. The colours, a blending of blue and violet, accentuated the sooty darkness of her eyes, and with her hair newly brushed and silkily lustrous, she felt better able to cope with the demands that were to be made on her.

Downstairs again, she could hear Margot extolling the virtues of the paintings Helen's great-great grandfather had collected. 'There were so many wonderful artists around at that time,' she was saying effusively. 'Constable, Turner, Millet! And Gainsborough, of course.'

'Not to mention Hogarth and Lawrence and Reynolds,' put in Jarret Manning's dry tones. 'Are you trying to tell me something, Margot? I assure you, I did have an education of sorts.'

'Of course you did, darling,' Margot sounded a little put out, and Helen heard her mother murmur something about hoping the weather was a forerunner of the summer to come.

'Summers at King's Green are so peaceful,' she declared, obviously trying to change the subject. 'I'm afraid you may find them too peaceful, Mr Manning.'

'Strange as it may seem, I'm looking for that kind of peace, Mrs Chase,' he retorted in the curiously harsh tones of someone driven to defend himself. 'Unlike Margot, I find London lacking in stimulation, and I anticipate the coming summer with more enthusiasm than I've anticipated anything for—years.'

'*This* summer?' Helen heard the note of anxiety in her mother's voice as she reached the open doorway. 'Oh, but —I—er——'

Her words trailed away at her daughter's appearance, and there was genuine relief in her expression as she rose from the sofa. 'There you are, Helen,' she exclaimed weakly. 'I was beginning to wonder where you had got to.'

'Sorry.' Helen forced a polite smile that encompassed her mother and Margot, but only touched the outline of the man who rose courteously from the armchair he had been occupying. 'Is lunch almost ready?'

'Not—er—not until you've shown Mr Manning the house, dear,' declined Mrs Chase firmly, her eyes flashing messages only Helen could interpret. 'I—er—I should start upstairs, and Margot and I will walk in the garden. Do you think that's a good idea, Mr Manning?'

'If your daughter has no objection,' he essayed, inclining his head, and Helen saw that he was not smiling now.

Silently she led the way across the hall and up the shallow stairs to the first floor. She was conscious of him behind her, of Margot's antipathy at her exclusion, but she determinedly ignored the personalities involved, and began her recitation.

'The house was originally begun in the reign of Queen Anne, but its completion was at a much later date. Since then, of course, various alterations and additions have been made, and some major structural repairs were carried out in the late nineteenth century. Its design was partly attributed to a man called Nicholas Hawksmoor, a contemporary of Vanbrugh, who as you know designed Blenheim Palace, and Castle Howard in Yorkshire, but we don't think it likely, and the fact that it took so long to complete takes it out of his lifetime. The name—King's Green—is attributed to the fact that in the early nineteenth century, when my great-great-grandfather was alive, the Prince Regent was reputed to have stayed here, on his way to Bath, but again——'

'Can we cut the thesis?' Jarret Manning's cool tones were as incisive as his words. 'I realise showing me around your home is obviously distasteful for you, and believe me, I can do without the guided tour.'

Helen was too stunned to answer him, and ignoring her offended expression, he opened the door to their left. 'A bedroom, right?' he suggested, glancing about its generous proportions. 'Very nice. Next?'

Pressing her lips together, Helen showed him all the bedrooms on the first floor, including her own, although she had made sure to put all her belongings away so that nothing should signify that this room was hers more than any of the others. The adjoining bathrooms she left to him, saying only that some of the bedrooms had been made over when the plumbing was modernised.

'There is a second floor,' she added stiffly, after he had admired the master suite which was presently unoccupied. 'We don't use it, so I expect it may be very dusty, but it's habitable if one needs more rooms.'

'I don't expect to,' Jarret remarked dryly. 'I see you have some central heating. I hope it wasn't installed when the Prince Regent came to visit.'

'No. It was installed after the second world war——' began Helen seriously, and then stopped when she realised what he had asked. The fact that he had caught her out so easily was irritating, and she indicated the narrow passage that led to the second floor staircase with evident resentment.

'Don't you ever relax?' Jarret enquired, accompanying her back along the gallery to the first floor landing, and when she didn't answer this, added: 'I suppose these lighter patches on the walls are where your—great-great-grandfather's paintings used to hang, is that right?' indicating the oblong squares visible between the panelled doors. 'What happened? Are they in storage, did they fall to pieces—or have they been sold?'

'I imagine you know the answer to that, Mr Manning,'

Helen declared stiffly, disliking his perspicacity. 'Had we a valuable collection of paintings to sell, we would hardly be selling the house, would we?'

'Not to a philistine like me, no,' he agreed solemnly, and she glanced sideways at him, sure that he was mocking her again.

'Why do you want King's Green, Mr Manning?' she demanded, halting at the head of the stairs. 'It—it's not your —your scene really, is it? Don't you want a—a pad nearer town?'

He grinned at this, an outright humorous grin that unexpectedly reacted on her like a blow to the solar plexis. She had reluctantly admitted his attraction before, but she had had no idea how irresistible his smile might be. Now, with the lighter creases beside his eyes deepening to reveal laughter lines, and the thin lips parting over slightly uneven white teeth, he was devastating.

'Oh, Helen!' he gulped, and the suppressed amusement in his voice briefly distracted her from the realisation that he had used her name. 'How would you know what my— scene is? And as for my having a *pad*—God!' He shook his head, and adopting a distinctly Bogart-like accent, added: 'Stick to your own territory, sweetheart!'

Helen felt a second's overwhelming impulse to giggle, but then common sense came to the rescue, and the awareness of what she was doing here and his part in it sobered her instantly.

'I don't know what you mean, Mr Manning,' she affirmed, with all the contempt she could muster. 'Shall we go downstairs?'

'In a minute...' He, too, had sobered, and as she moved to the head of the stairs his cool fingers closed about her arm. They successfully prevented her from moving away from him, and within their grasp she was conscious of his nearness and the disturbing magnetism his smile had generated. 'Tell me something,' he said, his thumb massaging her flesh almost without his being aware of it, 'what did I do to arouse so much resentment? I didn't ask to come here. I was invited. I was given the obviously mistaken impression that your mother wanted to sell the house, but if she doesn't then I shan't lose any sleep over it, *Miss* Chase.'

Helen held up her head. 'I—why—my mother does want to sell the house,' she admitted unwillingly.

'And you don't?'

'It's not my house to sell.'

'But if it were?'

Helen moved her shoulders helplessly, avoiding those blue eyes which seemed to have the cutting strength of steel. 'I—I expect I might have to,' she conceded, and with an exclamation he let her go.

'But not to me,' he inferred coldly, and she turned away from him to descend the stairs without giving him a reply.

Several rooms opened off the hall below. The drawing room, the music room, the dining room, the library—Helen did not know which to choose after their *contretemps* upstairs, and she waited for him to join her before making a decision. Jarret, however, seemed in no hurry to continue, and she had to wait some minutes while he examined the carving on the balustrade.

'Grinling——' began Helen reluctantly, only to have him interrupt her words.

'—Gibbons. Yes, I know,' he finished sardonically. 'Only Gibbons died in 1720, so how do you account for that, if the house wasn't completed until much later?'

Helen's face flamed. No one had ever questioned the authenticity of the carving before, and it was disconcerting to have him do so. It was true that the likelihood of Gibbons having completed the carving was in some doubt, and her father's assessment had been that it had probably been a pupil of Gibbons who accomplished the work.

'I—it's open to speculation that—that perhaps it was a pupil of Gibbons who completed the carving,' she admitted. 'But the style is his, and that's what's important.'

'Is it?' He descended the final few stairs to stand beside her. 'A connoisseur might disagree with you.'

Helen tilted her chin, annoyed that she still had to look up to him, despite her five feet six inches. 'Are you a connoisseur, Mr Manning?' she enquired as coolly as she could, and the humour in his expression annoyed her almost more than his sarcasm had done.

'You obviously don't think so,' he said, pushing back his hair with lazy fingers, his eyes far too knowing for her peace of mind. 'Shall we go on?'

As he had already seen the drawing room, Helen opened the doors into the dining room, standing back as he passed her to walk thoughtfully round the well-proportioned room. The panelled window embrasures overlooked the gardens at the side of the house, and attracting as it did the early sun, it provided a warm oasis on colder mornings. It had always been one of Helen's favourite rooms, and she waited with some reluctance for his verdict. It was an elegant room, the beige walls hung with panels of moiré silk, the carpets, with their distinctive design, brought back many years ago from the Caucasus. Much of the furniture was not original, however, although the dinner service residing in the long serving sideboards was Worcestershire porcelain. Ruched curtains framed long windows, and were matched in the deep blue cushions of the chairs that faced one another across the hearth.

'Do you use this room often?' Jarret queried, indicating the damask cloth and silverware which Mrs Hetherington had laid ready for lunch, and Helen hesitated.

'If—if you mean, do we give many dinner parties nowadays, the answer is no,' she replied at length, watching him push his hands into the pockets of his pants, unwillingly aware of the strong muscles of his thighs. 'I—er—the room is used by—by the family most days.'

'The family?' He arched his brows.

'My mother and me.'

'Ah!' He nodded his head. 'I gather you have no brothers or sisters.'

'No.'

'And your father's dead.'

'Yes.'

Helen resented this interrogation, but she didn't see how she could refuse to answer him, and with an obvious gesture she stepped back into the hall. It was another few seconds before he joined her, and her features had set in controlled lines. It was as if he was deliberately delaying her, and she wished her mother or Margot would appear and take this unwanted duty from her.

'The music room,' she declared shortly, throwing open the white panelled doors that led into a smaller, but equally attractive room. Here, one or two pictures still adorned the walls, portraits mostly, of long-dead Chases, whose likenesses would be of little value to anyone else. The carpet was Chinese, the grand piano reflected the warmth of the bowl of primroses that adorned it, and several pieces of eighteenth century mahogany gleamed with the patina of age. There was a small *escritoire*, a folding, gate-legged table, and a walnut bracket clock, whose ticking filled the quiet room with a steady rhythm.

'Do you play the piano—Miss Chase?' Jarret asked, strolling towards the stringed instrument which dominated one corner of the room.

'I used to,' she admitted, her words clipped and unwilling, and with a wry smile he seated himself at the piano and ran his long fingers over the keys.

At once she recognised the melody of a popular tune of the day, mellowed to a lilting refrain that tugged at the heartstrings. Then, just as she was considering making the scathing comment that he was abusing the age of the instrument, he switched to a Chopin prelude, and drew the very soul from the poignant phrase.

His eyes sought hers as he finished with a final sweep of the keys, and feeling obliged to say something, she tried not to sound as if she was envious. 'You're very accomplished,' she averred, glancing meaningfully towards the doors again, and his rueful grin denoted his acknowledgement of how reluctant she had been to compliment him.

'Faint praise?' he murmured, as he passed her into the hall, and she closed the doors behind them with a distinctive click.

The library was a cooler room, having the benefit of the north light, but seldom welcoming the sun. Nevertheless, the book-lined walls were warming, and the desk set squarely before the windows was an ideal place for anyone to work.

'Did your father use this room?' Jarret asked casually, wandering over to the desk and running his fingers over its tooled leather surface.

'Yes.'

As always, Helen was non-committal, but this time Jarret persisted. 'What did he do—your father?' he asked, propping himself against the side of the desk and folding his arms. 'A country gentleman, was he? The local squire? Or did he have to work for his living like the rest of us?'

Helen was shocked into speech. 'I don't think my father's affairs are anything to do with you, Mr Manning,' she declared, preparing to make her exit, but his next words arrested her.

'As I see it, there has to be some reason why you dislike me so much, *Miss* Chase,' he observed pleasantly. 'I'd like to know what it is, that's all.'

'And—and you think learning about my father's occupation will help you?' she exclaimed.

'Let's say I'm interested in your background, as you're obviously interested in mine.'

'What do you mean?'

'Oh, come on ...' He rested his chin on his chest, looking up at her through the thick length of his lashes. 'You think I'm coarse and uneducated, thoroughly unsuitable to own King's Green!'

Helen's lips worked silently for a moment, then she said: 'When my father inherited King's Green, we owned the land for—for miles around. He—he was the squire, yes, but he worked hard for the estate, and only the high cost of living and the taxes he had to pay forced him to sell most of it.'

'I see,' Jarret nodded, but Helen had to disabuse him.

'However,' she went on, 'if you think I—I object to—to you because I think you're socially inferior, you couldn't be more wrong!'

'No?'

'No!' Helen swallowed before continuing. 'What—what I do object to is—is Margot Urquart bringing her—her boy-friends here and pretending that they have the money to buy a place like this!'

She realised she had gone too far long before Jarret's dark features mirrored his contempt. She didn't know what had possessed her to speak so candidly, unless it was his scornful comments about her father. She did know practically nothing about him, after all, and although she suspected Margot was helping to finance his property speculation, she had no way of proving it.

'So that's what you think,' he commented flatly, his lips curling with dislike. 'My, my, what a devious little mind you have, to be sure! You really think I would let Margot *buy* me a country retreat?'

Having gone so far, Helen had no choice but to go through with it if she wanted to save her self-respect. 'Why not?' she asked now, lifting her shoulders. 'She's bought everything else, hasn't she?'

He was off the desk and confronting her before her shaken senses could acknowledge her mistake. He had been close before, when he had detained her at the top of the stairs, but not as close as this, nor breathing down upon her with all the fiery ferment of his anger. His breath was not unpleasant, and it was flavoured by the Scotch her mother must have offered him, but its heat was unmistakable, combined as it was with the ice-cold glitter of his eyes.

'You little——' His harsh tones cut off the expletive with brutal vehemence, and Helen, who had never suffered such an assault before, shrank back in alarm. 'What the hell do you think gives you the right to pass moral judgment on me, or Margot? What is it to do with you how we live or how we act? And if Margot chooses to spend her money in a way that suits her best, why should she have to defend herself to you?'

Helen shifted unsteadily under his gaze, momentarily numbed by the fierceness of his attack. 'I—I—I don't care what Margot does, as—as long as she doesn't expect—us to—to condone it,' she stammered, struggling to recover her dignity. 'And—and intimidating me isn't going to make me—change my mind, Mr Manning,' she added bravely.

'No?' Unexpectedly his eyes dropped to the modest neckline of her dress, and it was all she could do to prevent herself from clutching the collar about her throat. 'Then perhaps I should give you a sample of what you're missing, mmm?'

Helen gulped. 'Don't you dare——' she began chokingly, and then felt her words stifled at the source as his mouth descended over hers.

He held her, his hands gripping her shoulders without respect or gentleness, the narrow fingers digging into her soft flesh. She was not crushed against him, but she was aware of the hard strength of his lean body, and ridiculously embarrassed by the pressure of his legs against hers. She had never been kissed in anger before, never experienced the wholly possessive abrasion of raw emotion, and while her mind repulsed the savagery of his embrace, her senses swam beneath the undoubted skill of his expertise. He was no callow youth, attempting to seduce her with clumsy force, but an experienced man, making her fully aware of his needs—and her own. And that was the most upsetting thing of all. Until this moment she had not known she possessed such needs, or that she could be aroused in quite this fashion. It shed a whole new light on the prospect of her marriage to Charles, and with the remembrance of her fiancé, sanity asserted itself.

With a superhuman effort she wrenched herself away from Jarret Manning, and summoning all her strength she raised her arm to deliver the slap he deserved. But although he was gazing at her with a curiously speculative frown marring his lean features, he had obviously not been as emotionally disturbed by what had happened as she was, and when she tried to slap him he parried the blow without effort.

'You—you——' she began impotently, and he offered: 'Cad?' with mocking raised eyebrows. 'Yes! Yes!' she cried, unaware that her rounded breasts were rising and falling with the intensity of her anger, and were drawing his attention to their delectable promise.

However, he seemed to think better of any further incursion, and rubbing the back of his hand across his mouth, as if to assure himself he was not exhibiting some betraying trace of her lipstick, he gestured with mock-politeness towards the door: 'Shall we continue?'

Helen found she was trembling, but without saying another word she turned into the hall, only to stop abruptly at the sight of her mother and Margot, just coming along the passage which led to the back of the house. In consequence, Jarret almost stumbled over her, and she heard the almost inaudible oath he uttered at the realisation of why she had halted.

'Going to tell on me?' he murmured by her ear, his tone derisive, but the look she cast at him over her shoulder was belittling.

'And embarrass my mother?' she countered scornfully, but was in no way gratified by the lazy insouciance in his eyes.

'Have you seen over the house, darling?'

It was Margot who hailed them, quickening her step so that she reached them seconds before Helen's mother, and Jarret inclined his head, permitting her to slide her arm possessively through his.

'Er—*Miss* Chase has done a good job of—making me feel at home,' he remarked, with a wry grimace, and Helen felt, rather than saw, her mother give her a quick speculative glance.

'And what did you think, Mr Manning?' Mrs Chase asked now as she reached them, and they all moved by mutual consent into the drawing room once more.

He seemed to take ages to reply, and Helen, stiff and uneasy, chided herself for allowing such a situation to develop. The man was obviously a rogue and an opportunist, and she had only fuelled his resources by giving him that kind of a hold over her.

'I like it,' he said at last, detaching himself from Margot's clinging arms and going to stand by the windows, looking out on the view Helen had been admiring earlier. 'But I don't know if it's what I want.'

'Darling——'

'It's not?'

Both Margot and her mother spoke at once, and Helen put her hands behind her back so that no one could see she had her fingers crossed. He was going to turn it down, she thought, with an overwhelming sense of relief, and then wondered why she felt such a hollow sense of victory.

Jarret turned then, drawing a case of cheroots from his pocket, and after gaining Mrs Chase's permission, put one of the thin cigars between his teeth. Lighting it, the flame cupped in his brown hands, he let his gaze rove to Helen's uncertain features, and then, extinguishing his lighter, he inhaled deeply before continuing.

'It's—bigger than I had in mind,' he admitted thoughtfully, while Margot made a little sound of contradiction that for the most part he ignored. 'And the grounds—I believe Margot told me there were forty or fifty acres.'

'Fifty-five, actually,' put in Mrs Chase hurriedly. 'But most of that is arable land belonging to the home farm. I explained about the Flynns, didn't I?'

'Oh, yes,' Jarret nodded, studying the glowing tip of his cheroot. 'But the price you're asking . . .' His eyes flickered to Helen's set face once more. 'Quite frankly, it's a lot of money to lay out without any previous experience of living in the country. I'm sure your daughter would agree with me. An urban-reared individual like myself may find life at King's Green a little too—unexciting, you know what I mean?'

Helen's cheeks burned, the more so because she could imagine what her mother was thinking. She thought she had put him off, when in all honesty she had done no such thing.

'I'm afraid Helen's ideas are rather out of date, Mr Manning,' Mrs Chase was saying now, with a reproving look in her daughter's direction. 'She persists in clinging to the past, and forgets that times have changed. As far as living in the country is concerned, Mr Manning, Thrushfold is only a couple of hours drive from the outskirts of London, or there's an excellent train service from Bristol, if you prefer it. I can't deny I'm looking forward to living in the city myself for a while, but I shall miss the peace and tranquillity of King's Green once it's sold.'

Jarret smiled, that devastating smile that could charm the birds off the trees, thought Helen maliciously, and then said: 'You know, you almost convince me. I feel I could work here, certainly, but I don't know. I'd have to think it over.'

'Of course.' Mrs Chase caught her lower lip between her teeth. 'As—as a matter of fact, I don't mind if you take several months to think it over. You see,' she hastened on, 'Helen is getting married in August, and I rather hoped she might get married from here. Her father would have liked that, and if we have to leave . . .'

'I see.' The amusement faded from Jarret's face, leaving it strangely sombre suddenly. 'Well now, that rather disappoints me.'

'Disappoints you?' echoed Mrs Chase doubtfully. 'I'm afraid I don't understand.'

Jarret shook his head, pushing one hand into the pocket of his jacket. 'I had hoped—if I decided to buy—that the sale might be completed in a month or so,' he admitted. 'You see, Mrs Chase, I do want to get away from London for a while, and the sooner the better.'

'Jarret's working on his fourth novel,' explained Margot unnecessarily, and received a scathing glare from him for her pains.

'I am working,' he conceded dryly, 'although whether it will ever transform itself into a readable manuscript is doubtful. However, that is the position, and perhaps it would be as well for all our sakes if I looked at something else.'

'Oh, please ...' To Helen's astonishment, her mother sounded almost disappointed now. 'Don't be too hasty, I beg of you.' She paused. 'Perhaps we could come to some mutual arrangement that would suit all of us.'

The sound of footsteps in the hall arrested any further conversation, and the housekeeper's grey head appeared round the door to announce that lunch was waiting on the table.

'Thank you, Mrs Hetherington.' Helen's mother moved towards the door. 'But before you go, I'd like to introduce Mr Manning, who we all hope may be the new owner of King's Green.'

Mrs Hetherington greeted the newcomer with only veiled antagonism, but Jarret was not dismayed. 'You're the housekeeper?' he guessed, irritating Helen by his obvious attempts to charm the old woman, and she nodded.

'Been here forty years all told,' she asserted, daring contradiction, and he grinned warmly.

'I'm very pleased to meet you,' he affirmed, shaking the gnarled hand that was offered with some reluctance. 'If I do decide to buy, perhaps we could come to some similar arrangement. I shall need someone to cook my meals and make my bed. I've been doing the latter myself, but I'm not very good at it.'

Helen would have said he was extremely good, but Mrs Hetherington was unaware of the double entendre. On the contrary, she was taken aback by his easy familiarity, and after a moment's hesitation muttered that she would have to see about that. But she was disarmed, and they all knew it, and Mrs Chase led the way into the dining room with evident satisfaction. All her problems seemed to be ironing themselves out, thought Helen moodily, so why did she feel as if all hers were only just beginning?

Mrs Hetherington had excelled herself with the lunch. A rich home-made soup was followed by roast duckling with green peas and new potatoes, and the fruit sponge to finish was as light as any she had made. Covertly Helen watched Jarret Manning tucking into the meal, clearly enjoying the wholesome fare, but Margot only picked at her food, avoiding anything fattening and drinking more wine than anyone else. Mrs Chase had to ask the housekeeper to bring a third bottle as Margot emptied the second, and Helen saw Jarret lean towards his companion and say something which provoked a sulky reaction.

'I suppose some of the dairy produce is home-grown,' he remarked a few minutes later, as Mrs Hetherington cleared the dessert plates, and Helen's mother was eager to explain.

'Naturally, we get all our milk and eggs and vegetables from the farm,' she said, 'but these days we buy our butter and cheese. There simply isn't the time to make our own, although of course the equipment is still there. It's very old-fashioned, I'm afraid, but it does work.'

'I'd be interested to see it,' Jarret commented thoughtfully, and Margot made a sound of derision.

'Of what possible interest is a butter churn to you, Jarret?' she exclaimed. 'Unless you're intending to become totally rural and self-sufficient!'

'The mechanics interest me,' retorted Jarret flatly, his blue eyes offering a warning even Helen could recognise. Then he turned to her mother again. 'Tell me, Mrs Chase, do you have any idea of the approximate running costs of the estate for—say—six months, for example?'

Mrs Chase ran her tongue doubtfully over her lower

lip. 'Well now,' she began slowly, 'we did used to have a bailiff who attended to that sort of thing for us, but what with the rising cost of living ...' She frowned. 'My solicitor could tell you, I suppose. His office is in Malverley. That's the nearest town, you see.'

Jarret nodded. 'But you have no idea?'

Mrs Chase glanced anxiously towards Helen, and her daughter gave her back look for look. If her mother expected her to tell Jarret Manning how much it cost to keep King's Green going, she could think again! It was hard enough, contemplating selling the house to him, without his having the nerve to ask how much it cost to run the place. What did he want? A balance sheet for the year? A guaranteed return on his interest?

As if realising what was going through both their minds, Jarret suddenly broke the rather awkward silence that had fallen. 'I'm afraid I've started this rather badly, haven't I?' he said, showing again the perception which Helen had resented earlier. 'You're thinking I want to protect my investment—that my question was levelled in an attempt to find out exactly what my outlay might be.' He shook his head. 'I'm sorry. That was not my intention, and if I've offended you, please accept my apology. I had something entirely different in mind.'

Mrs Chase managed a polite smile. 'That's quite all right, Mr Manning. We—I—well, I suppose I should be more familiar with estate matters, but I'm afraid I've relied on professional advice since my husband died.'

'I can understand that.' Jarret was at his most disarming, and Helen, seated across the table from him, felt her nails digging into the palms of her hands. What now? What exactly did he have in mind? And why did she feel this uneasy apprehension that whatever it was, it would disrupt the tenor of *her* life? 'But my proposition—or at least, the proposition which has just occurred to me—would involve a financial settlement to cover the next six months.'

'Your proposition, Mr Manning?' But Helen could see her mother's interest growing. 'I'm afraid I don't understand ...'

Jarret frowned, resting both elbows on the table and linking his fingers together. 'It's this,' he said slowly, and even Margot was watching him with something akin to curiosity. 'You say you don't want to leave King's Green until after—your daughter has got married?'

'Yes?'

'And I've already explained that I want to get out of London right away.'

'Yes?'

The tension around the table was almost tangible, Helen thought imaginatively, herself steeled for whatever was coming next. Margot had put down her glass and was playing with its stem, a sure sign of nervous anticipation, while Mrs Chase was pressing her lips together, endeavouring to contain her evident impatience.

However, Mrs Hetherington's arrival with the coffee prevented Jarret from continuing, and they all had to wait, chafing under the restraint, while the housekeeper served each of them. Then, just as Jarret was about to begin again, Margot chose to forestall him.

'You're not suggesting you become a lodger here, are you, darling?' she protested in scornful tones, and the atmosphere splintered like so many shards of crystal.

Helen's stomach churned as Jarret subjected Margot to the kind of contemptuous appraisal that was both pitying and malevolent. Margot sought refuge in her wine, her jerking shoulders revealing the indignant remorse she was trying hard to hide, while he expelled his breath on a long sigh of resignation.

'As usual, Margot has jumped to conclusions,' he said, making an apologetic gesture. 'Only in this instance there is a shred of truth in what she's saying.'

He paused, and Helen sensed he was looking at her now, but she refused to lift her eyes. Margot had been right then, he was actually suggesting he might *share* King's Green with them! *How dare he?*

'Before you make the same mistake as Margot, let me explain what I had in mind.' He produced his cheroots, and after putting one between his teeth, he went on: 'It seems to me we might both benefit from the scheme I have to put to you. You want to stay, and I need a place to work. I also need to be sure that leaving London is right for me.' He hesitated a moment before continuing: 'What I'm suggesting is that we do share the house—but only partly. All I need is the library and a bedroom. My meals could be served to me in the library, and to all intents and purposes the house would still be your own. However, for that— service, what I am prepared to offer is that I'll make myself responsible for all financial matters pertaining to the estate in that time, and in addition, perhaps we could come to some private settlement regarding the extent of the inconvenience caused.'

Helen was shocked, but her mother was stunned, and Margot looked positively green.

'You can't be serious!' she exclaimed, plucking at his sleeve in utter disbelief, and even Mrs Chase uttered a short laugh, as if to relieve the incredulity she herself was feeling.

'You're not serious, are you, Mr Manning?' she exclaimed, a worried smile coming and going on her plump features. 'I mean—why, that would be far too much for anyone to—to—consider.'

'Why?' He raised his eyebrows. 'I can afford it.' His gaze flicked Helen's unguarded face in scornful dismissal. 'And if, at the end of the summer, I do decide to buy, we can take it from there.' He shrugged. 'Believe me, I'll get as much out of it as you will. It gives me all the advantages of the place, without any commitment whatsoever.'

He was right—Helen could see that. But she was sickened at the thought. To have Jarret Manning in the house all summer long, to know that he was always there, always in the background. It was almost worse than having to leave the house immediately.

But naturally Mrs Chase did not see it like that. 'You really mean it?' she said shaking her dark head, and Jarret nodded:

'I really mean it.'

'Well, I think it's a ridiculous idea!' Margot was clearly not at all suited by these unexpected arrangements. No doubt she had expected Jarret to have the place to himself, thought Helen cynically, her lips tightening at the images this evoked. 'How much isolation do you think you'll get here, with the house constantly in use, and visitors coming and going?'

'We don't get many visitors these days, Margot,' Mrs Chase put in at this point. 'Mostly there's just Helen and myself, and Charles, of course, when he's not at the stables.'

'Charles?'

Jarret looked questioningly at Helen's mother, and she quickly explained. 'Charles Connaught is Helen's fiancé. His father owns the Connaught stables at Ketchley. Charles works with him, and they've produced some excellent mounts this winter.'

'I see.' Jarret's eyes drooped over Helen's face again, as he acknowledged this information, and quickly averting her gaze, she wondered what he was thinking. She doubted that Charles would have much in common with Jarret Manning, and dreaded his reactions if her mother chose to fall in with Jarret's suggestions.

'But it's not the same, is it?' Margot persisted, still pursuing her theme of isolation. 'I mean, you'd be interrupted for meals, or someone could barge in on you ...'

'There is a lock on the library door,' pointed out Mrs Chase rather irritably now, not altogether convinced of Margot's sincerity. 'And as far as meals are concerned, Mr Manning can make his own arrangements.'

'And you're prepared to consider this, I suppose,' Margot declared waspishly, transferring her attention to Helen's mother. 'I can quite see why——'

'Margot!'

But Margot ignored Jarret's warning tone. 'After all,' she continued, 'you're getting the best of both worlds, aren't you? The chance to remain at King's Green, and a wealthy benefactor to ease the tiresome burden!'

'Margot!' This time Jarret succeeded in silencing her. 'I don't see that it has anything to do with you what arrangements I make with Mrs Chase.'

'Of course not. You wouldn't,' exclaimed Margot tremulously, suddenly pushing back her chair and getting to her feet. 'It doesn't mean a thing to you that *I* arranged this meeting, that *I* introduced you to King's Green! My opinions have ceased to matter, haven't they?'

'No!' With a rueful grimace, Jarret stood up now, and attempted to reason with her. 'But I have to work here,

Margot, it's my decision, not yours, and—well, I'm grateful to you.'

'Grateful!' Margot made it sound like an insult. 'I don't want your gratitude, Jarret! I want——'

'Margot ...' Mrs Chase had risen now, and moved round the table towards her friend in a determined effort to restore the balance. 'There's no point in getting upset over this. I mean, does it really matter to you what Mr Manning decides to do?'

Margot opened her mouth as if to confirm that it did, and then closed it again as pride and indignation obviously warred within her. Helen, watching the older woman's display, was dismayed, and she knew her mother would find this exhibition hard to forgive, too. Of course, they didn't know anything about Margot's relationship with Jarret Manning, and she might have every justification for feeling put out, but on the other hand, what was she really objecting to? Surely—always supposing these arrangements did come off, which Helen herself viewed with a deal of suspicion—did the fact that she and her mother were to remain in the house over the summer mean that much? Jarret would be free to come and go as he pleased, and once she was married her mother would offer a very small obstruction to his occupation.

'I think perhaps we should be leaving,' Jarret said flatly, his lean features guarding his real feelings. 'Naturally you need time to consider this, Mrs Chase, and maybe consult with your legal advisers. Whatever, I'll give you my address and telephone number, and the address of my solicitors, and perhaps you'll let me know what you decide.'

'Yes.' Mrs Chase sounded doubtful. Then, as if afraid Margot might change his mind for him, she did the unforgivable thing so far as Helen was concerned. 'But I'm quite prepared to accept your proposition, on a trial basis —say, of a month—and if you'd like to have the necessary papers drawn up, I'll be happy to sign them!'

## CHAPTER THREE

THE gardens at Ketchley were perfumed with the early promise of summer. Although it was only the middle of May, already the hedges were bright with hawthorn blossom, and clumps of violets decorated the sheltered borders. There was broom, providing its own splash of golden brilliance, pink and white and purple pansies, and acres of buttercups in the paddock where Charles was exercising his latest acquisition. It was a chestnut filly, young and spirited, and he was not having an easy time keeping her obedient to the leading rein.

Helen scuffed her feet rather restlessly as she hung back from the perimeter of the fence, watching the filly's antics from a safe distance. It was strange, she thought, not for the first time, that in spite of her relationship with Charles he had not been able to squash her fears about horses. They terrified her—she freely admitted it. And in the early days she had never felt quite able to believe that Charles could love anyone who disliked his beloved animals so much. Of course, time and subsequent events had disproved her theory, and every day she tried to persuade herself that time would also remove her fears.

It hadn't, as yet, and this morning she waited somewhat impatiently for her fiancé to finish his work-out and come and talk to her. For all the bright sunlight, it was quite cold just standing around, and she stuffed her hands further into the pockets of her scarlet nylon jacket, and was glad she had not succumbed to her mother's suggestion to wear a skirt. Her navy corded pants were very welcome, and tucked into the tops of her boots provided a steadfast barrier between herself and the errant wind.

'What do you think?'

With her shoulders hunched, and her chin tucked into her chest, Helen had been unaware of Charles's approach, but her fiancé's arm across her shoulders brought her head up with a start.

'Have you finished?'

'For the present,' he conceded, smiling, his eyes warming appreciatively as they rested on her delicately-cut features.

Charles Connaught was a man in his middle thirties. A little above average height, with dark good looks, he was considered quite a catch in the rural area in which they lived, and Helen had always experienced a sense of pride in knowing he had chosen her. Apart from her aversion for horses, they had quite a lot in common, including a love for the countryside, as well as similar interests in art and literature. They had known one another for a number of years, but it was not until two years ago, when Helen was nineteen, and bridesmaid at a friend's wedding where Charles was a guest, that their relationship had developed.

Now Charles lifted his lips from hers to comment casually: 'You feel frozen! You should learn to ride, instead of hanging back like a lion-tamer's apprentice!'

Helen's eyes twinkled. 'I like the comparison,' she remarked, adding, with a shiver: 'And I am cold! I've been waiting almost half an hour.'

'Sorry.' Charles's apology was sincere. 'But I didn't expect you over this morning. I thought you said you were working.'

'I should be,' admitted Helen glumly, linking her arm with his as they walked towards the house. She and a school friend ran a craft shop in Malverley, and she enjoyed her work immensely. But this morning she had other things on her mind, and at the last minute she had phoned Karen and asked if she could manage without her.

'So what's wrong?' asked Charles now, frowning as he met her mutinous gaze. 'Not Manning again!'

Charles had taken the news that Mrs Chase was going to let rooms to Jarret Manning without much enthusiasm, but it was two weeks now since that revelation, and his work and subsequent events had served to rob it of any urgency. However, his doubts were rekindled by Helen's attitude, and he promptly stopped and demanded to know what had happened.

'Oh, ...' Helen scuffed the toe of her boot against the gravelled path. 'Well, if you must know, the final arrangements have been made. Jarret Manning moves in a week today.'

Charles's good-looking features expressed his disapproval. 'I don't know what your mother is thinking of,' he declared, slipping his arm about Helen's waist as they continued their stroll towards his parents' home. 'I mean, it's not as if the fellow was seriously committed to buying King's Green.'

'I think that's part of the attraction,' murmured Helen thoughtfully. 'Oh, Mummy talks of what she'll do when the house is sold, but quite honestly, I think she's really dreading moving out. After all, she's lived there for almost twenty-five years, and it's quite a wrench when you remember there've been Chases at King's Green for over two hundred years.'

'But surely she realises that someone like Manning isn't the kind of chap to move into Thrushfold,' exclaimed Charles, stepping behind her as they reached the porch so that she could precede him into the house. 'Damned Londoner! What does he know about King's Green and its traditions?'

Helen caught her lower lip between her teeth as she entered the hall, wondering what Charles would say if she told him exactly how knowledgeable the other man was. She knew she was deliberately avoiding mentioning her own conversations with Jarret in an attempt to put what had happened between them out of her mind, but she still felt the sense of guilt that came from deceiving her fiancé in this way. Yet how could she tell him, without provoking trouble for both herself and her mother, not to mention the humiliation to herself of confessing to his moral blackmail? All the same, her natural inclination to be honest was being strained, and she hoped that once Jarret was settled into King's Green she would be able to keep any other associations out of her thoughts.

Mrs Connaught met them in the hall. Charles's mother was a slim, attractive woman in her fifties, and she and Mrs Chase had a casual acquaintanceship which Helen knew Mrs Connaught hoped would be strengthened by her marriage. The Connaughts had been at Ketchley almost as long as the Chases had been at Thrushfold, and the joining of the two families was looked forward to with much anticipation.

'Come into the sitting room and get warm,' exclaimed Mrs Connaught, after greeting her prospective daughter-in-law with a kiss on the cheek. 'You look chilled to the bone, Helen. Charles, couldn't you have left that animal for once, and looked after your fiancée?'

'Oh, really ...' Helen didn't want to be the cause of a family argument. 'It was my fault really. I wanted to watch. But this is lovely!'

There was an open fire burning in the sitting room grate, and its warmth was very welcoming. As Helen entered the room, however, following Mrs Connaught, another man rose from the chair he had been occupying beside the fire and grinned irrepressibly across at her. It was Charles's younger brother, Vincent, and Helen uttered a delighted cry.

'What are you doing here?' she exclaimed, as he came across the room to greet her. 'I thought you were supposed to be in Vietnam or Thailand or somewhere!'

Vincent Connaught was a journalist, working for a national newspaper, and although his parents were proud of him, Helen also knew that both Mr and Mrs Connaught worried about the dangerous locations their younger son reported from.

'I've got a couple of weeks' holiday,' he explained now, taking advantage of his soon-to-be-brotherly status to plant a less than brotherly kiss on her parted lips. 'Mmm, your lips are freezing. It's just as well I know there's a warm-blooded woman underneath.'

'Thank you, Vince, that's quite enough of that,' declared his brother, putting his arm possessively about his fiancée's shoulders, and although Charles's tone was amiable enough, Helen sensed the restraint he was endeavouring to hide. There had never been much love lost between the two brothers, they were too dissimilar, and Charles had never learned how to distinguish when Vincent was being deliberately provoking.

'So—how are things with you?' the younger man persisted now, addressing his question to Helen. 'Come and sit down and tell me what you've been doing since I last saw you.'

'That was Christmas!' remarked Helen dryly, pulling away from Charles's possessive hold, and taking the seat his brother had been occupying. 'A lot can happen in five months, as you should know.'

'We'd all like some coffee, wouldn't we?' suggested Mrs Connaught now, determinedly ignoring the tension between her two sons. 'Helen? You'd like some, wouldn't you? Oh, and do take off that jacket. You won't need it in here, Vincent is endeavouring to sustain the kind of climate he's just left behind in Bangkok.'

'Is that right? Is that where you've been?' exclaimed Helen, in admiration. 'How exciting! How long were you there?'

'Long enough to get himself arrested,' put in Charles scornfully, removing his own sheepskin coat. 'Here, let me take your jacket, Helen. I'll just leave it over the chair here.'

Helen smiled at her fiancé, but she was interested in what Vincent had to tell her, and for the next few minutes she listened enthralled while he described the city that has been called the 'Venice of the East'. He spoke about the meandering delta-arteries that gave the city its distinction, and the wonderful palaces and temples. It was a whole new world from that of Thrushfold and the problems of King's Green, and for a while Helen was able to put her own troubles to the back of her mind. Vincent was not like Charles. They shared similar appearances, but that was all. He was much more easy-going, and although Helen would not have trusted him with her affections, she enjoyed their casual relationship.

It was Mrs Connaught who eventually brought up the subject of Jarret Manning. Helen reluctantly explained the latest development, but it was Vincent who chose to intervene, thus forestalling his mother's commiserations.

'Jarret Manning!' he echoed disbelievingly. '*The* Jarret Manning! He's coming to live in Thrushfold? Lord help us!'

'Vincent!' His mother looked reprovingly at him. 'What's it to you where this man lives?'

'But I know him!' protested Vincent impatiently. 'We used to work in Fleet Street together. Hell, this is great news! Where is he going to stay?'

Charles's mouth turned down at the corners. 'Helen has just explained,' he stated coldly, seating himself on the arm of his fiancée's chair. 'The fellow's renting rooms at King's Green.'

'Hardly renting rooms, Charles,' murmured Helen ruefully, while Vincent burst into delighted laughter.

'You mean he's staying with you, Helen?' he demanded. 'My God! No wonder Charles looks so sick about it.'

'Vincent, please!' Mrs Connaught flashed her elder son an entreating look, and in the few moments Helen had to collect her thoughts, an awful idea struck her. What if Jarret chose to confide what had happened between them to Vincent? What if it amused him to try and cause trouble between the brothers?

'Manning is not staying with the Chases,' Charles declared now. 'Inasmuch as he's not a—visitor.' He paused, clearly wondering how much he should explain. 'There is some possibility that he may buy King's Green at the end of the summer, but for the present Helen's mother is allowing him the use of the library.'

Vincent shook his head incredulously, and then turned to Helen. 'So he is staying with you.'

'He's staying in the house,' persisted his brother.

'That's splitting hairs, Charles, and you know it,' retorted Vincent tersely. 'So, Helen? Have you met him?'

'Of course she's met him,' exclaimed Charles, equally tersely. 'Mother, can I have some more coffee? This is almost cold.'

Ignoring the older man, Vincent came to squat by Helen's chair. 'You were saying something earlier about him moving in?' he said, despite his brother's obvious irritation. 'Did you say next week? I'm afraid I wasn't paying proper attention.'

'Yes. A week today,' agreed Helen, rather awkwardly, conscious of Charles's disapproval. 'Are you planning to contact him?'

'Well, I was hoping you might tell him where I am,' remarked Vincent, raising his eyebrows appealingly. 'I'd hate to intrude if he's coming down here to get away from it all. But you could give him this number, if you would.'

'Helen's not a messenger girl,' put in Charles shortly, and Vincent rose abruptly to his feet.

'Nor is she a dummy, dummy,' he retorted harshly, and Mrs Connaught stepped between them before something drastic took place.

'Really, you two!' she protested, trying to strike a lighter note. 'You can't be together five minutes without squabbling! I'm sure Helen will be only too pleased to let Mr Manning know that you were enquiring after him, Vincent, and as for you Charles—I think you could try and be a little more forgiving. Good heavens, your brother has hardly been in the house more than twelve hours!'

An uneasy truce ensued, but Helen knew better than to mention Jarret Manning again, although as Charles escorted her to her car he had something else to say.

'You know,' he said, after helping her behind the wheel of the sleek little Alfasud, 'your mother could change her mind about letting Manning stay in the house. After all, as you said yourself, it's only a trial period. Would you like me to have a word with her? I really can't believe she really wants her life disrupting in this way.'

Helen grimaced. 'You don't know Mummy,' she observed dryly, putting the little car into gear. 'She's almost looking forward to it. It's years since she's been so well off, and what with the wedding and everything...'

'*Our* wedding,' echoed Charles, with some satisfaction. 'But you know, my father is quite willing to shoulder that burden——'

'No chance,' retorted Helen ruefully, shaking her head. 'Mummy is far too independent for that.'

'Oh, well...' Charles straightened from bestowing a warm kiss on her cheek. 'Until this evening, then. You haven't forgotten we're dining with the Harveys?'

'No, I hadn't forgotten,' agreed Helen with a faint smile. 'See you later.' And letting out the clutch, she allowed the car to move smoothly away.

During the short journey to Thrushfold, however, her thoughts returned to the unhappy chance of Vincent's knowing Jarret Manning. Until then she had not known that Jarret had once been a journalist, and it was disconcerting to realise that she had entirely misjudged his occupation. Her concept of Margot acting as some kind of female Svengali lost credence in the light of his obvious literary experience, and her own remarks about their association made her cringe. Still, there was no denying that Margot was involved with him, and remembering that awful scene before they departed, Helen did not look forward to seeing either of them again.

It was almost lunchtime as she drove between the stone gateposts and accelerated along the drive to the house. The beeches and sycamores were almost in full leaf, shielding the curve of the track, and concealing until the last moment the sleek green Ferrari parked near the porch. Its smooth lines were dusty, but there was no mistaking its elegance, and Helen remembered well the unwilling admiration she had felt watching Jarret and Margot drive away in such a vehicle. Now, however, it made her feel like turning round and driving back to Ketchley, but even as the thought entered her head, Jarret himself emerged from the porch and saw her.

There was nothing for it but to stand on her brakes, and bring the little Alfa to an abrupt halt alongside the Ferrari. Then, unclipping her safety belt, she thrust open her door and got out to face him, hoping she did not look as disconcerted as she felt.

'Good morning.' Using the tone she generally reserved for trying customers, she offered the greeting, and Jarret responded with a non-committal 'Hi.' As she extracted her bag from the car and pocketed her keys, however, she was conscious of him watching her, and in the same acid tone she added. 'We didn't expect to see you until next week, Mr Manning. Is Aunt Margot with you?'

Jarret hesitated a moment, his mouth taking on a vaguely sardonic twist, and then he shook his head. This morning he had shed the more formal attire of his previous visit for mud-coloured Levis and a matching denim shirt, and with the sleeves rolled back over his muscled forearms he looked hard and more dangerous, somehow. In spite of his declared need to get away from London, he was remarkably tanned for someone who lived in the city, she thought sourly, wondering whether Margot had accompanied him to whatever holiday location he had chosen. Obviously he did not neglect his creature comforts, and for some reason this irritated her still more.

She expected him to make some scathing retort to her challenge, but all he did was open the door of his car and emerge seconds later with his arms full of books. 'I decided to make a start on the removal,' he remarked, indicating his burden, 'and your mother has kindly invited me to lunch.'

Helen moved her shoulders in an offhand gesture. 'Oh,' she said blankly. 'Oh, I see.' And then pressed her lips together with the thought that her mother might have taken the trouble to ring the Connaughts and warn her.

Circling the two cars, she walked rather stiffly into the house, just as her mother was emerging from the library. 'I've cleared the last two drawers now, Jarret,' she was beginning enthusiastically, and then halted in surprise when she saw her daughter. 'Oh—Helen! I thought you said you were lunching in town.'

Helen's nails curled into her palms, and she pushed her hands aggressively into the unzipped pockets of her jacket. 'No, Mummy,' she said, clearly and succinctly. 'I said I was going to see Charles, not to the shop, and I told you I'd be back for lunch.'

'Dear me, did you?' Helen was half inclined to believe her mother was deliberately prevaricating. 'Oh, well ...' Mrs Chase smiled. 'There's no harm done, is there?'

Helen's expression repudiated this remark, but her mother was already moving beyond her, her features warming perceptibly as their unexpected guest made his reappearance. 'I've emptied those drawers, Jarret,' she heard her mother say again, and the unmistakable familiarity made Helen's blood boil. Had her mother forgotten she was coming home for lunch? Had she invited Jarret Manning to join her because she expected the meal *à deux*? It was upsetting and unsettling, and Helen experienced the unpleasant sensation of feeling an intruder in her own home.

Leaving her mother to fuss over the visitor, Helen abruptly mounted the stairs, and strode along the corridor to her room. Once there, she closed the door and leaned back against it, viewing the familiar appointments with something less than satisfaction. That man was trouble, she had known it the minute she saw him, and it was infuriating to think that he had won over her mother without any apparent effort.

She sighed heavily and leaving the door, moved slowly across the room to the windows. Hetherington was working in the garden below her, the slight stoop of his shoulders evidence of the rheumatism he suffered in cold weather. He had been at King's Green since before she was born, and it was another source of anxiety to her that in less than three months she would have given up the right to concern herself in the affairs of her home. Without her presence, her mother would be completely in the hands of the man presently making himself at home in the library, and she would have no say in the matter.

Unzipping her jacket, she tossed it on to the bed, and then viewed her reflection without pleasure. Unlike her mother, who was inclined to be plump, Helen was tall and slim, and the corded pants she wore complemented the slender curve of her legs. Her blouse, a collarless design in honey-beige silk, accentuated the creamy texture of her skin, and she had left several buttons unfastened to expose the hollow of her throat. Her hair as usual hung thick and straight, framing her face with an ebony curtain, the central parting adding a Madonna-like purity. Sombre, as she was now, her face had a haunting quality, but it was animation that brought a true beauty, and until the advent of Jarret Manning she had seldom looked as solemn as she did now.

Expelling her breath with an audible sound of frustration, she turned back to the door again, realising that the longer she spent skulking up here, the more familiar her mother and Jarret Manning were likely to become. Surely she had the breeding and determination to handle a man like him, and despite his outrageous behaviour, she must show him that she had treated the affair with the contempt it deserved.

The hall was empty when she came downstairs, and the outer door was closed. Obviously, Jarret had completed his unloading, and she hesitated at the bottom of the stairs, wondering where her mother might be. The library door was ajar, and hearing sounds from there, she stepped lightly towards it, hoping to detect its occupants unobserved. However, her booted feet were difficult to muffle, and Jarret swung the door wide as she faltered just outside.

'Can I help you?' he asked politely, his tone as cool as hers had been earlier, and she moved her shoulders in an awkward gesture.

'I—er—I was just looking for my mother,' she declared, trying to sound casual. 'I thought she might be helping you unpack.'

'No.' His denial was crisp. 'As you can see, I'm all alone in here. But if you're curious to see how I'm using your father's study, then feel free to come and investigate.'

Helen held up her head. 'I can assure you——'

'Oh, come on!' His mouth was derisive. 'I know what you were thinking.'

'Do you?' Helen's indignation simmered inside her. 'I don't see how that's possible, when——'

'For God's sake!' He dragged his fingers through the silvery strands of his hair, tugging them down to rest at his nape. 'Can't we stop this back-biting, here and now? I don't know what you think I am, but I'm here to work —nothing else! Believe it or not, I can get along without —female companionship!'

Helen felt the colour mounting in her cheeks. 'I think you misunderstand me, Mr Manning——' she was beginning, when he turned his back on her, and she broke off in mortified humiliation as he returned to the books he had previously been sorting.

There was little else she could do but turn away too, and this she did, pushing her trembling hands into the pockets of her pants as she walked quickly into the drawing room. Fortunately, her mother was not there either, and she had a few minutes to compose herself before Mrs Chase came to announce that lunch was ready.

During the meal her mother talked almost exclusively to Jarret, and Helen was left to pick at her plate without much appetite. It was unusual for her; she invariably enjoyed her food. But today, Mrs Chase was too absorbed with her visitor to notice. She was asking him about his work, about the methods he used to gain information, and the tremendous amount of research he must do before actually settling down to the story. Jarret spoke quietly and authoritatively, patiently answering her questions with a distinct absence of conceit. For someone who only minutes before had been deriding her daughter, he was remarkably amicable, and Helen decided, rather grumpily, that his remarks to her had been a personal affront and not a generalisation.

When Mrs Hetherington came to clear, Mrs Chase turned to their guest once again. 'What time are you leaving, Jarret?' she asked, the warmth of her enquiry denying any need for haste, and he pushed back his chair with a thoughtful frown.

'I guess I may as well leave right away,' he affirmed, granting the housekeeper the benefit of his smile before getting to his feet. 'I have things I can be doing in town, and I hope to bring down another load the day after tomorrow, if you have no objections.'

'None at all,' exclaimed Mrs Chase, rising to join him. 'But I wondered if you'd like to see the gardens while you're here, and get a little idea of the general layout.'

'That sounds fine,' Jarret agreed politely, but Helen sensed he was not entirely enthusiastic. Maybe he had made arrangements to meet someone in London, or perhaps his patience with her mother's garrulity was wearing thin. Whichever, it amused her to think his plans were being thwarted in this way, and she almost choked on her last mouthful of coffee when Mrs Chase continued:

'I'd have suggested it earlier if I'd remembered Helen would be joining us for lunch. You don't mind showing Mr Manning the garden, do you, dear? I'm afraid I have to attend a meeting of the church committee, Jarret. We're organising at fête next month, and there's always too much to do and too few helpers.'

Jarret's smile was tight now, but Mrs Chase didn't notice, bustling after Mrs Hetherington to arrange about dinner. Helen was left to face their guest, and she had little doubt about his feelings as she rose abruptly to her feet.

'Look, we can scrub round the conducted tour,' he declared harshly, picking up the denim jacket that matched his pants and pushing one arm into the sleeve. 'I don't really have the time anyway, and I'm sure you have better things to do.'

Helen shrugged. 'As you like.'

'It's not how *I* like, is it?' he emphasised shortly, as he shouldered the jacket. 'I didn't start this vendetta, *you* did, and I'd as soon not suffer the hassle.'

Helen pursed her lips. 'What shall I tell my mother, then?'

'What do you mean?' He eyed her narrowly. 'Surely you're not afraid of what *Mummy* might say?' Then he sighed heavily. 'So what the hell! I'll get out of here.'

Helen felt uncomfortable. It simply wasn't like her to be so uncharitable, and while she insisted she had reasons to feel resentment towards him, hadn't she really brought what had happened on herself?

He crossed the room to the open doors, and she knew that any minute it would be too late. Once he had spoken to her mother, once he had said his farewells, there would be no opportunity for her to change her mind, and half reluctantly she said: 'Mr Manning?' just as he stepped into the hall.

He turned, and she could tell from his expression that he regretted the delay. 'Yes?' he said, and his voice was as impatient as his stance as he waited for her to explain.

Helen took a few steps towards him and halted again. 'It's just—well, I'm quite willing to show you the gardens, if you'd really like to see them,' she explained awkwardly, and cringed anew as she waited for his response.

There was silence for several seconds, and then, propping his shoulder against the frame of the door, he said: 'That's a grudging proposal, isn't it?'

It was not what she had expected, and she shifted her weight from one booted foot to the other. 'I'm merely stating that—well, if we are going to live in the same house, we can't go on—sniping at one another.'

'*If?*' He took up the word, and then shook his head. 'Isn't that what I said earlier?'

Helen sniffed. 'Maybe.'

'It is, and you know it.' He straightened away from the

door. 'But don't lose any sleep over it. I shan't.'

Helen sighed. 'And?'

'I've got to get back to town.'

It was too much! 'You really are a—a—swine, aren't you?' she exclaimed stormily. 'You get me to offer to show you around, and then you deliberately turn me down! What do you expect me to do—grovel?'

'Hey ...' Amusement softened his dark features now, and a trace of mockery lifted the corners of his mouth. 'I didn't ask you to do anything. Your mother did. But if you're so desperate to show me, then by all means, let's go!'

Helen's chest rose and fell in her agitation. 'I—I—you can go to hell!' she retorted resentfully, and swung determinedly on her heel and marched back to the table.

'I really do bug you, don't I?'

Without her being aware of it, he must have covered the floor space between them, because when next he spoke his voice was right behind her. It was disconcerting to know he could move so swiftly, and she gripped the edge of the table with both hands, wishing desperately that he would go away. She felt distraught and raw, and absurdly vulnerable, and not at all convinced she could hide her feelings in the face of his deliberate mockery.

'Please—leave me alone,' she got out jerkily, and with a muffled oath he put one hand on her shoulder and swung her round to face him. It was useless to struggle, he was far stronger than she was, but she kept her head bent, and only lifted it when his hard fingers beneath her chin forced her to do so. He looked at her intently for several minutes, the long lashes narrowing his expression, and then, as if amazed, shook his head.

'I guess I have to apologise, don't I?' he said, his voice low and disturbingly gentle. 'I'm not used to polite society, and you're far too serious, do you know that?'

Helen pulled her chin away. 'I don't need your sympathy,' she retorted, refusing to respond to the olive branch. 'And—and now, if you'll excuse me——'

'But I don't,' he interrupted her firmly, and there was no mistaking his determination now. 'You're going to show me the gardens, and then I'm going to buy you tea at one of those quaint little cafés in Malverley.'

'No——'

Helen started to argue, but he put his hand over her mouth and the touch of those long brown fingers silenced any protest she was about to make.

It started to rain as they drove into Malverley, and Helen, still uncertain she was doing the right thing, felt it was an omen. It was useless telling herself that all was well. She had done that for the last two hours without any conviction, and in spite of the apparent amicability of their present relationship, she distrusted the association, and she distrusted Jarret.

Nevertheless, their tour of the grounds immediately surrounding King's Green had been conducted without incident. Jarret was suitably impressed with the gardens, that soon now would be a veritable kaleidoscope of colour, and he had endeared himself to Mrs Hetherington's husband by revealing an apparently genuine interest in the greenhouses.

'My stepfather is a keen gardener,' he told the old man pleasantly, as they examined the sprouting tomato plants, and confounded Helen by discussing the various problems encountered in tomato growing, with all the familiarity of an expert. He had an easy way of speaking to people that put them on an equal footing, and Helen, who had already seen her mother and Mrs Hetherington being won over, had to stand by and watch it happen again.

Jarret himself professed a love for the country, for the wide-open spaces, and the mingling scents of plants and flowers. He certainly seemed at home, tramping at her side through the buttercup-starred paddock, squatting down to examine some unusual specimen of insect life. He was not afraid to get his hands dirty, and the casual Levis were stained with mud when they walked back to the house.

They didn't talk a lot, except about impersonal things, like the house and grounds, and the little summerhouse where Helen used to play when she was small. But occasionally she felt his eyes on her in a deeply personal appraisal, and it was at times like these that she doubted her ability to handle a man like him. He was a little like Vincent, she reflected, loath to mention that particular relationship, but Vincent had never frightened her, and Jarret Manning did.

Jarret parked the Ferrari in the market place at Malverley, and then half turned in his seat towards her. 'So?' he said. 'Where's the best place to have tea? You'd know better than me.'

Helen shifted uncomfortably beneath the blue gaze and lifted her shoulders in an indifferent gesture. 'There's the Green Maple café, or the Embassy Tea-rooms. Or the local coffee bar, if you'd rather.'

'The Embassy Tea-rooms?' His eyes glinted with amusement. 'No, I don't honestly think that's me. I don't know about the Green Maple, but I do think the coffee bar sounds interesting.'

Helen didn't know whether he was serious or not, and her expression mirrored her uncertainty. 'I—well——' she began, then broke off abruptly as his hand came out to stroke his knuckles down her cheek.

'So solemn!' he mocked lazily, as she flinched away from his fingers. 'What kind of guy is this chap you're engaged to? Don't you ever have fun with him? Don't you ever laugh, or fool around?'

'I suppose you think I do that all the time,' she retorted woodenly, tilting her chin, and with a wry grimace he thrust open his door and got out before she could say any more.

Helen herself got out with less enthusiasm. Malverley was not a large place, it was just a small market town, and because of the shop she and Karen were comparatively well known. It occurred to her now that in spite of the weather she would be extremely lucky not to be observed, and a sense of frustration gripped her at the thought of having to explain to Charles what she had been doing, consorting with the enemy.

Jarret was looking round the market place with narrow-eyed interest, his collar turned up against the sudden shower, and she found herself acknowledging his undoubted physical attraction. Long muscular legs looked good in close-fitting jeans, and the shortness of his jacket exposed the flatness of his stomach and the powerful strength of his hips. Unlike Charles, who seldom wore anything but tweeds and evening clothes, he suited the casual attire, and she didn't need to see the admiring glances of two teenage girls across the street to know that he would never be short of female company. It was a whole new experience for her, being out with someone other than her fiancé, but when he pushed back his hair suddenly and turned to face her, she was embarrassed that he had caught her looking at him.

However, after a pregnant pause, he relieved the situation by asking where the coffee bar was, and she quickly stammered that it was just across the square. 'It's not far,' she added, turning up her own collar, and managed to remain composed as he gripped her elbow and hurried her across to its lighted façade.

The coffee bar was full of students from the nearby sixth form college, who congregated there after school was over. The air was thick with cigarette smoke and the steam from damp clothes, but it was a friendly atmosphere and Helen, who had never been inside before, looked about her with curious eyes.

'Tea—or coffee?' Jarret asked, having squeezed her on to a table in a corner and ready to serve himself, and Helen bit her lip. 'I'd go for the coffee, if I were you,' he added, seeing her indecision. 'The tea in these places is usually pretty sick.'

'All right.' Helen nodded, and with a reassuring grin, he turned away to the bar.

While he was gone, Helen half unzipped her jacket, and tried to appear unconcerned that so many eyes had turned in their direction. But it was difficult to remain casual when a group of teenage youths were obviously discussing her potential, and staring blatantly at her, even when she tried to outface them.

'I shouldn't bother,' remarked an amused voice near her ear, and she looked up to find Jarret straddling a chair he had tugged to the table. Two cups of espresso coffee resided on the table in front of him, and she quickly took possession of one of them, wrapping her fingers around the bowl to hide their unsteady tremor.

'That—er—that didn't take long,' she said, and he shook his head.

'Age and experience,' he observed lazily, and she looked down into her cup in polite acknowledgement.

To her relief, the boys who had been staring at her earlier seemed to have lost interest, now that Jarret had joined her, and she was able to sip her coffee with less self-consciousness. Even so, their eyes had been replaced by Jarret's, and she had to steel herself not to turn away.

'So what is there to do in a place like this?' he enquired now, forcing her to attend him, and she traced the pattern of the table top with her fingernail as she answered.

'Not a lot,' she admitted slowly. 'There's one cinema, and a theatre that operates during the winter months. Oh, and there's the art gallery and the museum, and a skating rink ...'

'But no night life?'

'I—I think there are discotheques,' she said, frowning.

'But you've never been.'

'Not to a discotheque, no.' Helen shook her head. 'But I have been to parties where they've played disco music,' she added hastily, feeling a ridiculous compulsion to justify herself, and saw the mocking gleam in his eye. 'Malverley's not like London,' she finished huffily. 'If you want night clubs and bars and sophisticated entertainment, Malverley's not the place for you.'

'Did I say I did?' His eyes narrowed with lazy humour, and she conceded that he had not. 'No, I was interested, that's all.' He paused. 'Interested in how you come to be so —inexperienced.'

'Inexperienced!' Helen was indignant.

'Yes, inexperienced,' he repeated firmly. 'Untouched by human hand!'

Helen was affronted. 'I think you're insolent, Mr Manning,' she declared hotly, preparing to push back her chair, but the firm grip of his fingers on her arm prevented her from rising.

'Why?' he said now, holding her eyes with his. 'Why am I insolent? It's a compliment, isn't it, knowing I acknowleged your—innocence?'

'Not the way you say it, Mr Manning,' she retorted unevenly. 'Will you let go of my arm?'

'Not unless you promise to remain where you are,' he countered smoothly, and she seethed with indignation.

'What makes you think I'll do it even if I say I will?' she demanded, and his mouth twisted wryly.

'Because I don't think you'd lie to me,' he replied, releasing her wrist, and she rubbed the flesh defensively as she strove for control.

'You have no right to say such things—to me,' she got out now, pushing her scarcely-touched coffee cup aside. 'If you don't mind, I'd like to go home. Will you take me, or shall I call a cab?'

Jarret sighed, a deep frustrated expellation of his breath. 'I'll take you,' he said, pulling out his cheroots. 'But can I finish my coffee first?'

Helen shrugged, but she was loath to make a fool of herself by walking out on him now that the first flush of anger had cooled, so she remained where she was, hands clasped in her lap, inhaling the pungent fragrance of his tobacco.

'Did I understand your mother correctly,' he asked suddenly, 'you run a shop here in Malverley?'

Helen hesitated, and then she nodded, saying briefly: 'Another girl and I share the running of it.'

'I see.' He looked at her through the haze of blue smoke. 'Somehow I imagined you as a lady of leisure.'

'Doing good works and visiting the poor?' she countered shortly, angered by his assumption, and saw the teasing grin that crossed his face.

'Now that was much more human,' he assured her approvingly, and she pressed her lips together as she stared down at the table. 'So where is this shop?' he pursued, refusing to be daunted, and she lifted her head reluctantly to meet his probing smile.

'Why should I tell you?' she demanded. 'You'll find out soon enough if you live here.'

'If that's so, what harm is there in telling me?'

Helen sighed. 'It's a craft shop. In the Arcade.'

'Which is where?'

'Across the square.'

He inclined his head. 'Who is the other partner?'

'A friend of mine, Karen Medley-Smythe.'

Jarret grinned. '*Miss* Medley-Smythe?'

'Yes.'

He inclined his head. 'Interesting.'

'Why?' Helen had had enough of being reticent. 'Of what possible interest is it to you?'

Jarret shrugged. 'Oh, just getting to know my way around. You know—making friends and influencing people!'

Helen turned her head irritably to stare out of the window. The discouraging trickle of rain all but obscured her view, and she felt a curious sense of depression, out of all proportion to the circumstances. What was the matter with her, letting Jarret Manning get under her skin? He was deliberately trying to provoke her, and she ought to know better than to listen to him.

'Okay—let's go!'

Jarret's summons brought her head round with a start to find him already on his feet. Zipping up her jacket again, she brushed past him on her way to the door, and felt the momentary strength of his body against hers. It was all too reminiscent of that day in the library, when he had shown her exactly how unscrupulous he could be, and the darting look she cast up at his face did nothing to dispel the image. It was as if he knew exactly what she was thinking and was enjoying her discomfiture, and the anger this generated sent her barging across the room with a distinct disregard for anyone else's safety.

'That was well done,' Jarret remarked gravely, as he closed the door behind them, but Helen pretended she didn't know what he was talking about. 'At least three booted ankles and half a dozen bruised ribs, not to mention flooding the place with overturned cups of coffee,' he added. 'Yes, I think I can safely say that you'll be welcome there again.'

At this Helen's sense of humour refused to respond to the dictates of her conscience. She found it impossible to keep her face straight, and a bubble of mirth burst from her in choking laughter. She couldn't help it. It was as if all the tension of the past half hour had been exploded by his words, and she pressed both hands to her cheeks in helpless abandon.

'Did I say something?'

Jarret viewed her innocently, but she couldn't answer him. Instead she shook her head weakly, too breathless to reply, and it was several more minutes before her hilarity subsided. Then, wiping her eyes with her fingers, she was once more aware of the rain, and also of how wet they were both getting, standing there in the downpour.

'You're getting soaked!' she protested, sniffing to clear her nose, and he shoved his hands into the pockets of his jacket.

'So are you,' he countered, and she put up a hand to her damp hair before nodding her agreement. 'Come on,' he said, 'I think we'd better get into the car. I'd hate to be responsible for you catching your death of pneumonia!'

'I'm much tougher than I look,' she explained, as they half ran across the square to where the Ferrari waited, but the glance he gave her was disbelieving.

'Are you?' he said, unlocking the car door, and she recognised the scepticism in his tone as she slid inside.

Seconds later he joined her in the car, breathing deeply from the exertion. With the door closed behind him, he shouldered his way out of his jacket, dropping it on to the low rear seat, and then looked expectantly at her.

'Aren't you going to do the same?' he suggested, and although her hostility towards him was only temporarily suspended, she obediently unzipped the jerkin and pushed it off her shoulders. But it wasn't so easy for her to remove, and without asking her permission Jarret tugged the offending garment down over her arms, making the task that much simpler.

'Thank you.' Helen pulled her arms free and folded the jacket in her lap. 'At least it's warm in here. What lovely spring weather!'

Jarret took the jacket from her unresisting fingers. 'A farmer would doubtless say that the crops need it,' he remarked reprovingly, dropping the jacket into the back with his own. 'And you—a country girl—should know that.'

'I do——' she began, and then stopped again as she realised she was taking him too seriously. 'Oh, well, I don't have to like the rain, do I? And judging by your tan, you don't spend your holidays in this country either!'

Jarret grimaced. 'My tan, as you call it, was acquired almost a year ago, in Mexico. And it wasn't a holiday. I was doing some research at the time, and it was bloody hot for working, I can tell you.'

Helen managed not to flinch at his choice of adjective, and looped her fingers round one drawn-up knee. 'Mexico,' she said. 'That sounds exciting. How long did you spend there?'

'Three months.' Jarret shrugged. 'It was—interesting. But you wouldn't have liked it.'

'Why not?'

A trickle of rainwater began to run down her cheek from her hair, and to her confusion, Jarret wiped the drop away with his finger before answering her. 'Oh—it was all involved with the seedier side of the Mexican dream,' he remarked, smoothing his palm down over his thigh. 'You wouldn't want to hear about it. It's far removed from Malverley and the—er—Embassy Tea-rooms.'

'You're mocking me again!' she exclaimed, releasing her knee and straightening her spine, and his gaze drooped to the vulnerable curve of her mouth.

'No, I'm not,' he said, and his voice was curiously gentle. 'Only drug smugglers and traffickers seem a long way from garden fêtes and afternoon tea.'

'I'm not naïve, you know,' she retorted. 'I am aware of what goes on in the rest of the world. Just because we seem very middle-class and boring to you, it doesn't mean we bury our heads in the sand!'

'You don't seem at all boring to me,' he assured her huskily, and her skin prickled as he put his arm over the back of the seat. But all he did was lift his jacket and extract the case of cheroots from the pocket, and she clasped her hands tightly together as he lit his cigar.

With the cheroot between his teeth he started the engine and the Ferrari circled the market square before turning on to the road to Thrushfold once more. The rain was easing a little and the wipers kept the windscreen clear, but nevertheless Jarret covered the distance without excessive speed, content to let the powerful pistons dawdle.

'Where do you plan to live after you're married?' he asked unexpectedly, and Helen hesitated a moment before replying.

'Charles is buying a house at Ketchley, not far from his parents' home,' she yielded at length. 'It wouldn't be sensible to live too far from the stables, and I can easily drive into Malverley from there.'

Jarret crushed the remains of his cheroot in an ashtray. 'Do I take it you intend to go on working after you're married?'

'Initially,' she agreed, not altogether liking his questions. 'Surely you don't disapprove, Mr Manning. Isn't that the modern way of thinking?'

'Maybe.' He was non-committal. 'You're not afraid you may find circumstances altering your plans?'

Helen held up her head. 'If you mean am I not concerned that I might start a baby, then no. Charles and I both agree that we can afford to wait a few years, and—and—er—well, I intend to cope with that contingency when the situation requires it.'

A faint smile touched Jarret's lips at this, and she guessed he was amused at her rather stilted explanation, but talking about such things to a stranger was not something she was used to, and taking a leaf out of his book, she asked him how long it would take to drive back to London.

Jarret shrugged then. 'It depends how congested the roads are,' he replied. 'It should take a couple of hours, but I can spend that length of time trying to cross central London.' He paused. 'Do you ever come up to town?'

'Sometimes.' Helen was defensive. 'Mummy and I occasionally go up for a day's shopping, and before Charles and I were engaged I used to go to shows and exhibitions with Karen.'

'Mmm.' Jarret sounded unimpressed. 'But not with Charles, I gather.'

'Charles doesn't like London, Mr Manning.' Helen could feel her resentment reasserting itself. 'Not everyone does!'

'Oh, I agree.' Jarret raised one hand in mock apology. 'I was just satisfying myself about something.'

'About what?'

He glanced sideways at her. 'The kind of relationship you have with your fiancé.'

'The kind of relationship ...' Helen's voice trailed away. 'I'm afraid I don't understand.'

'It's not important.' He peered through the windscreen. 'This is the turn-off for King's Green, isn't it?'

'What? Oh, yes, yes.' Helen was impatient. 'Are you trying to be offensive, Mr Manning?'

'Offensive? Me?'

'Yes, you.' She licked her suddenly dry lips. 'What did you mean about my relationship with Charles? I want to know.'

Jarret sighed. 'Forget it. I don't even know the man!' He turned between the drive gates. 'At least the rain seems to be passing over. What's the betting I'll run into it again on my way back to town?'

'*Jarret!*'

In her confusion, she had used his Christian name without thinking, and his mocking expression revealed it had not gone unnoticed. 'Yes, Helen?' he responded, quite solemnly, and with a sound of frustration she slumped down in her seat.

'You enjoy aggravating me, don't you?' she exclaimed angrily. 'Why can't you answer my question? I've answered yours.'

Jarret brought the car to a smooth halt before the porch, and as she struggled to sit up he said: 'You wouldn't like my answer. Is that good enough for you?'

'No!' She reached for her jacket from the back seat, and tugged it on to her knees, straightening the sleeves and keeping the damp outer surface away from her. 'I'm not a child, Mr Manning. But keep your secrets, if they mean that much to you.'

'They don't.' His tone was flat now, and as she reached for the handle of the door he pressed a button that successfully prevented her from opening it. 'All right, *Miss* Chase —I was curious what kind of man would let you wear his ring without taking advantage of the facilities it affords him!'

Helen's dark brows drew together. 'The facilities ...' she

echoed faintly, and then comprehension dawned. 'You mean——'

'I mean—you don't sleep with him, do you, Helen?' he stated decisively, his eyes narrowing as hers widened. 'And that's a terrible waste!'

Helen could hardly speak. 'How—how dare you?'

'You asked me,' he reminded her mildly, and releasing the catch on the doors, he pushed his open and got out.

It was several seconds before Helen summoned the assurance to join him, and by then he had put on his jacket and disappeared into the house. She found him in the hall, tossing his keys impatiently in his palm, and at her look of outraged bewilderment he explained: 'Your mother's given me a key. And as she doesn't appear to be home, perhaps you'd offer her my apologies, and tell her I'll see her on Friday.'

'You're leaving?' she enquired coldly, and with a sigh of resignation he nodded.

'Look,' he said, as if feeling the need to justify himself, 'don't blame me because you didn't like what I said. I warned you you wouldn't, remember?'

Helen balled her fists. 'You—you had no right to—to speculate about— about such a thing ...'

'Oh, come on.' He shook his head. 'It happens all the time. Surely I'm entitled to an opinion!' He stepped in front of her and looked down at her with disturbing candour. 'I said it was a waste, and it is. You're beautiful, Helen, and if Charles can't see that, then he's more of a fool than I thought. I wouldn't let you run around without putting my brand upon you, and any man who does is just asking for trouble.'

Helen took a deep breath. 'Just—just because you have a distinct lack of morality, you judge everyone else by your own standards. I—I—Charles and I, we have a very good relationship, as it happens. He's a fine man, and I love him dearly—*oh*!'

She broke off abruptly, her words silenced once again by the warm possession of his mouth. As before, he had taken her unawares, but this time there was no anger in his kiss, only a sensuous, searching need for expression, and her knees buckled beneath its probing caress. She clutched at him helplessly, her hands finding the rough buckle of his belt, and his hands slid down her back to her hips, arching her towards him. Her lips parted, responding to the hunger he evoked inside her. His arms enfolded her closely against him, her breasts were crushed against the hard muscles of his chest, but through the mists of mindless emotion she was gradually made to feel the unmistakable effect she was having on him.

Her mind revolted, and with a superhuman effort she pressed him away from her. 'Let me go!' she choked, despising herself, and despising him for making her feel that way, and with a shrug he stepped back. He made no attempt to hide his arousal, running one hand round the back of his neck in faintly rueful self-derision, and she averted her eyes from the sensual reflection of his. He was completely without shame, she thought, mortified by her own behaviour, and furious with him for taking advantage of her.

'Will you please leave!' she got out at last, realising there was little point in crossing swords with him. He was not ashamed of what he had done, and she would have to bear her disgrace alone.

But Jarret shook his head now, aware of her feelings and impatient of them. 'Don't look so shattered!' he advised dryly, making no move to go. 'It wasn't so terrible, was it? It's quite normal, I do assure you, particularly in the circumstances.'

Helen knew she would live to regret it, but she had to ask: 'What circumstances?'

Jarret sighed. 'You're going to get married. You'll find out soon enough. Providing that hidebound boy-friend of yours doesn't make a mess of it.'

Helen gulped. 'Of what?'

'Of you!' exclaimed Jarret in a driven tone. 'God, don't you know anything? The way you kiss, I get the feeling you've never been aroused before, and God help you if he's as frigid as I think he is!'

Helen uttered a sound of outrage. 'Get out of here, Mr Manning! Get out, do you hear me?' She almost shouted the words in her distress, and then burned with embarrassment as her mother appeared in the doorway.

## CHAPTER FOUR

'DON'T you want to go home this evening?'

Karen Medley-Smythe's drawling voice was puzzled as she stood in the doorway to the small office that backed the showroom. The shop had been closed some fifteen minutes already, and as she herself had transferred the cash from the till to the safe, she could see no reason for her friend to be lingering over the accounts ledger.

'I'll be leaving presently,' Helen answered now, hoping the smile she forced to her lips would allay the other girl's suspicions. 'I just want to go over these figures again, and then I'll lock up. You go ahead. I don't mind.'

Karen caught her lower lip between her teeth. 'I haven't made another mistake in the ledger, have I?' she queried worriedly. 'I know my maths are appalling, but I did use the calculator.'

'Oh, no—no!' Helen was quick to reassure her. 'The figures are fine, honestly.'

'So why are you checking them?'

Helen sighed. 'Go home, Karen,' she urged, cupping her chin in one shapely hand. 'I'll see you tomorrow.'

But Karen refused to be moved without a more satisfactory explanation. 'Something's wrong, isn't it?' she exclaimed. 'Is it Charles? Have you two had a fight? Is that why you've looked a little strained since you took that day off?'

'No!' Helen gripped the edge of the desk tightly. 'No, of course not. Charles and I never fight. You're imagining things, Karen.'

'Am I?' The other girl sounded as sceptical as she looked. 'Well, something's amiss, and if it's not Charles, it must be Jarret Manning.'

'What do you mean?'

Helen could not have looked more indignant, but Karen was not convinced. Coming fully into the office, she draped her elegant length in the armchair opposite, and regarded her friend with provoking blue eyes. 'It is Jarret Manning, isn't it?' she persisted, pulling a pack of cigarettes from her bag and placing one between her lips. 'Of course! Today's the day he moves in, isn't it? That's why you don't want to go home.'

'You're letting your imagination run away with you, Karen,' retorted Helen crossly, getting up from the desk and pacing restlessly across the floor. 'It is the day Jarret Manning is moving into King's Green, I can't deny that, but as for thinking it has anything to do with my working late ...'

Karen lit her cigarette and inhaled deeply, watching her friend reflectively through the haze. She was an attractive girl, some three years older than Helen, and her blonde good looks had proved a distinctive foil for Helen's darker ones. She was unmarried, and since the death of her parents some five years ago had rented a flat near the centre of Malverley. She was well liked, and popular with the opposite sex, but for the past four years she had been hopelessly in love with a married man.

'So?' she said now. 'Tell me, if you're not avoiding Jarret Manning, what are you doing?'

'I've told you, I'm just going over the figures,' retorted Helen tautly. 'Honestly, Karen, must we have this inquest? I'm not questioning your book-keeping, I'm just checking the invoices.'

Karen grimaced. 'Really?'

'Yes, really.'

'Who are you kidding, Helen?' Karen tilted her head. 'What happened, darling? Did he make a pass at you?'

Helen's cheeks suffused with colour, and she crossed her arms deliberately across herself, as if they might provide a protection against whatever was to come. Then, realising she had to give some explanation, she said: 'I don't like the man. Is that enough for you? I can't imagine why Mummy agreed to let him share the house. It was bad enough when Aunt Margot came with him that first time, but last Friday he brought some American model, who spent the whole time pawing over him! He said he wanted to get away from it all, but it seems to me he just wants to move the location.'

'My, my, we are bitter, aren't we?' Karen exhaled smoke through amused lips. 'Was the model Vivien Sinclair? I read she was his latest girl-friend.'

Helen snorted. 'Where did you read that?'

'Where do you think? In the paper, of course, darling. Your Mr Manning is quite a scoop for the gossip columnists. They give him a hard time.'

'He probably deserves it,' replied Helen maliciously, dropping her arms and walking back to the desk. 'Anyway, now you know why I prefer to avoid him.'

'Do I?' Karen was annoyingly perceptive. 'I can't believe cool, collected Helen has been rattled by some empty-headed model!'

'She's not empty-headed, actually,' muttered Helen, resuming her seat. 'Mummy told me that Jarret had told her that she was a college graduate or something, and only took to modelling after winning some beauty contest.'

'Jarret?' queried Karen teasing, and Helen bent her head.

'All right,' she conceded heavily, 'he did—make a pass at me.' She lifted her head. 'Now will you go home?'

Karen frowned. 'Oh, Helen ...'

'What's the matter?'

The other girl shook her head, and then squashed out her cigarette with impatient fingers. 'You worry me sometimes, do you know that?' she retorted.

'I? Worry you?'

'Yes.' Karen looked at her squarely. 'You're so—vulnerable, somehow. So open to being hurt. Do you know, there are times when I wonder if you've ever known what it's like to feel deeply—about anything.'

Helen moved her shoulders awkwardly, a little hurt by the other girl's candour, and as if regretting her outburst, Karen forced a smile. 'Don't take any notice of me,' she said, putting her cigarettes back into her handbag. 'I'm no counsellor to give anyone advice. Goodness knows, I haven't organised my own life with any degree of success, have I?'

Helen sighed, resting her elbows on the desk and studying her friend sympathetically. 'How is John?' she asked, glad of the distraction, and Karen's eyes grew reflective as she spoke of the man she loved.

'He's fine,' she said, a reminiscent smile tugging at her lips. 'We spent the weekend at Stratford, and I can't remember enjoying Shakespeare so much before.' She shook her head. 'He's so crazy, Helen. We took a boat on the river at one o'clock in the morning, and made love in the shade of a clump of weeping willows!'

Helen's tongue circled her lips. 'I think you're the crazy one, Karen. What if—what if you got pregnant? What would you do then? You know he has four children already. And he's refused to get a divorce.'

Karen gave a resigned shrug. 'He can't get a divorce, Helen—his wife is a Catholic. And besides, how could he leave Audrey to bring up four children alone?'

Helen made a confused gesture. 'I don't understand you, Karen, I don't honestly. You say he can't leave his wife to bring up their children alone, and yet you're perfectly prepared to run the risk of putting yourself in the same position without the benefit of a wedding ring!'

'I take precautions,' Karen retorted patiently. 'And if you think John and I could stand the same kind of relationship you and Charles have, you're very much mistaken.'

Helen shifted uncomfortably. 'My relationship with Charles has nothing to do with it.'

'Doesn't it?' Karen looked disbelieving. 'I sometimes wonder what you're saving yourselves for!'

Helen was not offended, but she had to defend herself. 'Charles and I both believe that a honeymoon should be just that!' she declared. 'What's the point of getting married at all, if you've already anticipated the wedding night?'

'Oh, Helen! What a lot you have to learn!'

Helen sifted the papers on the desk with a careless hand. 'Why is it that people always think that they know best?'

Karen sighed. 'What if you're incompatible?'

'Incompatible?' Helen managed to sound almost amused. 'What do you mean—incompatible? We love one another.'

'Oh, I'm sure you do, but loving one another and actually sharing love can be two very different things.'

Helen made an irritated gesture. 'And of course, you know all about that.'

'John wasn't the first man I went to bed with,' stated

Karen frankly. 'But he's the only man I've ever *wanted*.'

'Want! Want! What has wanting to do with love? What you're talking about is lust!'

'No, I'm not.' Karen leaned towards her. 'Helen, listen to me, are you sure you and Charles——'

With an abrupt movement Helen got to her feet. 'You've convinced me!' she declared, cutting the other girl off before she could say any more, and Karen stared at her blankly.

'Convinced you?'

'Yes. That I'm a fool to hang about here, just because Jarret Manning has invaded my home! Why should I care what he does? I'll be leaving in less than three months. Mummy can have him all to herself.'

Karen shrugged and relaxed again. 'Jealous?'

Helen gasped. 'Of Mummy?'

'No. Of Jarret Manning,' retorted Karen dryly. 'You've been the apple of Mummy's eye for the past ten years, haven't you?'

Driving home, Helen remembered Karen's words with a sense of irony. If she only knew, she thought grimly. She and her mother had shared an uneasy truce since that scene in the hall, and the memory of her mother's words to her after Jarret had left still stung in her mind. Mrs Chase knew nothing about what Jarret had done to her, of course. All she had seen was another example of what she saw as her daughter's discourtesy, and she had lost no time in making her conversant with her present financial position.

'Without Jarret's generosity, I might well have had to accept the Connaughts' offer to assume responsibility for the wedding. Now I shan't have that anxiety, and as you're the one who is going to benefit, the least you can do is to be civil to the man!'

There had been other words about her lack of gratitude for what her mother had done for her, of how selfish she had become, and how little she considered anyone's feelings but her own, and Helen had not argued. She had been too stunned to produce any defensible alternative anyway, and it had been easier to hide her real feelings.

Jarret's second visit had been shorter, but no less memorable for all that. Instead of coming in the morning as he had done before, he had arrived in the early evening, just after Helen had succeeded in convincing herself that he was not going to come at all. And Vivien Sinclair was with him.

Mrs Chase had been relieved to see him, of course. Like her daughter, she had begun to have doubts about his future intentions, and had even voiced a terse rebuke to the effect that if he had changed his mind, Helen ought to be ashamed of herself.

In the event, it appeared that Vivien had had a modelling assignment earlier in the day, and as Jarret had promised to bring her with him, he had had to delay his departure. The American had proved to be a friendly girl, but Helen had kept out of their way as much as possible. To her relief, her mother agreed to show Vivien over the house, and it was only when they came into the drawing room for a drink before leaving that Helen had had to face them. Even then, Vivien had done most of the talking, curled beside Jarret on the sofa, her scarlet-tipped fingers continually straying over his shoulder or his knee, letting them know in no uncertain manner exactly what their relationship entailed.

Helen drank her sherry, and joined in the conversation only when spoken to, and as Vivien addressed most of her remarks to Mrs Chase, that was not often. Jarret, likewise, had little to say for himself, but his smile was lazily indulgent when it rested on his companion, which seemed to satisfy her. Helen thought he looked tired, when her eyes strayed irresistibly in his direction. He lounged on the comfortable sofa, his head resting against the dark green velvet upholstery, long legs splayed indolently across the carpet, and while she suspected he was no less harmless than a sleeping tiger, he was obviously prepared to let Vivien take the initiative. They had left without his having said more than two words to her, and only the knowing mockery in his eyes signified his awareness of the control she was exerting.

Remembering this now as she turned between the drive gates, Helen's fingers tightened on the wheel. She couldn't help wondering if he intended continuing his relationship with Vivien at King's Green, whether he expected them to accommodate her when she chose to pay him a visit. The prospect was irritating enough, without the inevitable suppositions it engendered, and she prayed the next three months would soon pass.

The green Ferrari was not at the door and briefly her heart lifted, but then she saw it parked under the archway at the side of the house. It was in the entry to the yard and stable block, and she guessed her mother had allocated him one of the empty garages. These days only her Alfa and her mother's Triumph occupied the buildings which had once accommodated half a dozen traps and carriages.

However, the Ferrari did block her way most successfully, and she was obliged to park her car beside the porch. Walking into the house, she was convinced that even the atmosphere was different, and finding Jarret flicking through the telephone directory in the hall seemed the last straw.

Realising the best method of defence was attack, she took a stand. 'Your vehicle is blocking the entry,' she announced, as her arrival caused him to glance round, and his expression darkened ominously.

'Move it, then,' he advised, thrusting his hand into the pocket of his black cords and bringing out his keys. 'Here!' He tossed them towards her. 'Make yourself useful.'

An automatic reflex made her catch the keys, and she stared at them disbelievingly for a moment before saying helplessly: 'I can't drive your car.'

'Why not?' He had resumed his examination of the directory. 'You've passed your test, haven't you?'

'Well, yes—but——' She sighed frustratedly. 'You know I can't do it.'

Jarret looked up again. 'Scared?'

Helen squared her shoulders. 'Of damaging it—yes, I am.'

Jarret shook his head. 'I'll take the responsibility for that. Go ahead. It's quite easy really.'

Helen stood, undecided, the weapon of defence having been taken out of her hands once again. Then, realising that if she refused she would appear foolish or childish or both, she turned about and went out.

The Ferrari was not locked, and still with some misgivings she opened the door and got in. Despite her height, her feet did not even touch the pedals, and she took several minutes to adjust the seat. Then, satisfied with its position, she inserted the key in the ignition.

The engine fired at the first attempt, and she felt a thrill of excitement coursing through her at the thought of the power under her hands. Holding the wheel as if it was likely to be wrested from her fingers, she inched the car forward, finding its smoothness of acceleration easy to control. It was like taking hold of a wild-cat and finding only a purring kitten, and encouraged to experiment, she allowed it a little more freedom. It was a mistake. Like any caged creature, it yearned for escape, and her brief indulgence almost ended in disaster as the Ferrari accelerated towards the stable wall. She found the brakes just in time, but even after the vehicle had stopped, she found she was still shaking.

Then, lifting her head, she saw Jarret's reflection in the rear-view mirror, leaning against the arched entry. He seemed to be half doubled over, and for an awful moment she thought she had hit him, although how she might have done so, she couldn't imagine. But suddenly she realised he was laughing, almost doubled up with laughter in fact, and her trembling reaction gave way to angry indignation.

Thrusting open the door, she got out and stormed towards him. 'I suppose you'd have found it hysterical if I'd buried myself in the wall!' she burst out furiously, but he shook his head, suppressing the mirth that had gripped him.

'What?' he said, in mild reproof. 'And smashed up almost thirty thousand pounds' worth of machinery!' and a cry of impotence broke from her. 'No,' he went on soberly, 'I admit, I did have a few bad moments while you were practising your emergency stop, but I could tell you had everything under control.'

She stared at him then, anger and prejudice, and half tearful indignation warring in her expression. Was he serious? No, of course he wasn't. He was making fun of her again, but suddenly the humour of the situation was too much for her. It was no use. She wanted to remain serious, she wanted to be angry with him for laughing at her, but the image of the Ferrari racing madly for the wall with herself panicking desperately inside it, trying to find the brakes, was just too much to ignore. And as before, she found herself giggling helplessly, allowing all the tense nervous reaction to evaporate.

'Are you all right?' Jarret said at last, as she struggled to achieve some semblance of sobriety, and she nodded vigorously.

'I'm sorry,' she said, wiping her eyes with the tips of her fingers. 'It's really not at all funny.'

'Isn't it?' He regarded her with wry amusement. 'I could have sworn you found it so.'

'Well, I did—that is, you made me laugh!' she accused, pulling a face at him. 'Is the car all right? I didn't do any damage, did I? I don't think I did.'

Jarret strolled towards the vehicle, extracted the keys, and closed the door she had left open in her fury. Then he came back to where she was waiting, shaking his head at her anxious expression.

'Come on,' he said. 'It's okay there for tonight. It's not blocking anyone's entry, is it?'

Helen shook her head, feeling slightly chastened by his remark, and they walked back to the house in silence. All the same, she was intensely conscious of him beside her, and the conflicting emotions he aroused made her feel keyed-up and restless. In the hall again, Jarret returned to his study of the telephone directory, but Helen stood irresolute for a moment, not at all decided what to do. She guessed her mother would be in the kitchen, helping Mrs Hetherington organise dinner, but she didn't really feel like going in search of her. Instead, she went upstairs to her room, aware that the incident outside had shown her how difficult it was going to be for her to remain indifferent to Jarret, and feeling distinctly dissatisfied with herself and with life in general.

Fortunately she was going out for dinner, and a long soak in the bath and a change of clothes restored her equilibrium. Charles was calling for her at seven o'clock, and she spent a satisfying length of time applying a delicate make-up, and choosing what she was going to wear.

She eventually decided on a calf-length dress of dark red velvet, its low round neckline complimented by elbow-length puffed sleeves. It's lines were stark and dramatic, accentuating her dark beauty, and the simple gold chain she wore around her throat was all the jewellery she needed. That and her diamond engagement ring, of course.

She heard Charles's car arrive as she was fastening the chain about her neck, and a feeling of anxious apprehension forced her to sink down on to the side of her bed for a minute, to restore her ruffled composure. She knew Charles was hoping to meet Jarret this evening, so that he could compare his reactions with hers, but somehow the prospect of being present at their meeting was something she would rather avoid. She still had not mentioned Vincent's identity to Jarret, and while she doubted Charles would say anything, there was always the chance that Jarret himself might connect the names. It was fully another five minutes before she descended the stairs, and then it was her mother she encountered first in the hall below.

'So there you are!' Mrs Chase's tone was the cool one she had adopted of late. 'Charles is here and waiting for you. I was just about to come and find you.'

'I'm sorry.' Helen was polite, and her mother sighed.

'You might have let me know when you got back,' she added. 'You were late, weren't you? It was after six when I heard the car.'

Helen nodded. 'I had some book-keeping to do after the shop was closed,' she explained, reluctant to dissemble but unable to avoid it. 'I—er—I expect Mr Manning told you I was home.'

'Yes, he did, when I asked him. But I'd prefer not to have to ask about your whereabouts in future.'

'Sorry.' Helen said the word again, and with an impatient wave of her arm her mother disappeared in the direction of the kitchen.

Charles was alone in the drawing room, pacing short-temperedly before the hearth, obviously annoyed that she had not been there to greet him. Helen, who had expected Jarret to be with him, felt a little put out herself, and her fiancé's first words did not improve the situation.

'I thought we agreed on seven o'clock!' he remarked,

making no effort to return the tentative kiss she bestowed on his cheek. 'It's now nine minutes past the hour, which gives us precisely twenty-one minutes to get to the Arrowsmiths'.'

Helen stifled her protest, not wanting to argue with him, and said with assumed lightness: 'I doubt if the Arrowsmiths will turn us away if we arrive at a quarter to eight, Charles. Seven-thirty is just a guideline.'

'Nevertheless,' Charles fingered his bow tie, 'I expect punctuality from other people. The least I can do is try to return it.'

'Oh, don't be so pompous!' Helen made the retort without really thinking, and instantly regretted it. 'I'm sorry, darling, but it's not that important, surely. Besides,' she glanced behind her apprehensively, 'I thought you wanted to meet—Jarret Manning.'

'I did. I do.' Charles lifted his chin, as if his collar was too tight. 'Only as you can see, the fellow isn't around.'

'I expect he's in the library,' said Helen doubtfully, half wishing Jarret would appear, but he didn't, and with her mother's reappearance, Charles said that they were leaving.

In the hall, however, as her fiancé was helping her on with the lambswool jacket she sometimes wore in the evenings, the library door opened, and Jarret stood looking at them. He hadn't changed. He was still wearing the black cords and matching waistcoat he had been wearing earlier, the sleeves of his dark blue open-necked shirt turned back over his forearms.

'Oh, I'm sorry,' he said politely, his smile encompassing all of them, even her mother who was hovering in the background. 'Are you just leaving?'

Helen knew it was up to her to perform the introductions, and this she did, watching the reactions of both men with interest, unwillingly aware that despite her fiancé's more formal attire, Jarret seemed the most self-assured.

'Manning.' Charles's greeting was the usual one to someone he considered inferior to himself. 'Settled in, have you? You'll find this a very pleasant place to work, I'm sure.'

Jarret's eyes had a sardonic gleam and Helen herself

cringed for Charles's patronising tone. 'I'm sure I shall, Connaught,' he responded amiably enough. 'Particularly when everyone is so friendly. One gets the feeling one is really welcome.'

'Oh, yes, well——' Charles was not quite sure how to take this. 'Grand part of the world to be in. Travelled a bit, you know, but I'm always glad to be home again.'

'I'm sure you are.'

Somehow Jarret had succeeded in putting Charles on the defensive now, and Helen was amazed at the transition. 'Anyway, we have to be going,' he asserted, urging Helen towards the door. 'Very nice to meet you, Manning. You must come over for a drink one evening—Helen will show you the way. I know my brother will be pleased to see you again. I expect Helen told you he's home for a couple of weeks.'

Helen went crimson with embarrassment and Jarret's eyes seeking hers in frowning interrogation did nothing to assist her. 'Your brother?' he echoed, and Charles nodded.

'Vincent. Vincent Connaught,' he said, and Jarret's brows ascended.

'Vince Connaught is your brother?' he exclaimed, shaking his head disbelievingly. 'Well, what do you know!'

'Helen!' Charles turned to her now, as if her omission meant something to him. 'Helen, didn't you give Mr Manning Vincent's message? He was saying only the other day that he'd heard nothing from you.'

Helen licked her lips. 'I forgot,' she said, and despite Jarret's challenging look, she refused to admit otherwise. 'I—er—Mr Manning only arrived today, Charles. I—I haven't had time.'

'You didn't tell me Vincent was home either,' her mother put in at this point. 'How is he, Charles? Wasn't he out in the Far East, the last time I was speaking to your mother?'

'He was.' Charles explained the situation, and Helen averted her eyes from the impatient accusation in Jarret's. Any minute, she expected to hear him ask why she hadn't mentioned it that afternoon they had spent together, but instead he remained silent, only the brooding slant of his mouth an indication of censure to come.

To her relief, Charles's explanation was brief, and a few minutes later they had said their farewells, and he was helping her into the Range Rover. Then, circling the vehicle, he joined her, putting the Rover into gear and starting down the drive before he spoke.

'That was rather thoughtless, wasn't it?'

The accusation should have come from Jarret, and either way, Helen was in no mood to respond lightly to it. 'What was thoughtless, Charles?' she enquired now, deliberately prevaricating, and he cast a reprimanding look in her direction.

'Not telling Manning that Vincent would like to get in touch with him.'

'I didn't know you were so concerned about Vincent, or his friends,' retorted Helen tightly. 'And as I pointed out inside, the man only moved in today.'

'But didn't you say he'd already made a couple of visits, to bring down his books and personal belongings?' countered Charles, turning on to the Malverley road. 'Couldn't you have told him then? You mentioned something about showing him over the grounds.'

'Does it matter?' Helen was fast losing patience. 'Honestly, if I'd known it meant that much to you, I'd have made a special point of informing him.'

Charles sighed at this, and made a conciliatory gesture. 'Of course, it's not that important,' he conceded now. 'And perhaps you were right not to mention it. After all, we don't want the fellow arriving at Ketchley at all hours of the day and night.'

'I doubt that's likely,' remarked Helen dryly. 'And in any case, you have invited him.'

'Only for a drink,' her fiancé protested. 'And I could hardly avoid that.'

Helen shrugged. 'Oh well, let's talk about something else.'

Charles frowned. 'I can't understand your attitude, Helen. The man seems civil enough.'

'Civil!' Helen was scornful. 'Didn't you think he was rather insolent?'

'Insolent?' Charles considered this. 'No. No, I can't say I thought he was insolent. A little conceited perhaps, but that's to be expected, I suppose.'

Helen turned to stare out of the window. In all honesty, she knew that Jarret was not conceited. Many things he might be, but believing his own publicity was not one of them, and for a man with such literary charisma he was amazingly unassuming about his work. However, to admit this to Charles would promote exactly the kind of discussion she most wanted to avoid, and deciding enough had been said on the subject, she began asking Charles about his horses. He was easily diverted. They were the great love of his life, and listening to him expounding the merits of one and another of them, she wondered if she would ever get to care about them as he did. It seemed unlikely, but then he had no interest in the shop, and the working aspects of their life together were entirely apart from their personal relationship. All the same, she couldn't help wishing she was not so timid, and that Charles showed a little more pride in her business acumen.

## CHAPTER FIVE

IT was a little after eleven when she arrived home, and throughout the journey she had been planning how she could avoid a possible confrontation with Jarret. She was sure he would be waiting up for her, ready to do battle over why she had chosen to withhold Vincent's message, and while there was a certain masochistic satisfaction in anticipating his anger, common sense warned her of the dangers of challenging a man like him.

Consequently, she invited Charles in for a cup of coffee, only to discover she had wasted her time. Her mother was alone in the drawing room, engrossed in the gruesome outcome of a late-night movie on television, and in no mood to indulge in small talk. Instead, Helen was obliged to make the coffee and serve it in silence, and not until Charles had taken himself off home did Mrs Chase volunteer the information that Jarret was out.

'He phoned Vincent after you'd gone, and they arranged to meet at the pub in the village,' she offered crisply, during a commercial break. 'He's got a key, so I'm not worried. Go to bed, if you want to. This film doesn't finish until after midnight.'

So Helen went to bed, but not to sleep. Even after she heard her mother come upstairs, she still lay awake, and it was not until she heard the powerful throb of the Ferrari's engine, some time in the early hours, that she completely relaxed. Even then her slumbers were dogged by a recurring nightmare, in which Jarret was pursuing her on the back of one of Charles's horses, and she awakened in the morning with a headache, resolving not to drink so much wine in future. She refused to attribute her dreams to her anxieties over Jarret, and went down to breakfast feeling distinctly raw.

There was no sign of their guest, of course, and as she munched her toast and drank several cups of strong black coffee, she reflected rather sourly on the advantages of working at home. Obviously, Jarret could lie in this morning after his late night, and the hours he chose to work were his own, not dictated by shop or office requirements. He didn't have to drive the twelve miles to Malverley with a thumping headache, or face a series of customers with smiling courtesy. He could stay in bed all day if he wanted, and feel fresh and invigorated this evening when she would be as limp as a wet rag.

She was surprised therefore when Jarret appeared as she was pouring her fourth cup of coffee. The fact that even unshaven he looked as relaxed and self-confident as he had done the night before did nothing for her assurance, and when he lounged into a chair at the table, she wished she had forgone the final indulgence.

'Good morning,' he said, after her gaze had slid away from him, and she responded politely, keeping her head down. 'What's wrong with you this morning? Charlie give you a hard time?'

Helen's head jerked up at that. '*Charles* and I had a very pleasant evening,' she retaliated, and added recklessly: 'Must you come to the table in that condition?'

'Oh—this?' He ran exploring fingers over the shadow of his beard. 'Does it offend you? I'm afraid I'm not used to encountering a beautiful woman at the breakfast table.'

'No?' She heard the mockery in his voice, but couldn't help rising to it. 'I should have thought you were.'

'Would you?' The mocking look in his eyes deepened. 'But then you don't know a lot about me, do you?'

'Enough,' she retorted, picking up her coffee cup, and he toyed thoughtfully with the knife beside his plate.

'Vince and I had quite a reunion last night,' he went on. 'In spite of your obstruction.'

'Drinking!' declared Helen scathingly, and a lazy smile touched his lips.

'Yes—drinking,' he agreed blandly. 'Was that what you were trying to save me from?'

'Me?' Helen could not have been more astounded. 'It's nothing to do with me if you choose to ruin your health. I was merely expressing an opinion of the kind of reunion you probably had.' She put down her coffee cup, and pushed back her chair. 'And now, if you'll accept my apologies, some of us have work to do——'

He stepped into her path as she came round the table, getting up lithely from his chair and successfully blocking her exit.

'Mr Manning——' Her automatic protest was silenced by the anger in his expression, and despite her dislike of him she couldn't help but be aware of his disturbing sexuality.

'Don't patronise me, Helen,' he advised her harshly. 'I work, believe me, I work! And damned hard sometimes, so don't go getting the idea I came down here to take a rest-cure. I didn't. I intend to finish this book, and when I do, there's another all lined up and waiting for me.'

Helen was trembling, as much from the painful throbbing in her head as from his aggression, and as if suddenly becoming aware of her pallor, Jarret's eyes narrowed.

'Are you ill?' he demanded, spreading cool fingers on her hot forehead, and although she flinched away from him, he had glimpsed the bruised darkness of her eyes. 'What is it?' he persisted. 'I don't frighten you that much, do I?'

'You don't frighten me at all!' she denied hotly, turning aside. 'If you must know, I have a headache, that's all. I intend to take some aspirin before leaving.'

'You're driving to work with a headache?'

Helen nodded. 'I have to.'

'At the risk of being accused of chauvinism, why don't you take the morning off?'

Helen shook her head. 'I can't. It's our busiest day. I can't leave Karen to handle it alone.'

Jarret frowned. 'Okay, so I'll drive you.'

'You!' Helen could not have been more surprised.

'Why not? You're not fit to handle a car. Take your tablets, and meet me out front when you're ready.'

'I—I can't ...'

Jarret had walked towards the door, but now he halted, one hand raised in resignation against the door jamb. 'Why can't you?'

Helen felt wretched. 'You ... you haven't had breakfast ...' *and I've been rude to you, and I've been thinking bad thoughts about you, and I didn't give you Vincent's message*, her conscience silently appended, though she did not voice these protests.

'So what?' Jarret shrugged. 'I can survive. Believe it or not, I have been known to miss a meal now and again.'

Helen took a couple of steps towards him. 'It's very kind of you, but——'

'God! It's not kind at all,' he snapped. 'I'd do the same for anyone. Do you have a coat to get or anything?'

Helen glanced down at her businesslike skirt and waistcoat, the ruffled jabot of her blouse the only touch of femininity, and nodded. 'A jacket,' she conceded, and he inclined his head.

'Okay. Five minutes. Right?'

'Right,' she agreed reluctantly, and he swung about and walked towards the front entrance. Obviously he considered his sweater and jeans adequate protection against the mildly misty day outside, and when Helen emerged a few minutes later, having swallowed the aspirin and feeling slightly better, the Ferrari was idling at the door. Jarret pushed open the door from inside, and she quickly folded herself into the seat beside him, casting him a nervous smile as she fastened the safety belt. She had not seen her mother to tell her that Jarret was running her to work, but it couldn't be helped. No doubt she would find out soon enough.

The drive was soon negotiated, and they turned on to the road to Malverley, keeping a steady pace that was quicker than Charles's negotiation the night before, but without giving the powerful car its head. The conditions were just not suitable as dozens of commuters made their way to their offices, and Jarret seemed quite content to remain in the stream.

'So,' he said, after there had been several minutes of silence, 'why didn't you tell me about Vince?'

Helen had expected it, and yet when it came, she was not prepared for it. 'Oh—you know what I said,' she murmured awkwardly. 'I forgot.'

'Now you didn't really expect me to believe that, did you?' he argued. 'I could tell that last night. You were waiting for me to contradict you.'

Helen sighed. 'All right, so I didn't tell you on purpose.'

'But why didn't you tell me? Where was the harm?

Vince tells me you and he are good friends, so it's not because you disapprove of him——' He broke off suddenly as another thought struck him. 'Unless—unless it's me you disapprove of.' He uttered a short laugh. 'You know, I never thought of that.'

Helen pressed her lips together. 'And you know that's not the answer either,' she muttered in a low voice. Then, with another sigh, she shook her head. 'If you must know, I put off telling you because—because I was—afraid you might discuss me with him.'

Jarret frowned. 'Isn't it natural that we might?'

Helen hunched her shoulders. 'I suppose.'

'What you really mean is—you were alarmed in case I told Vince I'd kissed you, weren't you?' Jarret commented flatly. 'You need not have worried. Vince and I got over those sort of confidences when we left our teens.'

Helen glanced surreptitiously at him, and then resumed her study of her fingernails. 'I'm sorry.'

'Yes.' His acknowledgement had a resigned sound. 'So am I.'

Helen felt small. 'Well, at least you know now,' she murmured, but was in no way reassured by his silent concurrence. It had not been her intention to diminish her own credibility, and she wished she had just delivered the information and risked its outcome.

The arcade where the craft shop was situated opened into a small private mews, and it was here Helen directed Jarret to take her, deciding he would find it easier to turn in the mews than in the busy market square. However, when he pulled up to let her out, he did so by parking the Ferrari at the kerb, and as she turned to thank him for driving her she saw he was getting out, too.

'I'm interested to see this shop where you work,' he remarked, closing and locking his door. 'And in meeting your partner, of course.'

Helen's brief burst of remorse evaporated. Obviously his offer to drive her to Malverley had been motivated more by curiosity than compassion, and for some reason best known to herself she wished she did not have to introduce him to Karen.

But she could say none of this. She merely tightened

her lips as she began to walk along the arcade, supremely aware of his lean stride matching hers. Of course, Karen might not be there this early in the morning, but as the older girl had only to walk across the square, it was hardly a convincing supposition.

The shop was small, as indeed were all the shops in the arcade, but every inch of the showroom was filled with a variety of goods, from leather purses and fringed waistcoats to hand-painted pottery and sparkling glassware. The idea for the store had been Helen's, but Karen had suggested the kind of thing they sold, and her frequent buying trips to Belgium, France and Italy had produced the varied selection of hand-made items that attacted residents and visitors alike. Lately, too, they had branched out into hand-printed scarves and jewellery, and already Karen was suggesting that when another shop in the arcade came vacant, they might consider clothes.

Helen only needed to push the heavy glass door to know that her friend was already there. Karen opened up as soon as she arrived, her joking comment that they might conceivably attract customers on their way to work proving profitable, and now Helen led the way into the shop with an intense feeling of frustration.

'Is that you, Helen?'

The older girl's voice heralded her appearance in the doorway that led to the rear of the premises, and her brows arched significantly when she saw her friend was not alone. Helen, aware of Jarret behind her, sensed their mutual appraisal and said, rather tautly:

'Mr Manning drove me to work, Karen. And he was interested to see the shop.'

'Really?' Karen smiled and came round the glass display cases to shake hands. 'I've heard a lot about you, Mr Manning, though I must confess, little of it was from Helen.'

'Don't believe all you hear,' Jarret responded modestly, releasing her fingers more slowly than Helen thought necessary. 'I, on the other hand, know nothing about you, which must give you an advantage.'

'Oh, I wouldn't say that,' Karen laughed, at ease with him at once, though she viewed Helen's tense face with some anxiety. 'Have you settled in at King's Green? Helen told me you were moving down yesterday. I expect you'll find it very quiet after London.'

'I hope to,' Jarret averred, looking round the shop as he spoke. 'This is very attractive. Do you do all the displays yourselves?'

'Yes.' Karen moved to straighten a heavy glass paperweight, and took the opportunity to cast a reproving frown in Helen's direction, out of sight of Jarret's gaze. 'We weren't very professional when we started, but we've learned by trial and error, and after three years...'

'And who does the buying?' he enquired, bending to examine a leather wallet.

'Karen!' Helen chose to reply, her response curt and vaguely hostile, and his expression mirrored his comprehension.

'Of course,' he said, but there was a wealth of meaning in those two words and Helen half wished she had let Karen answer him.

'Helen is a much better book-keeper than I am,' Karen put in apologetically, conscious of the animosity Helen was exhibiting and trying to relieve the situation. 'Besides, her fiancé wouldn't like it if she was continually flying to Rome or Paris in search of merchandise, whereas I...' She moved her shoulders expressively.

'I gather you have no troublesome fiancé,' Jarret remarked, ignoring Helen and smiling at the other girl, and Karen shook her head.

'Unfortunately, no,' she agreed, though her tone implied otherwise, and Helen felt the headache which had briefly eased, throbbing again with increased vigour.

'Well, I suppose I'd better be going,' Jarret said at last, and Helen let out her breath in a weak sigh. 'I can't keep you girls from your work any longer. It's been nice meeting you, Miss—er——'

'Karen,' said Karen firmly, and he grinned.

'Karen,' he agreed. 'Goodbye for now.'

'Goodbye.'

Karen inclined her head, and Helen, who had been supporting herself against one of the display cases, was obliged to lift her chin. 'Thank you for the lift,' she said stiffly, meeting his eyes with an effort, and he acknowledged her words with a hard stare.

'What time do you close?' he asked, reaching for the curved handle of the door. 'Five? Five-thirty? I'll pick you up whenever you say, if you'll just give me some idea——'

'I can get the bus home,' declared Helen, interrupting him, and saw the perceptible signs of his impatience.

'What time?' he repeated, between tight lips, and Karen made a helpless gesture.

'Five-thirty tonight,' she offered, ignoring Helen's outraged face. 'Any time after five really. Helen stayed late last night.'

'Five o'clock, then,' said Jarret crisply, pulling the door open. 'See you!' and he was gone.

There was a pregnant pause, and then, as if determined to get her say in first, Karen exclaimed: 'What was all that about? Honestly, Helen, I don't understand you! The man drives you to work, and you act as if he's committed a crime or something.'

Helen said nothing. She brushed round the end of the display units, and went into the office, dropping her handbag down on the desk before taking off her jacket. As she hung the jacket away on a hanger in the corner, Karen followed her into the office, and at her reproachful expression Helen's antipathy faded.

'I know, I know,' she said wretchedly, looping her hair behind her ears with trembling fingers. 'I know I acted badly, but—well, I've got a headache. That was why—he drove me to work. Or at least, that was his excuse.'

'What do you mean—his excuse? What other excuse could he have?'

Helen shook her head. 'He wanted to see the shop—to meet you.'

Karen gave her an old-fashioned look. 'Oh, yes? And he drove the dozen or so miles to Malverley and back again, just for those reasons?'

'Why not?'

'At nine o'clock in the morning? You've got to be joking, Helen.' Karen gave her friend an impatient stare. 'Can't you accept that he might have been considering you—your feelings, your health? I think you treated him abominably, and I think deep down inside you, you think so, too.'

Helen drew a deep breath. 'I don't like him, Karen. Isn't that good enough for you?'

Karen sighed. 'But why don't you like him? I think he's dishy.'

Helen forced a wry smile. 'You would!'

'Well, he is.' Karen helped herself to a cigarette. 'You have to admit, he's very attractive.'

Helen shrugged. 'All right, he's attractive.'

'And sexy.'

Helen turned away. 'Is that all you can think about? There has to be more to a man than—than that!'

'Oh, I agree,' Karen nodded. 'But it will do to be going on with.'

Helen heard the sound of someone entering the shop, and indicating that Karen should carry on with her cigarette, she went to the door. But as she passed the other girl, she couldn't resist saying dryly: 'What about John?' and Karen made a face.

'Just because I've bought a book it doesn't mean I can't look at other covers,' she retorted irrepressibly, and Helen relaxed a little as she went to serve the first customer of the day.

However, by lunchtime the headache which had troubled her on and off since breakfast time was no better, and Karen, aware of Helen's pale face, suggested that she ought to go home.

'I can manage here for once,' she assured her, when the younger girl protested, and Helen eventually gave in.

'Shall I call a cab?' Karen asked, as she put on her jacket, but Helen shook her head.

'I'll get the bus,' she insisted, picking up her handbag. 'I've done it before, and the walk from the bus-stop will do me good.'

Karen sighed. 'How about calling home?' she ventured. 'At the risk of having my head bitten off, I'd say your new house-guest would probably——'

'Don't finish, Karen,' Helen advised wearily, walking to the door. 'I'm sorry about this, believe me. But I'll see you tomorrow.'

In the event, there was a fifteen-minute wait before the next bus to Ketchley, which would drop her off at Thrushfold, and she began to wish she had driven herself in that morning. But truthfully, she was glad she did not have to concentrate on driving, and when the bus did turn up, she settled into her seat with some relief.

The journey to Thrushfold took approximately half an hour, stopping as it did at every wayside halt, and making various detours into off-the-track villages. But eventually it set her down at the Black Bull, and she breathed a sigh of relief as it trundled away.

The day had blossomed from a misty morning into a sunny afternoon, and she shed her jacket as she walked up the village street. It was more than half a mile to King's Green, but she refused to be daunted, even though the heat made her head throb.

She had progressed perhaps half that way, leaving the outskirts of the village behind and following instead the country lane which led to the house, when she heard the powerful motor behind her. Convinced it was Jarret and that Karen must have rung him after all, Helen felt an overwhelming sense of despair. She couldn't face Jarret now, she thought desperately, she couldn't, and without looking back, she scrambled up the bank and through the hedge, emerging into the fields some distance from the house. Hot and dishevelled, she waited to see if the car went by, but to her horror it stopped, and even as she hurriedly began to put some space between herself and its occupant, a puzzled voice called:

'Hey—Helen! Helen, what's the matter?'

Helen turned, albeit reluctantly, to face her fiancé, and Charles ducked through the hedge to reach her. In his tweeds and open-necked shirt, he was endearingly familiar, and she felt a twinge of guilty culpability as she acknowledged her earlier suspicions. What would he think if he knew she had been attempting to avoid another man, particularly when her reasons for doing so were so abysmally inadequate?

'Oh—hello, Charles,' she said now, hands holding her jacket linked behind her back, assuming an attitude of wide surprise. 'What are you doing here?'

Charles frowned. 'I might ask you the same question,' he retorted, striding across the turf towards her. 'Sneaking through the hedge as if you were trying to avoid me!'

'I wasn't!' Helen could at least be truthful about that. 'I—I just thought I might take a short cut.'

'Just as you heard the Range Rover?' queried Charles sceptically, and she realised she wasn't going to find it easy to convince him.

'Oh, Charles...' Now she grasped his sleeve, shaking her head apologetically. 'I didn't know it was you, really.'

'But why aren't you at the shop?'

'For the same reason as I scrambled through the hedge,' she replied honestly. 'Ask Karen, if you don't believe me. I had the most awful headache, and she suggested I came home, and that was why I was walking up the lane.'

'But where's your car?'

Helen sighed. 'At home.' She paused, and then realising that nothing less than the truth would suffice, she went on: 'Jarret Manning ran me to work this morning. I—I had the headache then, you see, and he said I shouldn't drive.'

'So he drove you,' remarked Charles, rather tersely.

'Yes. Yes.' Helen moistened her upper lip. 'I didn't want him to, but he insisted.'

'Yes.' Charles sucked in his cheeks reflectively. 'He's quite an insistent person, your Mr Manning. As I know to my cost.'

'To your cost?' Now it was Helen's turn to look confused. 'What do you mean—to your cost? What did he do?'

'It's not exactly what he did that matters,' responded her fiancé grimly. 'It's what he encouraged Vincent to do that I'm concerned about. That's why I'm here now. I intend to see him, to have it out with him. That idiot brother of mine could have broken his neck!'

Helen's head was hammering so hard, she felt almost giddy, but she had to know what all this was about. 'Please,' she exclaimed, weakly. 'What happened? How could Vincent have been hurt? I don't understand.'

Charles sniffed before continuing. 'It was last night,' he said. 'You know, of course, that Manning met up with Vincent.'

'Yes, Mummy told me.'

'Yes, well, apparently they got drunk. The first thing I knew about it was the noise the horses were making. They woke me up. Then, of course, I heard the shouting.'

Helen stared at him. 'What shouting?'

Charles sighed. 'That man—Manning—he'd encouraged Vincent to ride Poseidon.'

'The new stud?' Helen was appalled.

'Yes.' Charles shook his head. 'You know what a vicious beast he can be. I wouldn't even try to ride him myself. I warned Vincent about him days ago, but you know how pig-headed he can be.'

Helen gazed helplessly at him. 'But what makes you think —Manning is involved?'

'He was there, wasn't he? Vincent never would have had the nerve to ride Poseidon without encouragement. And why didn't he stop him, that's what I want to know? As it is, the damn animal has caused pounds worth of damage. It's lucky he didn't lame himself, or I'd have been suing Manning and Vincent both for several thousand pounds!'

Helen's shoulders sagged. 'And—and that's where you're going now? To—to see him?'

'Manning? Yes. Come along, I'll give you a lift. Unless you prefer to tramp across the fields?'

'Oh, no. No, I'll come with you.' Helen was only too eager to escape the brilliant glare of the sun, but as Charles put her into the seat beside him, he still had one further question to ask.

'You never did tell me why you dived through the hedge like that,' he said, swinging himself in beside her. 'Who did you think it was? Manning?'

Realising it would be easier to admit to avoiding her mother's house guest, Helen nodded. 'It didn't really matter,' she said, prevaricating just a little. 'I didn't honestly feel like talking to anyone.'

'Including me?' demanded Charles huffily, but she hastily denied his claim.

'Of course not. Just—just anyone else,' she finished lamely, and hoped she did not look as deceitful as she felt.

King's Green was dreaming in the afternoon sunshine, a mellow, creeper-hung building, its rows of windows reflecting the burgeoning beauty of the tall oaks that shaded the courtyard. The heavy door stood wide to admit the maximum amount of air, and bees throbbed about the entrance, busy in the overhanging blossom that sweetly scented the porch.

Charles brought the Range Rover to a halt, and Helen quickly scrambled out without waiting for his assistance. It had occurred to her that Jarret might be out, and the absence of any sign of the Ferrari seemed to confirm this supposition. However, her mother must have heard their approach, for now she came out of the porch to greet them, her brows meeting anxiously as she looked at Helen, and her first words dispelled any hope that Jarret had not returned to the house.

'Oh, Helen,' she exclaimed, and it was the gentlest tone she had used to her daughter in weeks. 'Jarret told me how unwell you were feeling this morning. You should have rung up. I'd have come to pick you up, without bothering Charles.'

Helen glanced awkwardly at her fiancé who had heard most of this speech, and then began to explain. 'I came home on the bus, Mummy,' she murmured, loath to arouse any further antipathy between them. 'I—er—I met Charles in the lane.'

Mrs Chase looked confused. 'But I thought you expected to be at the shop all day. I naturally assumed——'

'I'm afraid I'm here on rather different business, Mrs Chase,' Charles intervened at this point. 'It—er—it has to do with your house guest, Manning. Is he about?'

'Jarret?' Mrs Chase looked even more puzzled now, and with a sense of resignation Helen said:

'I did come home because I have a headache, Mummy. But Charles wants to speak to—to Mr Manning, that's all.'

Mrs Chase spread her hands in rather a bewildered gesture, and then indicated the open doorway behind her. 'Jarret is at home, of course,' she admitted doubtfully. 'But he's working, and he asked me not to disturb him, even for lunch.'

'I'm afraid this matter is urgent, too, Mrs Chase,' insisted Charles woodenly. 'I'm a busy man, I really can't spare the time to come here on a fool's errand. I'm sorry I have to involve you, naturally, but as he's staying here, I really have no choice.'

Helen's mother shook her head a little helplessly. 'You'd better come in,' she said, leading the way into the house. 'He's working in the library, as you know.' She paused, studying her daughter's pale face. 'Helen, you'd better go and lie down—you look dreadful. I'll come and see you after—after Charles has gone.'

'Yes, you do that, my dear,' approved her fiancé, approaching the library door and subjecting the panels to a heavy tattoo. 'I'll ring you later to see how you're feeling. And don't forget, it's the gymkhana on Saturday.'

Helen could have done without being reminded at this particular moment of her obligation as Charles fiancée. Charles was the chairman of the local committee which organised the yearly event, and while in ordinary circumstances she managed to hide her misgivings, right now she could not suppress the grimace of dismay that crossed her face. It was as well the library door opened just then, distracting Charles's attention from her lack of enthusiasm.

Jarret himself looked less than pleased at the interruption. He had shed the sweater he had been wearing earlier in favour of a collarless sweat shirt, and its sombre colour did little to lighten his equally sombre expression. His eyes moved swiftly over Charles and Mrs Chase, coming to rest on Helen's pale face, and then turning with a lightning change of direction back to her mother.

'Yes?' he said, the terseness of his query evident in the single syllable, without any need to elaborate his impatience at this interruption.

'Oh, Jarret.' Mrs Chase spoke uncomfortably. 'I'm sorry if we're being a nuisance, but—but Charles wanted to speak to you and——'

'I can handle this, Mrs Chase.'

Charles was ineffably self-confident, and Helen, lingering in spite of herself, felt an anxious surge of apprehension. Did he really know who he was dealing with? she wondered. Had he even considered that Jarret was not his brother's keeper, and would most likely say so in no uncertain words?

'It's about last night, Manning,' he continued now, squaring his shoulders in an unconscious effort to maintain the upper hand. 'I'm sure you know to what I'm referring.'

'Yes.'

That was all Jarret said, and Helen, hovering at the foot of the stairs, was riveted to the spot.

'Yes—well——' Clearly, Charles had not expected so monosyllabic a reply. 'You must realise that a certain amount of damage was caused.' He paused, and when Jarret still said nothing more, but just stood regarding him with cool hard enquiry, he went on: 'Aside from the obvious recklessness of trying to mount Poseidon, Vincent could have suffered some serious injury, not to mention the fact that that animal is worth a considerable sum of money!'

Jarret inclined his head. 'And what do you want me to do about it?'

'What do I want you to do about it?' Charles was obviously staggered now, as much by his apparent success in winning his point as by the cool indifference of the question. 'I—why——'

'Will a hundred pounds cover the damage?'

Jarret's offer was delivered in such a mild tone that Charles was completely deceived, and instead of accepting the olive branch, such as it was, he lost his head.

'A hundred pounds!' he echoed, his voice rising as his temper expanded. 'Who do you think you're dealing with? Some snotty-nosed trainer grumbling about some nag not worth the candle? Poseidon is a prize stallion, not that I'd expect *you* to know anything about that! He's a thoroughbred—a temperamental thoroughbred, and psychologically he could have been marred for life! You and Vincent, you're both the same, utterly thoughtless, utterly irresponsible!'

Jarret's mouth hardened into a thin line, and even across the hall, Helen could see the steely glitter of his eyes. 'Why, you pompous hypocrite,' he said slowly. 'You goddamned puffed-up little weed! Who the hell are you calling thoughtless and irresponsible? If you're not sufficiently capable of keeping your brother in order, why in heaven's name do you think I should be?'

There's going to be a fight, thought Helen weakly, horrified by the deterioration of the situation. Charles had never come up against anyone like Jarret Manning before, and his whole attitude had been one of aggression right from the start. Instead of accepting that he had made his point, that at least it was not going to cost him anything to get the stalls repaired, he had jumped in with both feet, and now there seemed no way of retrieving his dignity. Charles was not a fighter. He was a country gentleman. And although he was more heavily built than Jarret, she doubted he would stand a chance if it came to blows.

'For heaven's sake!' It was Mrs Chase who came between them as Charles's features suffused with hectic colour. 'Can't we at least be civil about this? Charles, really—I didn't know you intended to start a row of this magnitude, or I would never have allowed you to—to do so.' She looked helplessly at Jarret, not quite knowing what to say to him, and under her appealing gaze, the fury in his face subsided.

'I'm sorry,' he said, but his words were addressed to Helen's mother, not to Charles. 'I regret I'm not always polite when my work is being interrupted.' He flashed a glance at the other man, and then saw Helen still hesitating at the bottom of the stairs. His eyes narrowed slightly, as if calculating her reactions, before turning back to her mother. 'Perhaps you would explain to—Connaught here that my offer still stands. He can even send the bill to me, if he likes, and I'll see that it's paid. More than that, I don't see what I can do.'

He didn't wait to see the relief in Mrs Chase's face, or the blustering indignation in Charles's. He simply stepped backward and closed the door, leaving them all in various stages of stunned incredulity.

Helen's mother recovered first, urging Charles across the hall and into the drawing room, only noticing her daughter's presence as she turned away.

'What are you doing, hanging about down here, Helen?' she demanded testily, clearly disconcerted to find she was still there, and Charles cast a resentful look in his fiancée's direction.

'And this is the man you allow to drive you to work!' he declared, with justifiable wrath.

'The man *Mummy* invited to stay here,' Helen reminded him shortly, unable to let that go undefended, but her mother just tossed her head.

'A storm in a teacup!' she exclaimed, marching into the drawing room. 'A lot of fuss over nothing. And you, Charles, should have known better than to start it.'

Charles was outraged. '*I* didn't start it!' he asserted. 'You don't know what happened last night.'

'Yes, I do.' Mrs Chase was not at all put out by his anger. 'Vincent was over here earlier on this morning, apologising to Jarret for making a fool of himself.'

'What?'

'It's true.' Mrs Chase was complacent. 'You know what he's like, Charles. Vincent never could drink a lot, and since when did he need encouraging to do anything?'

Charles clenched his fists. 'Manning was there. He should have stopped him.'

Mrs Chase looked at him squarely. 'Could you?' she asked pointedly, and as Charles's expression began to falter, she added: 'I suggest we have a nice cup of tea, and forget all about it.'

## CHAPTER SIX

IT was impossible, of course. None of them could forget that the antipathy between Jarret and Charles had flared into open conflict. It meant that the casual relationship which Mrs Chase had hoped would exist between her future son-in-law and her house guest never materialised, and Helen had to avoid all mention of the other man when she was with her fiancé.

Not that Jarret intruded into her life. On the contrary, since that first morning when things had gone so abysmally wrong she had had little opportunity to show her own opinion of him. He did not appear again at breakfast time, and as she frequently lunched in town, only dinner presented any problems. But again Jarret asked to be excused, taking his meals in the library, leaving the tray outside to be collected by Mrs Hetherington. It was a convenient, if unsatisfactory, arrangement for all of them, and during the following weeks Helen learned that three people could live in a house without really sharing it. Just occasionally she heard the sound of music emanating through the thick walls of the library, and guessed Jarret was taking a break from working, but for the most part the only sound was the faint click-click of the typewriter.

She heard from Charles that Vincent had left again only days after his reunion with Jarret. She had known there could not be too many days of his holiday left, but she was surprised and a little upset to think he had gone away without saying goodbye. Still, after the furore there had been, perhaps it was all for the best, and she had enough to do, now that Charles had been given the keys to their new home. Most evenings they spent at the house, choosing colour schemes and measuring for curtains and carpets, and Helen endeavoured to recover the enthusiasm for her coming marriage, which lately seemed to have been dissipated by her mother's antagonism and her own uncertainty. Not that she was uncertain of her love for Charles, she told herself severely, only of his demands on her, and the growing awareness that perhaps their association did lack physical expression. She could not entirely dismiss the remembrance of her reactions to Jarret's lovemaking, and while she might condemn his sexuality, she could not deny her unwilling response. Perhaps Karen was right, she thought doubtfully, maybe she too needed a more physical relationship.

The following evening she drove to Ketchley in a rather emotional frame of mind. It was three weeks since Jarret had moved into King's Green, and this evening, for the first time in weeks, he had joined her mother and herself for dinner. He was apparently going out, judging by his dark brown denim suit, his tie knotted neatly over a matching beige shirt. Even his hair was slicked back by the dampness of his shower, and her suspicions had been realised when her mother had asked him what time he expected to be home.

'Not too late, I hope,' he assured her smilingly, and watching his lean features relax in response, Helen was stricken by the realisation that she resented his intention of taking time out. He was supposed to be here to work, she thought indignantly, disregarding the fact that that was precisely what he had done for the past three weeks.

Although she had hung around after Mrs Hetherington had cleared the table, her mother had not said if she knew where he was going, and as Jarret himself had already departed, Helen had had to stifle her curiosity. She refused to ask the question, and as she and her mother had still not entirely resolved their differences, she left the house feeling distinctly fretful.

Charles was waiting for her when she arrived at his home, and after a brief word of greeting to his parents she climbed into the Range Rover for the drive to Petersham. The house Charles had bought lay on the outskirts of this tiny hamlet, only two miles from his parents' home, and for the first time Helen felt no pride of ownership as he turned between the iron gateposts.

The house was reasonably new, built just before the last war, and considerably modernised by its last owner. There was an Aga cooker, and oil-fired central heating, and the four bedrooms and two bathrooms would be ample for their needs. The present decoration was rather old-fashioned, however, and in these weeks before their wedding Charles intended to employ a firm of interior designers to alter it to their taste.

Inside, it was chilly, in spite of the heat of the day, but the electric fires in the main reception rooms soon dispelled the draughts, and Helen endeavoured to pay attention to what Charles was saying.

'So we've decided the main colour scheme should be green and gold in the hall, and beige and brown in the drawing room,' he said, checking the clipboard in his hand. 'Did you have any further thoughts about the dining room? I think blue is a little cold, don't you?'

Helen sighed, unbuttoning the jacket of her cream suede slack suit, loosening a further button of the silk shirt underneath. She felt discontented and restless, her blood prickling hotly under her skin, her senses alive to an urgent dissatisfaction, and certainly in no mood to discuss colour schemes. Karen had hinted that now they had a place of their own, where they could be alone together, Charles would probably become more demonstrative, but so far he seemed totally indifferent to their isolation. If anything, he seemed to avoid a more tangible contact, and was quite happy debating interior decorating. It was irritating and frustrating, and she wondered if he was afraid to show his feelings too strongly.

'I was speaking to Martin Coverdale the other day, and he says he can let us have a dining room suite at cost, if we care to go and have a look round his warehouse,' Charles went on, diligently ignoring her apparent lack of interest. 'I think that's jolly good of him, don't you? I mean, he has some damn good stuff and——'

'Oh, can't we talk about anything else than furniture these days!' Helen broke in abstractedly, torn by her emotions, by the way she was feeling, and her own inability to handle it. 'I mean——' she pushed her silky hair back behind her ears, leaving her hands cupping her neck, '—why don't we ever talk about *us*? Ourselves! Our feelings for one another! And not just—just paint and wallpaper and— and household articles!'

Charles looked astonished, but then, recovering his composure, he said: 'I should have thought that was our primary consideration at the moment!' in an offended tone.

Helen sighed. 'Well, it shouldn't be. What about us, Charles? Why don't we ever talk about ourselves, about our relationship? Why don't we ever *do* anything about it?'

Charles looked slightly embarrassed now. 'What is there to do?' he protested. 'We love one another, we both know that——'

'Do we?'

'What do you mean—do we?' Charles made a play of putting his fountain pen back into his pocket. 'Of course we do, Helen. I don't know what's the matter with you.'

'Karen says there should be more to our relationship than—than there is.'

'Oh, Karen does, does she?' Charles could look at her now, secure in his condemnation of the older girl. 'And I suppose she knows all about it. Where does she get her information, I wonder? Through her association with John Fleming, I suppose.'

Helen gasped. 'You know about that?'

'I should think half Malverley knows about it. They're not exactly discreet, are they?'

'They're in love.'

'Love!' Charles snorted derisively. 'I doubt either of them knows the meaning of the word.'

Helen's lips trembled. 'Well, at least they show their feelings for one another. They're not afraid to exhibit their emotions or lose control now and again.'

'And you think I am?' asked Charles coldly.

'Well, aren't you?' Helen sniffed. 'I mean, you never kiss me as if you couldn't bear to let me go. You seem quite content to wait. It makes me wonder sometimes.'

'Does it?' Charles's mouth had thinned to a straight line, and she could tell he was very angry. 'It doesn't occur to you that I might be constantly controlling myself, keeping my feelings in check, respecting you too much to—to take advantage of you?'

Helen hunched her shoulders, a little uncertain now. 'I—why—I don't know,' she mumbled, and he put down his clipboard on the stairs, and came purposefully towards her.

His hands descended on her shoulders and he jerked her towards him, his mouth seeking hers with fierce urgency, and she felt an unexpected sense of dismay. It wasn't that he hadn't kissed her before, he had, many times, but never in this rough, unfeeling way. She thought at first it was anger that was dictating his behaviour, but as his kisses grew harsher and more demanding, she realised he was becoming aroused by this savage display. His mouth, hot and wet, assaulted hers, and crushed against his strong body, she had little opportunity to protest. If she had needed any confirmation that Charles was a normal male with normal masculine needs, she had been given it, but what appalled her most was his apparent indifference to her lack of response. He was concerned only with his own needs, his own satisfaction, and as the embrace continued she felt herself growing cold inside. What had begun as a desire for reassurance had become a struggle for survival, and she was exhausted when he at last let her go.

'Well?' he said thickly, looking down into her flushed face with triumphant eyes. 'Are you satisfied now? I want you, Helen, never doubt that. But I'm prepared to wait until I have the right to take what's mine.'

Helen shuddered with revulsion. She could hardly bear to look at him. Did he really believe his selfish lovemaking had satisfied her? Did he really think those hot greedy kisses had aroused anything other than disgust inside her? She felt she wanted to scrub all traces of his caresses from her, and turning aside, she sought to hide her horror from him.

'What's the matter? Embarrassed you, have I?' Charles demanded, secure in his own self-confidence. 'Well, you asked for it, Helen. I'm only a man, not a machine. And you're a very beautiful woman, you know that.'

'I—I—perhaps we ought to go,' she ventured, wiping the back of her hand across her lips, and was appalled to hear his amused laughter.

'Why?' he countered. 'Don't worry, I can control myself. Now, let's consider the kitchen. I think those dark red tiles are rather effective, don't you?'

With the greatest difficulty Helen managed to sustain her composure for the rest of the evening, but she was enormously glad she had driven herself to Ketchley and could therefore avoid Charles's accompanying her home. She wanted to think, and she couldn't do so in his bombastic presence. Even so, driving back to King's Green, she was intensely aware that at present the prospect of giving Charles exclusive rights to do with her body as he wished filled her with revulsion.

It was a shadowy night, the moon obscured by successive banks of cloud, giving only a fitful light as she drove up the lane towards her home. The trees that interspersed the hedges cast elongated phantoms across her path, and occasionally a large insect flew into her headlights sacrificing itself for that brief moment of glory.

She drove through the drive gates, glancing at the clock on the dash. It was only a few minutes after half past ten, and she breathed a little sigh of resignation. At least Charles didn't believe in late nights, and she had had no difficulty in convincing him that she wanted to be home before the pubs turned out.

She left the car in the stable yard, noticing as she did so that the Ferrari was back. Her surprise was tinged with relief, and as if needing to dispel this emotion before going into the house, she wandered across to the paddock fence. Wherever Jarret had gone, it had not been to London, and her brows drew together as she realised she had not known he had friends in the area. Unless he had met up with Vincent again ... Yet if he had, she doubted he would have been home so early, and curiosity made an unwelcome addition to her already troubled thoughts.

Resting one foot on the lowest rail, she supported her elbows on the top of the fence, cupping her chin on her knuckles as she gazed blindly into the darkness. If only she hadn't encouraged Charles to make love to her, she thought wryly, she would not feel so uneasy now. Karen was wrong. Some people needed to be married before they could share a real relationship, and no doubt Charles would have behaved far more sensitively if she had not pretended she wanted him to seduce her. All the same, she could not entirely dispel the thought that perhaps it was she that was at fault, and the fear that she might be the one who was frigid surfaced.

She had been so intent on her thoughts, she had given no heed to the possibility that she might not be alone. Besides, apart from Jarret and her mother, there was no one else at the house, and she would have heard either of them crunching across the gravelled forecourt. Therefore it was with a sense of real horror that she felt the cold dampness of something brushing against her cheek, and when she lifted her head to encounter dark soulful eyes, she let out a shriek of pure terror. As she threw herself back from the fence, the horse, for that was what she saw it was now, neighed in protest, and she lost her footing and sat down with a bump on the stony ground.

There was the sound of someone coming now, she realised, as she probed her bruised rear with a gentle hand, and she lifted her head to voice her complaints as Jarret strode up to her. He was still wearing the denim pants he had been wearing earlier, but he had shed his jacket and his tie, and unbuttoned the neck and sleeves of his shirt, and in the filtering moonlight he looked dark and vengeful.

'What the hell do you think you're doing?' he demanded, hauling her up with no evidence of sympathy, assured by her belligerent expression that she was all right. He moved to the fence then, calming the animal with soothing noises, and then turned back to her again, as she brushed the dust from her pants. 'Screaming like that!' he muttered, anger giving way to impatience as he succeeded in controlling himself. 'I thought someone had attacked you. I might have realised you'd shout before you were hurt!'

'I am hurt,' she protested, gazing up at him infuriatedly. 'And where has that animal come from? We don't have any horses at King's Green. Is it yours? Did you put it there? You have no right to graze an animal in our paddock without first gaining permission!'

'I have permission,' he retorted flatly. 'Your mother granted it. And naturally, I assumed she'd told you.'

'Well, she didn't.'

'Obviously not. And I'm sorry, if that's any consolation. But I didn't know you were going to go mooching about the paddock at this time of night, did I? Where's that damned fiancé of yours? Charles—what's his name? I thought you and he were spending the evening together.'

'His name is Charles Connaught, as you very well know. And we have spent the evening together. This just happens to be the night, or hadn't you noticed?'

Jarret shook his head. 'I don't call ten-thirty *night*, but if you do, that's your affair. Anyway, you're not really hurt, are you? Only your pride. What happened? Did he make a pass at you?'

Helen pursed her lips as they walked back to the house. 'He—he touched my cheek,' she admitted, shuddering at the recollection. 'And I don't like horses, Mr Manning. I—I never have. And I wasn't mooching about the paddock, I was just leaning on the fence.'

Jarret nodded. 'Your mother told me you were afraid of animals——'

'Not animals. Just horses.'

'—but I guess part of that is due to ignorance.'

'Ignorance?' Helen glanced at him as they entered the lighted hall, and the sound of his record deck came flooding clearly through the open library door. 'You have a cheek!'

'I mean it.' Jarret was indifferent to her objections. 'No one need be afraid of anything they know about and understand. If you like I'll introduce you to him properly tomorrow, and who knows, maybe you'll get to like him.'

Helen shivered. 'I don't think so.'

'As you like,' Jarret shrugged, and strolled towards the door of his room. 'By the way, your mother is out. She left a message with Mrs Hetherington. She was invited to a bridge evening at the vicarage, and she's not back yet.' He paused in the doorway, his expression wry. 'Apparently she hasn't realised how late it is!'

Helen pursed her lips. He was mocking her again, and with a sigh she turned away towards the kitchen. She would make herself a cup of something hot and take it up to bed. She had a new paperback that she wanted to read, and she didn't feel particularly tired.

'Are you hungry?'

Jarret's query halted her and she turned back. 'A little,' she admitted cautiously, and he indicated the room behind him.

'Mrs Hetherington supplied me with a tray of coffee and sandwiches before she retired for the night. She seems to think I'm in some need of fortification. Anyway, you're welcome to share them, if you want to. Despite Mrs H's beliefs, I'm not hungry.'

'She just likes making a fuss of you,' Helen conceded, with an expressive wave of her hands.

'It's as well someone does,' he commented dryly, and she glimpsed a momentary vulnerability in his unguarded eyes.

Helen hesitated. 'I—er—I will share your sandwiches, if you don't mind,' she said, giving in rather rashly to a feeling of sympathy for him, that as the door closed behind her was quickly dissipated. But she was too worked up to go to bed yet, and the idea of being alone with her troubled thoughts held no temptation for her.

'Good,' was all he replied, and after she had entered the lamplit library, he closed the door behind them with a definite click.

She had not been into this room since his occupation, and now she looked about her with genuine interest. The desk was obviously where he did most of his work, and apart from the typewriter and a pile of manuscript, there were notepads and reference books, and various rubbers and pencils. Beside the desk were boxes of typescript and carbon paper, and rolls of ribbon for the powerful-looking machine, as well as a tape-recorder and spools of cassettes, and an overflowing wastepaper basket.

The music she had heard was coming from an expensive-looking record deck, and now she could see that he had installed speakers at either end of the bookshelves, which accounted for the high fidelity quality of the reproduction. There was an enormous pile of long-playing records, and a smaller one of singles, and the sound that was presently emanating from the speakers was one of her favourites of the moment.

'Billy Joel,' she said, indicating the empty sleeve. 'I have one of his singles. Even Charles—well, I mean—my fiancé —likes his music,' she finished lamely.

Jarret nodded, making no comment, indicating the tray of sandwiches on the table by the empty fireplace, silently offering her the food. Helen thanked him, and helped herself to one of Mrs Hetherington's turkey sandwiches, perching on the edge of one of the armchairs that flanked the fireplace, munching rather nervously as he crossed the room and abruptly silenced the record player.

'Oh, don't do that!' she protested, half turning in her seat to look at him, but the expression on his face caused her to shut her mouth.

'I feel like something else,' he explained shortly, replacing Billy Joel with the haunting inflection of the Carpenters, and Helen hugged her knees as she recognised another favourite of hers.

'So tell me,' he said at last, propping his hips against the desk. 'How was your evening? Am I wrong, or do I detect a certain restraint in your attitude towards your worthy fiancé?'

Helen flushed. 'You're wrong!' she answered at once, reaching for another sandwich, even though she wanted to run from his questions. 'Charles and I had a very pleasant evening, thank you.'

'I'm pleased to hear it. Is that why you've got that ugly mark on your neck? Or is Horatio responsible for that?'

Helen's hand went automatically to her throat, and with trembling fingers she felt the tell-tale scar Charles's teeth had left. It was horrible to think he had left his mark on her like this, and she could imagine what Jarret must be thinking.

With burning cheeks, she faltered: 'Hor-Horatio? Who—who——'

'The monster in the paddock,' Jarret remarked flatly. 'Old Horatio. You know—the warhorse?'

'Oh...' Helen caught her lower lip between her teeth, replacing the half eaten sandwich on the tray. 'Is—is that his name?'

'It's my name for him,' agreed Jarret. 'So? I don't believe he would attack a lady. That isn't Horatio's way.'

'He didn't. That is——' Helen broke off awkwardly, and got to her feet. 'I—I think I'd better be going. It—it is quite late, and—and Mummy will be home shortly.'

Jarret straightened from the desk and stepped into her path. 'It's not that late,' he averred quietly. 'And you were in no hurry to go to bed until a few moments ago. What's the matter? Did I touch on a sore spot? I'm sorry. I didn't know you—er—went in for that sort of thing.'

'I don't.' Helen's face blazed, but unable to sustain that cold blue gaze, she bent her head to stare unseeingly at the Oriental pattern of the carpet. 'Thank you for the sandwiches, but I really must be going . . .'

'If I thought he'd hurt you——' muttered Jarret, his hand curving unexpectedly over the line of her jaw, hiding the unsightly contusion with his fingers, and Helen's whole body stiffened. 'Relax,' he said, exerting the lightest of pressures to draw her towards him, and as the music changed to a poignant rhythm, added: 'Dance with me . . .'

Helen's anxious eyes sought his and what she found there seemed to melt her resistance. Almost hypnotically, she allowed him to draw her into his arms, to rest his chin against her temple and envelop her in a warm embrace.

It was hardly dancing. They scarcely moved around the confined circle of carpet, but it was an excuse for him to hold her in his arms, and although she knew she was crazy to allow it, her overheated senses repudiated any denial. After Charles's abrasive conduct, it was almost comforting to succumb to such an undemanding attachment, and she badly needed to be reassured on that score.

At one point his hands shifted from the small of her back, sliding under the jacket of her suit to spread against the thin silk of her shirt. Her flesh tingled at the awareness of how narrow was the barrier between her skin and his, but when a few moments later he separated the shirt from her pants and probed the cool hollow of her spine, she felt no sense of embarrassment. She did know she ought to protest, that she ought to tell him he had no right to touch her so familiarly, but the music was seducing her, drugging her with feeling, arousing emotions that Charles in his ham-fisted fashion could never have inspired.

Her arms were around his neck, her fingers coiled in the silky hair that grew on his nape, and she was overwhelmingly conscious of the smooth skin beneath that roughened surface. He smelled so good, she thought, a mingling of shaving cream and lotion, of body heat and his musky male odour that filled her nostrils like some enervating intoxicant, and made her weak with longings she didn't know how to fulfil. She only knew her breasts were hard where they were crushed against his chest, and there was a curious aching feeling in the pit of her stomach.

Jarret lowered his head to her shoulder suddenly, turning his lips against her neck, and saying huskily: 'He tried to make love to you, didn't he?' and when she automatically started to protest, he went on: 'What happened? Did he go at that like a bull at a gate, too? I guess he would. He has about as much sensitivity as a rhinoceros!'

Helen succeeded in drawing back from him sufficiently to look into his face, and her own was flushed and indignant. 'You have no right to say such things!' she exclaimed unsteadily. 'You don't know what he's like.'

'I can hazard a guess——'

'And you'd be wrong!'

'Would I?' Jarret did not sound convinced. 'Okay, so I'm wrong. Forget it. Let's dance.'

'No!'

'Why not? Is there something you would rather do?' The blue eyes were soft and lazy, and looking into their infinite depths was like drowning. Helen was overwhelmingly conscious of their situation—of the lamplit room, of Jarret's hands lightly gripping her waist, of his shirt half open down his chest, and the instinctive awareness of her own response to him. Why hadn't it been like this with Charles? she asked herself despairingly. Why couldn't it have been him who made her feel so breathless, so weak at the knees, so ridiculously aware of her own sex and its fulfilment?

As it was, she was betraying everything she had ever believed in by letting Jarret hold her at all. And of course, he knew exactly how to arouse her. Unlike Charles, who had saved himself for the woman he loved, the woman he intended to make his wife, Jarret Manning had experimented wherever the opportunity presented itself, and it was this experience she was confusing with sensitivity.

'I must go,' she said quickly, trying to turn away, but the hands which only moments before had been holding her so lightly now tightened their grasp.

'Not yet.' Jarret's eyes dropped from hers to her mouth, and then lower to the rapid rise and fall of her breasts. 'Talk to me.'

'I—I don't think it's talking you want, Mr Manning,' Helen got out chokily, and then pressed her lips together frustratedly as his curved into a sardonic smile.

'Really?' he mocked. 'So tell me—what do I want?'

'Oh, Jarret, please ...' She couldn't stand much more of this double talking. 'I have to go. Save your line in seduction for—for Vivien and—and Margot. I—I already have a boy-friend.'

'A *boy*-friend!' he echoed huskily, his hands moving up over her rib-cage to rest just below her breasts. 'Oh, Helen, you really are an old-fashioned girl, aren't you?'

'Please——' She despised herself for pleading with him, but she had to save her self-respect. 'Let me go, Jarret. Don't make me hate you!'

She thought he was going to ignore her, and for several seconds the erratic beat of her heart was suspended. But then, with a muffled oath, he released her, turning away to push both hands through the hair at his temples, extending the gesture into a weary flexing of his shoulder muscles.

Helen swallowed the panic in her throat, and with trembling fingers pushed her shirt back into the waistband of her pants. She felt exhausted, and in spite of her relief that he had let her go, strangely deflated, too. The inconsistencies of her own feelings were a constant source of anxiety to her, and although only minutes before she had desperately wanted to get away, now she was curiously reluctant to leave him. As he turned back to look at her, her heart wrenched inside her, and the dark torment in his eyes was more than she could bear.

'Oh, Jarret——' she breathed, hardly aware of covering the space between them, but when his hands sought the soft flesh of her upper arms and pulled her towards him, she knew there was no drawing back.

Her mouth parted under his without conscious volition. If she was subconsciously aware that Jarret's lips were just as demanding as Charles's had been, she also knew that there the similarity ended. With Charles there had been only a selfish need to satisfy his own ambitions, whereas Jarret took her with him every step of the way, coaxing a smouldering response that inevitably ignited into a burning passion. She had been unaware of her own sensuality, but now an instinctive reaction had taken over, so that she responded to his kisses without constraint, arching her body against his, promoting an intimacy between them that she had never known before with any man.

'*God*—Helen!' he muttered once, lifting his mouth from hers, but she went after him with her lips, seeking and finding their target, and his brief moment of withdrawal was stifled by his own urgent needs.

She felt his fingers between them, loosening the buttons of her shirt, exposing her pointed breasts to his narrow-eyed appraisal, and almost intuitively she tugged his shirt apart and pressed herself against him. Her whole body felt on fire, awash with a yearning longing to feel his flesh against hers, and his moan of satisfaction was uttered against her mouth.

'You're beautiful,' he muttered, 'but you don't know what you're doing to me——'

'I know what you're doing to me,' she countered, and his groan of protest was half rueful.

'What am I doing?' he breathed, and her tongue appeared in unknowing provocation.

'You make me—want you,' she whispered, hardly understanding what she was saying, and she felt the shudder that ran through him as he buried his face in the hollow of her neck.

'I want you,' he conceded in a smothered voice, and she pressed herself closer, feeling the stirring muscles against her thigh.

'I—I never knew it could be like this,' she confessed, half wonderingly, and his mouth parted hungrily over hers.

Almost without her being aware of it, he had drawn her down on to one of the huge velvet armchairs, and now its softness enveloped them like a cushioned embrace. She was half on his knees, half crushed against the corner of the chair, the silky texture of the upholstery sensuous against her naked flesh.

'Let me look at you,' he insisted, sliding the concealing folds of her shirt from her shoulders, and an aching longing to please him swept over her. 'I want to taste every inch of you,' he muttered, caressing the tilted curve of her breast, his voice thickening as he pulled her hands down to his body, encouraging her to give in to the impulses she had to explore him as he was exploring her. She had never felt this way before, never felt any particular curiosity about Charles whatsoever, but it was different with Jarret. His lean brown body fascinated her, and she wanted to touch him just as much as she wanted him to touch her. His skin was taut and smooth, hard and muscled, and not as hairy as Charles's coarser flesh.

'I want to look at you, too,' she murmured, when his mouth found hers once again, and his response was huskily rueful.

'I'm not half as interesting as you are,' he protested, against the shell-like cavity of her ear. 'But I can't stop you.'

'No, you can't,' she agreed, equally huskily, and he crushed her under him with an increasing urgency.

The sudden peal of the telephone bell was like a cold knife slicing between them. Its insistent ringing reacted on Helen like a sobering draught, and a feeling of intense confusion enfolded her in a wave of heat. It occurred to her how terrible it would have been if her mother had chosen to walk in on them with as little discrimination as the telephone bell had exhibited, and her awareness of her own state of undress filled her with hot embarrassment.

'Let it ring,' Jarret groaned, as she began to struggle beneath him, but Helen moved her head vigorously from side to side.

'It—it must be Mummy,' she exclaimed. 'And she'll know I must be home by this time——'

'Pretend you're asleep,' muttered Jarret, against her throat. 'Do you really want to leave me?' he demanded, looking down at her with eyes darkened by emotion, and she knew that deep inside her, she didn't.

'I—I have to,' she wailed, knowing her mother would demand a satisfactory explanation if she did not answer it, and also knowing that there must be some serious reason for her to ring so late.

'All right.' With an abrupt movement, Jarret levered himself up and away from her. 'I'll answer it.' He snatched up his shirt and shrugged into the sleeves with evident impatience. 'But don't move, I'll be right back.'

Helen managed a tremulous nod, and with a gesture of frustration, he threw the library door open and strode across the hall. Struggling into a sitting position, Helen looked down at her swollen breasts without conceit. She felt charged with emotion, and her lips parted almost disbelievingly as she recalled the last hour in Jarret's arms. She felt really alive for the first time in her life, alert to every nerve and sensation in her body, throbbing with expectation of what was still to come, and weak with the knowledge of her own sexuality. She had thought she might be frigid. How wrong she had been! It was Charles's clumsy groping that had frozen her natural responses, and now she knew how it could be, she would never have that anxiety again.

Through the mists of her sensually-induced lethargy, she became aware that Jarret was taking longer than he should have done, and the first faint twinges of alarm gripped her. What if something was wrong? What if there had been an accident? Surely Jarret should have let her know by now.

Unwillingly, she slid her feet to the floor and stood up. Her legs felt incredibly unsteady, but she managed to slide her arms into her shirt and looked round blankly for her jacket. It was on the floor, where Jarret had pushed it from her shoulders, and she bent to pick it up as she walked towards the door.

She heard his voice as she paused in the open doorway, and even in those confused seconds she realised he was not talking to her mother. He was too relaxed for that, and even as her brows drew together in anxious disbelief, she heard his low laugh.

'No, nothing important,' she heard him say, through a haze of shocked incredulity. 'I'm glad you rang. It's good to know you haven't forgotten me. What? Oh, yes, in a couple of weeks, I hope. You have? That's great! So why don't you come down here? That would give us plenty of time to——'

Helen's whole body felt chilled. She could guess exactly who was on the other end of the line, and the whole episode the call had interrupted seemed suddenly incredibly sordid. Her behaviour was not without reproach, on the contrary, she felt almost sick with shame at the awareness of what she had done, but somehow she had believed that Jarret had been as emotionally involved as she had. Now it was obvious he regarded her as just another in his long line of conquests, and she wanted to curl up and die when she recalled how close she had been to calling off her engagement.

She had heard enough. Pressing the back of her hand to her lips, she fled across the hall and up the stairs, paying no heed to his abrupt ejaculation. She only wanted to get away from him, and his frustrated: 'Helen, *for God's sake*!' did not halt her headlong flight. He need not interrupt his telephone call for her, she thought bitterly, almost running along the corridor to her room, and she blessed the heavy oak door and the key which she turned with trembling satisfaction.

She was still standing there, pressed against the inner panels, when she heard his footsteps pounding along the corridor to her door and presently the angry hammer of his fists.

'Helen! Helen! For God's sake, I know you're in there. Open the door, there's a good girl. I want to talk to you.'

Helen said nothing, but her head moved from side to side in silent negation. What did he think she was? How could he go from one woman to another without the least compunction?

'Helen!' His voice was hardening now, and she could hear his impatience. 'Helen, don't let's make a drama out of this. Open the door. I have something to tell you. Stop acting like a schoolgirl. This is important!'

But still Helen made no response, and his anger exploded.

'Helen, open this bloody door! I mean it. If you don't I'll break it down!'

'Try it,' she breathed, but her words were not audible to him, and at the other side of the panels she heard his savage oath.

Seconds later there was the thud of someone's shoulder being applied to the task, and then another string of oaths as the door resisted even the violent assault of his boot.

'Helen—*please*!'

When oaths produced no reaction, he tried pleading, but although her senses craved the reassurances only he could give, she kept her lips pressed tightly together. She heard him shoulder the door once again, and this time she heard his groan of agony as the solid panels repelled his efforts. A sob of hysterical laughter rose in her throat at the farcical aspects of the situation, and if it hadn't been so horribly serious she might have found it very amusing. As it was, she felt only sick remorse, and tears burned painfully at the back of her eyes.

'Helen ...' He was getting tired, she could hear it, and there was a weary appeal in his voice. 'Helen, who in God's name do you think it was? At least let me explain.'

Her shoulders sagged. She wanted to—oh, how she wanted to, she thought tremulously, but if she opened the door there would be no turning back, and could she live with herself after that?

She hesitated, her lips parting to say something—anything, when she heard the sound of a car coming up the drive. It had to be her mother. No one else would arrive at King's Green at this time of night, and weariness overwhelmed her. It was too late now to do or say any of the things she had anticipated, and presently there was another sound—that of Jarret's footsteps receding along the corridor.

## CHAPTER SEVEN

THE morning light disturbed her, which might have been natural in ordinary circumstances, but after only a couple of hours of sleep Helen felt hardly confident to face the day. Her head felt muzzy, and her eyelids were sticky, and when she crawled out of bed to view her reflection in the mirror of the dressing table, she winced at the puffy swellings beneath them. Still, what could she expect after the storm of weeping she had indulged in? she asked herself miserably, and turned away to the bathroom to take a cold shower.

It was a hazy June morning, the sun filtering through clouds that would presently clear to give another warm day. It was not a day for working, but Helen was looking forward to going in to the shop. At least it would get her out of the house, and if she could hide the ravages of the night before from Karen, time, too, to consider what she was going to do.

She dressed in beige cotton pants, teaming them with a sleeveless cotton vest, whose warm apricot colour would, she hoped, distract from the pallor of her cheeks. Make-up had hidden the worst of the damage, and she was reasonably assured her mother would notice nothing amiss.

She was right. With the church fête only days away, Mrs Chase was too absorbed with the final arrangements she had to make to pay much attention to her daughter's unnaturally withdrawn demeanour, and Helen carried her toast and coffee into the dining room with a sigh of relief.

It was short-lived. She had only been sitting there about five minutes when a sound alerted her to the fact that she was no longer alone, and looking up she saw Jarret had entered the room and closed the door behind him. He was leaning back against it, as she had leant against her door the night before, and the connotations were unmistakable.

He was wearing a black leather suit—close-fitting pants that hugged his muscular thighs and a jerkin-length jacket which, with a matching silk shirt, added to his air of brooding vengefulness. In those first few minutes Helen gave no thought to his unshaven jawline, or the haggard hollowness of his eyes, only panic asserted itself, and the painful awareness of her own vulnerability. How could she handle him in her present state of nervous tension when she had fared no better the night before?

After subjecting her to a moment's appraisal, he straightened away from the door and came towards her. Now she began to see the ravages in his face, ravages that he could use no cosmetics to disguise, and her blood started to race wildly through her veins. He looked so pale, even the darkness of his skin seemed faintly transparent, and the blue eyes were bruised and sunken.

'Helen,' he greeted her flatly, pulling out a chair and straddling it. 'How are you?'

Helen's tongue circled her lips. 'How—how are you?' she got out jerkily. 'You—you look awful!'

'Thanks.' He flicked over the napkin beside him. 'You don't look so brilliant yourself.' His eyes darted upward. 'Did you sleep well?'

'Yes.' Helen's response was automatic, but when he exposed her to another of those penetrating stares, she felt the hot colour run helplessly up her cheeks and he knew she was lying. 'I—well, no,' she conceded, unable to withstand his scathing contempt. 'I slept very badly, as it happens. But that—that was hardly surprising in—in the circumstances, was it?' she finished rather contentiously.

'I'm not arguing, am I?' he countered, folding his arms along the back of the chair and resting his chin on his sleeve. 'I could say it served you right, but I won't.'

Helen gasped. 'You could say it. But you know it's not true.'

'Isn't it?' His eyes were narrowed and intent. 'Or are you so naïve you don't know what you did—to *both* of us?'

Helen pushed back her chair and got to her feet. 'I don't intend to sit here and listen to—to that kind of—of abuse!' she declared, and he tilted his head back to look at her.

'Why not?' His lips twisted. 'Doesn't it fit in with that totally unreal conception you have of the relationship between a man and a woman?'

'You have no right to say that to——'

'I have every right,' he snapped, getting abruptly to his feet. 'There's a word to describe what you did, but I won't use it because—God help me! I don't think you realised exactly what you did do.'

Helen held up her head. 'And—and what did you do?' she countered. 'Leaving me to speak to—to some other female——'

'I spoke to Jim Stanford!' stated Jarret coldly '*Jim* Stanford,' he repeated. 'My publisher—who also happens to be my agent. Who the hell did you think I was talking to? *Margot?*'

Helen was desperately trying to digest this. 'Your—your publisher?' she echoed. 'At—at half past eleven at night? You can't expect me to believe——'

'It was only half past six in New York,' stated Jarret harshly. 'God Almighty, Helen, what do you take me for? Some kind of male nymphomaniac? Lord, don't you know anything? I wanted you—*you!*' His voice thickened abruptly. 'I still do, damn you!'

Helen trembled, linking and unlinking her fingers as she tried to absorb what he had just told her. He had not been speaking to a woman, after all. That split conversation she had heard had been with his publisher, and what she had taken for assignations were in effect business appointments.

'Is—is that really true?' she breathed at last, and he gave her an impatient look.

'Is what true? That I want you?' He moved his shoulders in an offhand gesture. 'I guess you got under my skin. I'll get over it.'

Helen pressed a hand to her churning stomach. 'I meant —I meant—it really was your publisher?'

'Oh—yes.' He pushed his hands into the narrow pockets of his pants, unconsciously disrupting her efforts to remain detached. 'He wanted to be the first to tell me that *Devil's Kitchen* is going to be made into a film.'

'Oh, Jarret!' Helen couldn't prevent the thrill of excitement that coursed through her. 'That's wonderful news! You must be very pleased.'

'I was,' he conceded with another offhand gesture, and Helen's excitement died beneath a wave of remorse.

'That—that was what you wanted to tell me,' she

breathed, catching her lower lip between her teeth. 'And I thought——'

'I know what you thought,' he interrupted shortly, and she was silent. 'Anyway, I just thought I'd clear the matter up,' he continued, nodding towards her untouched toast and coffee. 'Get your breakfast. You look as though you need it.'

Helen glanced down at the table and then up at him again. 'Like I said, you don't look so—so good yourself,' she ventured, and his mouth took on a sardonic curve.

'Haven't you ever seen a hangover before?' he queried, his tone vaguely scornful, and she shifted rather uncomfortably. 'I got—stoned,' he added, changing the word he had been about to use at the last moment. 'You know— as in out of my mind.'

'Oh, Jarret!' There seemed nothing else she could say, and he lifted his shoulders and let them fall again in a dismissive shrug. 'At least I lost consciousness,' he mused, his gaze flickering over her swollen lids. 'You look as if you had a rough time.'

'I did.' She made no attempt to deny it, but although he acknowledged her husky confession, he made no move towards her. Instead he turned and strolled towards the door, and she realised that so far as he was concerned, the matter was closed.

'Jarret!' She could not let him go like that, but when he turned she hadn't the faintest idea what she was going to say to him.

'Yes?'

'I—well, I'm sorry about—about last night,' she offered.

'Yes. So am I,' he conceded with a wry smile, and without another word he left her.

Helen sank down into her chair again rather heavily. Her legs seemed to have lost the power to support her, and with a sense of anguished frustration she realised the last few minutes had also robbed her of what little appetite she had had.

Reaching for the coffee pot, she poured a measure of the strong black liquid, and then holding the cup between her cold hands, she tried to assimilate her reactions. It was crazy, this feeling of raw vulnerability, this painful aching void inside her that craved a fulfilment it could never attain. No matter how guilty Jarret made her feel, she had to remember that everything that had happened last night had been at his instigation—and it was all wrong! She was engaged to Charles. She owed him everything, and Jarret nothing. The way Jarret had treated her, she should be despising him this morning, not secretly regretting the interruption which had saved her from making an even bigger fool of herself.

Finishing the coffee, she left the table and went to tell her mother she was leaving, and then reversed her Alfa out of the stable yard. The air was sweet with the scent of lilac blossom, and breathing deeply, she determined to put all thoughts of Jarret Manning out of her head.

But as she drove across the forecourt she was visibly reminded that it would not be easy. Jarret himself was watching her manoeuvrings, seated on the back of one of the most beautiful animals Helen had ever seen. The night before she had been unable to distinguish its colouring, but now she saw it was a warm reddish-gold colour, with a white star on its nose, and the lean muscled lines of a thoroughbred.

She was obliged to halt. The horse was standing squarely in her way, and even as she stood rather reluctantly on her brakes, it shifted with evident nervousness. Jarret controlled it easily, running his long brown fingers over its ears before dismounting. He swung himself to the ground with the minimum amount of effort, as lean and muscled in the tight-fitting leather outfit as the powerful animal beside him, and Helen felt the familiar tightness in her chest that his nearness promoted.

Tossing the horse's reins over the pommel, Jarret strolled towards the car, bending to her open window with lazy indolence. 'Come and meet Horatio,' he said, and she knew from his tone that that was not really the animal's name. 'Come and apologise for frightening him half to death last night.'

'I can't.' Helen's response was abrupt. 'I—I'm late. I have to get to the shop——'

'I'm sure your worthy assistant can cope for a few extra minutes,' Jarret retorted, ignoring her palpitating breath.

'Come on. He's very gentle with ladies.'

'No.' Helen shook her head. 'No, I can't. I'm sorry, Jarret. He—he's a lovely animal, I can see that, but I—I can't——'

'Of course you can.' He was immovable. 'He'll be most offended if you turn him down.'

'Oh, stop this!' Helen's fine control was wearing thin. 'I don't want to meet your—your animal. I have to get to work, and that's where I'm going——'

'I think not.' Without asking her permission, Jarret opened her door, and the cooler air flooded in around her bare ankles. 'Come along. We're waiting.'

'No!' Anger came tremulously to her rescue. 'You have no right to do this, Jarret. I'm not a child, and I have no intention of being treated like one. If—and I say *if*—I ever do decide I need a closer relationship with a horse, then I'll ask Charles to arrange it.'

Jarret's lips twisted. 'No, you won't. You're going to get out right now and come and meet Horatio——'

'No, I won't!' Helen was adamant, but even as she made to start the car again, Jarret's fingers closed round her arm, and the power in his fingers numbed the strength in her hand.

'Now,' he said, maintaining a mild expression even while she could see the steely brilliance of his eyes, 'do you get out under your own steam, or do I assist you?'

Guessing what manner his assistance would take, Helen thrust her legs over the valance of the car and allowed him to draw her to her feet, but she hung back as he would have drawn her after him.

'Oh, please . . .' she whispered, and there was real fear in her voice now. 'Don't make me do this, Jarret. I—I'll do anything—anything——'

'Anything?' he mocked, and she sniffed rather tearfully.

'Anything,' she insisted, and he expelled his breath in an impatient sigh.

'That won't be necessary,' he informed her harshly, letting her go so violently she almost lost her balance. 'Go on, get back into your cage. You'll feel safe there. I won't deprive your fiancé of your doubtful pleasures. Go and bury yourself in the sand. You buried your head long ago!'

'Why, you—you——'

Helen could not think of an expletive suitable to describe the hatred she felt for him at that moment, but Jarret only turned and walked back to Horatio, swinging himself into the saddle with a lithe movement.

'So—okay,' he taunted. 'What are you going to do now? Attack me?'

Helen pursed and unpursed her lips, her hands clenching and unclenching at her sides. 'You—you're a pig!' she declared, her vocabulary no match for his. 'You think you can say—and do—anything you like to me!'

'And can't I?' he mocked. 'Oh, little girl, what a lot you have to learn!'

'I—I hate you!'

'That's healthy anyway.' He dug his heels into Horatio's sides and turned the horse towards her. 'Going to come with me?'

He was incorrigible, and she had no defence against him. Besides, as Horatio began to move towards her, other emotions took possession, and stumbling slightly she tumbled back into the car, slamming the door behind her. She heard his mocking laughter as she wound up her window, but without waiting for him to humiliate her further, she swung the wheel and describing a large semi-circle around him, she took off down the drive.

Karen had already opened up the shop when Helen arrived, and she had the kettle boiling ready to make some coffee. She grinned cheerfully when she saw her friend, but her smile turned to an anxious expression as she took in Helen's evident distraction.

'Hey!' she exclaimed, taking tthe other girl's arm and urging her into the privacy of the office. 'What's happened? You look awful!'

'Oh ...' Helen shook her head, unwilling to discuss her problems with Karen. 'I—er—slept badly, that's all. Is that coffee you're making? I could surely use a cup.'

Karen gave her another considered look, and then with a shrug went to make the coffee. 'You're late,' she said. 'I thought you must have slept in, not the other way about.'

Helen sighed, making a display of examining some invoices on the desk. 'Oh, you know how it is,' she said. 'The more time you have, the more you take. Has the mail come?'

'Not yet.' Karen stirred sugar into the cups, before handing one to her friend. 'There you are. I hope it's all right. The milk has gone sour, so I've used that powdered substitute.'

'It's fine.' Helen sipped hers with real relief. 'Mmm, just what I needed. The traffic was really bad this morning.'

Karen nodded, perching herself on a corner of the desk. 'Did you go to the house last night?'

'The house?' For a moment Helen's mind was blank, and Karen stared at her disbelievingly.

'The house. Your house. Yours and Charles's. At Petersham.'

'Oh!' Helen moved her shoulders in a helpless gesture. The hours she had spent with Charles seemed so incredibly distant as compared to the subsequent time she had spent with Jarret, and for a moment she had been unable to think beyond the events of the library. 'Oh, yes,' she added. 'We—er—we were choosing colour schemes for the kitchen. I—er—Charles thinks red tiles are attractive.'

Karen pulled a wry face. 'Memorable indeed!'

Helen sighed. 'We have to get the house decorated, Karen.'

'Oh, I agree. But what a waste of all those empty rooms.'

Helen shook her head. 'Honestly, Karen, there's more to marriage than sex!'

'So you say,' her friend conceded lightly. 'So—what did you decide?'

'Decide?' Once more Helen's mind was blank, and Karen reached for her cigarettes with mild impatience.

'About the kitchen,' she exclaimed. 'You just said——'

'Yes, I know, I know.' Helen gathered herself with difficulty. 'I—I don't think we decided anything definite.'

'You don't *think*?'

'Karen, what is this? The third degree?' Helen endeavoured to sound amused. 'What did you do with your evening? Did you go and see that film you were talking about? I'll have to try and persuade Charles to go to the cinema sometimes. I never seem to go these days.'

Karen lit her cigarette with careful deliberation, and then

she said casually: 'No, I didn't go to the pictures, Helen. As—er—as a matter of fact, I had a date.'

'Oh?' Helen arched her dark brows. 'With John?'

'No.' Karen's tongue circled her lips. 'With Jarret Manning, actually.'

'What?' Helen could not prevent the shocked exclamation, and Karen, watching her, saw the revealing colour come and go in her cheeks.

'Yes, I thought you'd be surprised,' she went on blithely. 'I would have told you, but I know how you feel about him, and—well, it seemed easier this way.'

Helen sought for composure. 'I—I didn't know you knew him that well,' she got out at last, trying to absorb this turn of circumstances. But all she could think of was that if they had had a date, it had been over earlier than surely Karen could have anticipated.

Karen shrugged, still observing her closely. 'He rang me a week ago,' she explained. 'He wanted to know if I knew a stables hereabout where he might be able to buy a mount.'

'But Charles——'

'Yes, well, obviously he didn't want to contact Charles. I told him about Burt Halliday.'

'I see.'

'Anyway, he contacted Burt, and Burt knew of this bay gelding that would be ideal, and I guess you know, he got the horse last night.'

Helen nodded.

'So he invited me out for a drink to celebrate,' Karen finished, drawing deeply on her cigarette. 'Naturally I accepted.'

'Naturally.' Helen's tone was bitter, and Karen eyed her mockingly.

'What's wrong? Do you disapprove? I don't see why you should. At least Jarret isn't married.' She paused. 'He told me quite a lot about himself, actually. He's not half as self-conscious as you'd have me believe.'

'I'd really rather not talk about Jarret Manning, if you don't mind,' retorted Helen shortly. 'Did you unpack those onyx figurines? I had a customer in here yesterday who——'

'Helen!' Karen cast her eyes heavenward. 'You're not

fooling anyone, you know. I know you're not indifferent to my going out with him, so stop pretending you are. Oh, I realise he's something outside your normal range of acquaintances, and I also accept that you're going to marry Charles, come hell or high water, but can't you at least be honest with *me*? For God's sake, he's not interested in me! Oh, I don't deny, I'd like to think he was. But he's not. It's you he's hooked on. But whether that's just another way of saying he wants to go to bed with you, I don't know. I only know he spent half the two hours we were together asking questions about you, and the other half trying to convince me what a lucky devil he'd been in making a success of his writing. He's not a bit conceited, if anything, he underplays his part, and I wish to hell it had been me who attracted him!'

'Karen!' Helen was shaken, but her friend was unrepentant.

'Well, it's true,' she declared snappishly. 'He's nice, really nice, and if you were really honest you'd admit it.'

Helen licked her dry lips. 'I don't know what you're suggesting, Karen, but——'

'I'm suggesting you stop behaving like a frustrated virgin, and act like a grown woman. Are you going to tell me you don't find him the least bit attractive, because I won't believe you.'

'Then there's no point in telling you, is there?'

'Helen!' Karen pressed out the stub of her cigarette with a heavy hand. 'Can't you see? It's this very—opposition you have to him that proves you're not indifferent.'

'All right, all right.' Driven beyond reason, Helen looped her hair behind her ears with trembling fingers. 'I do find him attractive. But as most women seem to, I'm not so different, am I?'

Karen sighed. 'The difference is—he finds you attractive, too.'

'Did he say so?'

Karen snorted. 'He didn't have to.'

'Oh, Karen!'

'Oh, Karen—nothing. I've seen the way he looks at you, remember? That first morning he brought you to the shop——'

'But that was weeks ago.'

'So what? At a guess, I'd say you were the reason he was so keen to take over King's Green.'

'But that's ridiculous! He knows I'm engaged to Charles.'

'Oh, Helen! When will you learn that two and two don't necessarily make four?'

Helen bent her head. 'I think we ought to leave this topic——'

'Why?'

'Why?'

'Yes, why?'

'Because—oh, because it's getting late, and we have things to do. You haven't forgotten that consignment from Bruges, have you——'

'You really won't listen to reason, will you, Helen?'

'Reason? *Reason?*' Helen pressed her lips together. 'What's reasonable about getting involved with Jarret Manning?'

Karen sighed. 'I don't know.'

'You see! Karen, I know you mean well, but honestly, Jarret Manning and I have nothing more to say to one another.'

Karen got up from the desk, and then she hesitated. 'So you have no objection if I see him again?'

Helen's fingers sought the edge of the desk. 'Wh-why should I have?'

'It was just a question,' said Karen mildly. 'Okay, what do you want me to do?'

Helen caught her lower lip between her teeth. 'Oh, I—I—let me think.' Despite her affirmed indifference, the other girl's words had left her feeling horribly faint. It was useless telling herself that it was just because she had had nothing to eat that morning. Deep down inside her, she could feel a knife turning slowly, and nothing could erase the knowledge that Karen would have no qualms when it came to a more intimate relationship ...

## CHAPTER EIGHT

DURING the following days Helen waited with a sense of foreboding for Karen to tell her Jarret had invited her out again. But she didn't, and she tormented herself with the thought that perhaps the other girl did not intend to tell her. Jarret himself seemed engrossed in his work, but after she had gone out of an evening she could not be absolutely sure that he stayed at home. She could hardly ask her mother. Although Mrs Chase liked Jarret, she would not give her approval to his conducting an illicit relationship with her daughter, and in spite of her defence of her house guest, she was really very fond of Charles.

For Helen, caught in the web of her own uncertainties, it was a terrible time. When she was with Charles, she was able to convince herself that everything was all right, that nothing had changed, that their marriage would be as successful as she had always imagined it would. But when they were apart, she was plagued with doubts, torn by the certain knowledge that Charles would not suffer a neurotic wife, and troubled by the awareness that she might not be able to respond to him. If only she could talk to him, she thought, try to make him understand what it was she was afraid of. But any attempt at an intimate discussion provoked an embarrassed rejection, and she was left feeling more and more conscious of their lack of mutual understanding. For Charles, that side of their marriage was a closed book, only to be opened between the sheets of their marriage bed, and Helen could not pursue the point without promoting the kind of display she most wanted to avoid.

The following week, she left work early one evening to do some shopping before she went home. She had promised Charles she would collect some wallpaper catalogues from the design centre, and she wanted to buy some tights and some make-up and visit the hairdresser for her monthly trim. This regular appointment kept her hair in good condition, and stopped it from growing longer than she wanted. She thought its present length was enough to handle, and as she invariably washed and dried it at home, it paid to keep the ends neat.

The small town was not busy at that hour of the afternoon. It was another warm day, although slightly overcast, and most people had done their shopping early to make the most of the sunshine. In consequence, she completed her purchases in ten minutes, and arrived at the hairdressers in good time for her appointment. Sally, the girl who always attended to her, was not busy either, and the wash and trim were soon accomplished, and a junior employed to blow it dry. It was quite pleasant sitting there, the open door providing a welcome draught, and Helen was almost sorry when it was over.

She drove home slowly, trying not to think of the problems that going home had come to mean to her, and parked the car by the porch, in readiness for her trip to Ketchley that evening. As she got out of the car she thought she could hear voices, but Horatio's whinny of welcome drowned any other sound, and she turned towards the horse in unwilling admiration.

'I know you're beautiful,' she said, grimacing across the space that divided them as Horatio leaned over the paddock rails. 'But I'm not the person you should be welcoming. You're too big and too aggressive for me. I don't like horses.'

Horatio shook his head, the movement sending the silky gold threads of his mane flying, and Helen felt a ridiculous sense of communion. 'It's no good, you know,' she persisted, closing the car door and pocketing the keys. 'I'm not a friend, so there's no point in pretending I am. You stick to —to your master. He likes you. I don't.'

Horatio did nothing. He just stood there looking hopefully at her with those dark soulful eyes that had so startled her that first evening Jarret brought him home, and almost involuntarily, Helen found herself taking a few steps towards him.

'Are you hot?' she asked, feeling no real sense of embarrassment in speaking to the horse. No one could hear her, and at least he did not answer back. She could see the way his tail was flicking his hide, dislodging the troublesome flies the heat had attracted, and she wondered suddenly if

Jarret had remembered to fill his water trough.

Horatio watched her approach without moving. Helen, realising she was as close to him as she had ever been to any horse, felt an increasing sense of pride in her own achievement. Maybe this was what she had needed all along, she thought, an opportunity to test herself, to try alone what she had never dared to try with anyone else. After all, what could he do to her? He was on one side of the fence, and she was on the other, and so often Charles had explained to her what intelligent beasts they were. The idea of being able to tell her fiancé that she had actually stroked a horse made her stretch out her hand towards his muzzle, and her fingers spread tentatively against its velvety nose.

It was an exquisite moment, a moment of immense satisfaction, when all the doubts and fears she had nourished seemed to melt away. It wasn't frightening at all, it was exhilarating, and her breath escaped on a choking sob of relief.

But it was spoilt by the increasing sound of the voices she had heard before, or one voice at least, shrill and accusing and totally out of control. She turned her head bewilderedly, wondering if her mother and Jarret could be having some kind of altercation, but not really believing it, and saw Margot Urquart appear in the open doorway. Seeing Margot like that was like sustaining a solid blow to the solar plexis. Somehow Margot was the last person she had expected to see, but even as she started to avert her head, the sun glinted on something Margot was carrying, something that was very heavy and which the older woman was finding it difficult to hold on to. Blinking, Helen saw in amazement that it was Jarret's typewriter, the strong, heavy-duty portable machine he had brought to King's Green with him, but while the conviction was dawning that there was something seriously amiss, Margot suddenly flung the machine with all the force she could muster on to the gravelled sweep of the forecourt. It all happened so quickly, Helen had no time to voice any objection, and even though she could now see Jarret behind Margot, his attention had been distracted by her own closeness to the horse. And before he could drag his eyes from her and back to Margot, the deed was done.

Horatio was startled by the sudden uproar. Backing off from the rails, he made his own audible protest, but Helen was too shocked to be alarmed. Margot must be out of her mind, she thought, unable to conceive of anything which might have caused her to react so violently, and the outcome was so appalling, she felt glued to the spot.

'Now you'll have to come back to London, won't you?' the other woman was shouting hysterically. 'You'll have to get another typewriter from the apartment, or buy a new one. And I doubt a little place like Malverley will sell a sophisticated machine like that!'

Helen felt terrible. She did not want to be an onlooker to this unprovoked display, but there was no way she could escape without being observed. Margot seemed deaf and blind to anyone's feelings but her own, and any sudden move on her part might precipitate the kind of verbal abuse she most wanted to avoid.

Jarret was standing perfectly still, listening to her. When the expensive typewriter had bounced off the forecourt, he had thrust his hands into the back hip pockets of the jeans he was wearing, and since then he had neither moved nor said anything. He had made no attempt to examine the machine presently residing on its side on the gravel, and Helen, who had seen the glitter of the metal fragments which had been flung from it, guessed he knew it would need more than an overhaul to repair it.

The unexpected sound of a car approaching up the drive motivated Helen to turn towards it, but it was not her mother's Triumph that accelerated towards the house. It was Jarret's Ferrari that swung round in an arc on the forecourt and came to rest beside Helen's Alfasud, and she looked in surprise at the strange man who thrust open the door and got out from behind the wheel. Unlike herself, he did not seem at all surprised to see Margot, though his face took on an appalled expression when he saw what had happened, and his first words were ones of accusation.

'My God,' he muttered, turning to look at Margot's flushed and angry face. 'Did you do this? What the hell for? I'd never have brought you if I'd suspected—you must be out of your tiny mind!'

'Leave it, Jim.' It was Jarret who answered him, his eyes

flicking briefly in Helen's direction. 'Did you get some cigarettes? Good. Let's go and have a drink. I guess we could all use one.'

'But damn it, Jarret——'

The man's instinctive protest was revealing, but it was Margot who interrupted him. 'Don't you walk away from me, Jarret Manning!' she cried, almost sobbing in her fury. 'You're not going to walk away from me. I—I'll ruin you before I let you go!'

'You never had me, Margot,' Jarret responded in a driven tone. 'For God's sake, don't do this to yourself!'

'To myself? To me? I'm doing nothing I'm ashamed of,' she averred. 'But you—you're going to be sorry!'

'For God's sake, Margot!' The other man spoke again now, and Helen realised that this must be Jarret's publisher, Jim Stanford. 'Can't you see? You're only making an exhibition of yourself.' He seemed to see Helen for the first time and cast an embarrassed look in her direction. 'Can't you pull yourself together, woman!'

'You—you're as big a fool as he is, Stanford!' Margot spat out the words contemptuously. 'You think you're such good friends, don't you? I wonder how you'd feel if you knew your wife was not above trying her hand at adultery with your good friend Manning!'

This was awful. Helen felt both sickened and appalled. She wanted to put her hands over her ears and not listen to any more of Margot's crudeness, but there was a fearful fascination in her malicious revelations that kept her riveted to the spot. She dared not look at Jarret. She was afraid of what she would see in his face, and she looked instead at Jim Stanford, waiting for the shocked disillusionment which she was sure would come.

But there was no anger in the older man's features, only a weary acceptance, and with cold resignation he said: 'I know Jo's faults as well as you do, Margot—I've lived with her for almost twenty years. Don't try to come between us, because it simply won't work. Save your accusations for someone who needs them. I don't.'

The two men turned abruptly towards the house, and Helen expelled her breath on an uneasy sigh. What now? Would Margot turn on her, or could she conceivably steal away without further embarrassment? Surely Margot had to give up now. If she had driven down with Jim Stanford, and it seemed the only explanation, she would have to drive back with him, and there seemed no point in aggravating an already difficult situation.

Margot turned towards the house and Helen's shoulders sagged. But her hopes that Margot was going to follow the two men were short-lived. Instead, she circled the Ferrari and jerked open the driver's door. Even if Helen had wanted to stop her, she would have had no time to do so, and although she automatically started forward, the older woman gave her no chance to intervene. The ignition fired and the powerful sports car began to accelerate down the drive, and Helen shrank back appalled as it passed her with Margot hugging the wheel.

The two men had heard the firing of the engine, of course, and they came out of the house as the Ferrari disappeared behind the concealing branches of the beeches that lined the drive. Jarret was first, his face grim as he realised what had happened, and Jim Stanford followed to stare morosely at the cloud of dust the tyres had churned up.

'I—er—I couldn't stop her,' Helen offered, needing to say something, and Stanford turned to her with a helpless gesture.

'I don't think it would have been politic to try,' he assured her tautly, his face revealing his anxiety. 'Hell, Jarret, what can I say?'

'Silly—bitch,' Jarret responded, raking long fingers through his hair. 'Where the hell do you think she's gone?'

'Would you believe—London?' Stanford sighed. 'God, I'm sorry Jarret. If she damages that car, I'll never forgive myself.'

'It wasn't your fault,' Jarret retorted dryly. 'And don't be so mercenary. She could damage herself, never mind the car.' He shook his head. 'Come on, I've poured you a beer. It'll help to cool you down.'

Helen hesitated, not quite knowing what to do, and as Jarret turned away, his eyes encountered hers. It was the first time she had looked at him fully since Margot's eruption from the house, and in spite of her condemnation of his part in the proceedings, she could not tear her gaze away.

Eventually it was Jarret himself who broke the contact, indicating the other man and saying offhandedly: 'My publisher, James Stanford. Jim, this is Helen Chase. My—er—landlady's daughter.'

'Oh, hello.' Stanford's acknowledgement of the introduction was brief, his thoughts obviously occupied with the whereabouts of the Ferrari, and Helen, about to hurry indoors and leave them, suddenly found Jarret's hard fingers about her wrist.

'You touched Horatio,' he said in an undertone. 'I saw you.'

'To your cost,' she retorted, disturbed in spite of herself by the unwanted intimacy, and he inclined his head.

'You might say that,' he agreed, his fingers invading her palm, and her breath caught in her throat.

'You don't imagine I could have stopped her, do you?' she exclaimed, annoyed that he could arouse her like this, but he chose not to answer her.

'I suppose I should—congratulate you,' he said instead. 'I imagine friend Connaught will be overjoyed when he hears you're no longer afraid of his four-legged meal tickets.'

Helen's head jerked up. 'Do you expect me to thank you?' she demanded, but he only grimaced.

'I've learned not to expect anything from you,' he essayed smoothly. 'I'd have to be pretty slow not to realise you're as afraid of showing your feelings as you were of old Horatio over there.'

'And you're certainly not that, are you, Mr Manning?' she countered, wrenching her arm away. 'Slow, I mean. Quite the reverse, I'd say.'

Jarret's face lost expression. 'If that's what you choose to believe,' he essayed flatly, and his lack of aggression was somehow more disconcerting than his anger might have been. He seemed determined not to argue with her, and she was left feeling distinctly let down.

Fortunately Stanford chose that moment to decide he would like the drink he had been offered, and the two men disappeared into the library as soon as they entered the house. Helen, not a little distrait, wished she could drown her sorrows so easily, but instead she went along to the kitchen in search of Mrs Hetherington's panacea, tea.

As it turned out, Helen drove Jarret's publisher to the railway station in Malverley later that evening. When her mother returned from the garden party she had been attending and discovered the events of the afternoon, she had insisted Stanford should stay for dinner, and he had been only too happy to agree. Mrs Chase also arranged for the pieces of Jarret's typewriter to be gathered from the drive, and they presently were residing in a cardboard box, awaiting delivery to a repairers. But it was Jim Stanford himself who insisted that Jarret should use his car until his own was returned to him.

'I'd never have borrowed the Ferrari if I'd known what might happen,' he exclaimed, after explaining to Helen and her mother how he had parked his own Mercedes in the stable yard when he and Margot arrived at lunchtime. 'It was hot, you see,' he explained, 'and you know how unpleasant it is having to undertake a long journey in an overheated vehicle.'

'It wasn't your fault, Jim,' Jarret said once again, but clearly Stanford didn't agree with him, and his enquiries as to how he might get to the railway station had encouraged Mrs Chase to suggest that Helen might drive him on her way to Ketchley.

'After all, you don't even know where the station is, do you, Jarret?' she pointed out reasonably. 'And Helen can easily make the detour, can't you, darling? So long as Mr Stanford doesn't mind riding in the Alfasud.'

'Helen can use the Mercedes, if she'd like,' he declared gallantly, his good humour restored after the satisfying meal Mrs Hetherington had provided, but Helen declined the offer.

'I—er—I know my own car,' she demurred, and after the two men had bade one another farewell, Helen took her seat at the wheel. She was intensely conscious that Jarret had not addressed one remark to her throughout dinner, and although she told herself she didn't care, deep down inside her she knew she did. It was useless to deny the fact that since he came to King's Green her life had taken on a new meaning, and no matter how she might crave ignorance of his affairs, her mind would not allow her to forget.

It was a heavy evening, the overcast skies lowering and deepening, and threatening a storm. Helen, making polite responses to Jim Stanford's conversation, pondered the advisability of driving to Ketchley at all, realising that the game of tennis Charles had suggested would most likely be rained off before long.

She was therefore taken aback when Stanford said suddenly: 'I hope you weren't too upset by Margot's behaviour this afternoon,' and when, startled, she began to protest that she had thought nothing of it, he went on. 'She's an hysterical woman, and ever since Jarret's first book was successful, she's convinced herself that he owes it all to her. He doesn't, of course. Oh, she drew my attention to the manuscript in the first place, I don't deny that, but if Stanfords hadn't published it, another house would. Have you read it?'

'No, I'm afraid not . . .'

'You should. It's well worth the trouble. Jarret has a distinctly professional approach and I suppose his work as an overseas correspondent is responsible. You knew he worked in Fleet Street before he became a novelist?'

'Well—yes——'

'Even so, no one could have anticipated the phenomenal success he's had.'

Helen moved her shoulders rather awkwardly. 'Why are you telling me all this, Mr Stanford?'

'I don't know.' He paused. 'I guess because I care about Jarret, and I wouldn't like to think I'd been responsible for Margot lousing things up for him.'

'I don't know what you mean!'

Helen was taken aback now, but Stanford didn't appear to notice. 'She begged me to bring her with me, you know, saying she hadn't seen him for months, pretending she'd been too busy to bother with him. God, if I'd only known!' He sighed. 'I guess women like her always need to latch on to success, don't they? Margot more than most. She's had a singular lack of success in her own personal life.'

Helen shook her head. 'Margot's my mother's friend,

Mr Stanford, not mine. And—and perhaps she's had—provocation.'

'Provocation?' He glanced sideways at her. 'You're not saying you feel sorry for her!'

'I—I might be.'

He made a sound of derision. 'You know, I got the impression earlier that you were as shocked by her behaviour as I was.'

Helen pressed her lips together for a moment. 'Well—yes. Yes, perhaps I was. But anyway, it's nothing to do with me, is it? I mean, Mr Manning's affairs are no concern of mine. I'm engaged to be married, Mr Stanford.'

'So what? My wife is my wife, but I know how she feels about Jarret?'

Helen was astounded. 'And don't you care?'

He shrugged. 'Jarret's not interested in Jo. If she throws herself at his head, can he be blamed for that?'

Helen blinked, and said no more. His words had disturbed her, but she had no right to question him. Besides, they reached the station a few minutes later, and there was no further chance to pursue it. Instead, she bade him a good journey and drove away.

Deciding she needed the reassurance of Charles's presence whether or not it was going to rain, Helen took the Ketchley road, but the storm broke before she reached the Connaughts'. Charles was watching for her and he opened the door as she sprinted from the car to the porch, helping her off with her jacket as soon as he had closed the door.

'What rotten luck!' he exclaimed, as she dried her cheeks with a damp tissue, and Helen nodded.

'I just felt like a game of tennis, too,' she said with a rueful grimace, but Charles looked blank at this.

'I meant it's going to be pretty heavy going at Exeter tomorrow,' he exclaimed. 'You know I've got two horses running. I told you. If this rain continues——'

'Oh, never mind about your horses, Charles,' Helen protested wearily, accompanying him into the sitting room. 'We were going to have a game, weren't we? Now we can't. And I'm sorry.'

Charles sniffed. 'I realise you don't like my animals, Helen, but I should have thought the least you could do is to show some concern for their welfare. Rain makes the track slippery or heavy or both——'

'I know that, Charles. And I'm not unfeeling, honestly.' Helen hesitated. 'As a matter of fact, I—er—I stroked Jarret's horse today. What do you think about that?'

'You did what?' Charles was suitably shocked, but she didn't altogether like his expression. 'You—*stroked* Manning's horse! When did he get a horse? You didn't tell me he rode.'

'I didn't know myself until a few days ago. He—er—he bought a gelding from Burt Halliday.' Helen seated herself beside the empty fireplace, wrapping her arms about her knees and saying quickly: 'Where's your mother? Surely she's not——'

'Burt Halliday!' Charles interrupted harshly, as she had half guessed he might. 'Manning bought a horse from him? That—that rogue! Well, I hope he got what he paid for!'

Helen shrugged, rather doubtfully. 'He—I—Horatio seems a sound animal,' she ventured, but Charles only snorted again.

'What would you know about it?' he snapped. Then, as if remembering what else she had told him, he added: 'How come you got close enough to the horse to stroke it?' His eyes darkened angrily. 'Perhaps I ought to ask whether Manning was riding the animal at the time!'

'No, of course he wasn't.' But Helen flushed all the same. 'He—he wasn't even there. I just—well, Horatio was there——'

'*Horatio!*'

'—and I—I felt sorry for him, because the flies were bothering him.'

'So you stroked it.' Charles was contemptuous.

'As it happens, yes.' Helen refused to be intimidated. 'I thought you'd be pleased.' Then, as Charles continued to look at her in that unpleasant way, she went on: 'You didn't say where your mother was.'

'She and Dad have gone to the theatre,' he declared shortly. 'I believe it's the local operatic group who are performing some musical or other. Anyway, she wanted to go, and Dad had to take her.'

'I see.' Helen felt a faint twinge of regret. She would have preferred Charles's parents to be at home this evening. Somehow she sensed he was spoiling for an argument, and she guessed his concern for his beloved horses was responsible.

'So you think you could learn to ride yourself now, do you?' Charles persisted, determined to make something of her confession, and Helen sighed.

'Some day—maybe,' she conceded, unwilling to be drawn into a dispute, and her fiancé came to stand looking down at her with cold angry eyes.

'When I think of the number of occasions I've tried to get you to make friends with my animals,' he said savagely, 'and Manning has only to produce some mangy nag and you're all over it!'

'That's not true!' Helen stood up abruptly, refusing to sit at his feet like some inferior being. 'I've told you. Jarret knew nothing about it.'

'Oh, it's Jarret now, is it?' Charles's lips curled. 'Well, well! I wondered how long it would take.'

'Oh, don't be silly, Charles.' Helen felt impatient with herself. 'Perhaps—perhaps you tried too hard. I don't know. I only know that the horse was there, and so was I, and I approached it. That's all there is to it.'

'Huh!' Charles thrust his hands deeply into the pockets of his tweed jacket. 'But I suppose you wouldn't like to repeat the exercise.'

Helen stared at him. 'I don't know what you mean.'

'I mean now. Here and now. You could show me how— how brave you are.'

Helen frowned. 'Is that necessary? Don't you believe me?'

'What if I said no?'

Helen caught her lower lip between her teeth. 'Oh, Charles, this is silly!'

'Why? Because I'm asking you and not Manning?'

'Jarret had nothing to do with it, Charles. How many more times?'

'Very well then.' Charles's chin jutted. 'Prove to me that you can enter the stables without panicking.'

Helen sighed. 'Really, Charles . . .' But his expression was unrelenting, and after a moment she moved her shoulders in a gesture of acceptance. 'All right, if it will please you. But don't expect too much, will you? I—I need a lot more time.'

Charles's face was unrevealing, and she felt an increasing sense of unreality as she put on her jacket once again. If only his parents had been at home, she would have felt less apprehensive. As it was, she felt distinctly uneasy, and half inclined to call the whole thing off and risk his anger.

It was possible to reach the stables from the house without going out into the storm. A covered walkway led from the back of the building to the centrally-heated block, and Helen, who had never traversed its sacred pavements before, felt a twinge of panic at the first scent of horseflesh. Keep calm, she told herself severely, but it wasn't easy, knowing that Charles expected so much of her.

The stables were gloomy in the grey light, only an occasional flash of sheet lightning bringing a shaft of brilliance to the shadowy passages and making the animals shift uneasily. Helen wished they could have chosen another evening, and she was relieved when Charles switched on the electric lights. The mingled smells of leather and clean straw served to distract her senses from other things, but when she saw the stalls and the narrow gangway between she had the strongest urge to turn and run.

'So,' said Charles, indicating the animal in the first stall, a spirited grey that tossed its head at their approach. 'This is Moonmist. What do you think? Could you handle him, do you suppose?'

'H-handle him?' Helen expelled her breath on a nervous laugh. 'Heavens, no! I—I couldn't handle any horse. Not—not yet, anyway.'

'What about Lacey here?' Charles stroked the neck of a gentler-looking chestnut, that whinnied its appreciation. 'She's harmless enough. Come and stroke her. She won't bite you.'

Helen hesitated, but another look at Charles's set face sent her forward, reaching out almost blindly towards the animal. If she failed now he would never forgive her, and it was with a weak sense of relief that she felt the silky coat beneath her fingers.

'Well, well...' Charles was impressed, but she didn't like his tone. 'I can hardly believe it. When did you say this miracle took place?'

'It's no miracle, Charles.' Bravely, Helen allowed the mare to nuzzle her fingers. 'It—it just happened. One minute I was terrified, and the next I wondered why I'd ever been so timid.'

'And what did Manning say?' inquired Charles caustically.

'Oh—he was surprised, of course——'

'You said he wasn't there!' Charles cut in coldly, and she realised he had deliberately trapped her.

'He wasn't,' she asserted, refusing to be bullied. 'But I told him.'

'Really?' Charles was absolutely furious. 'You told him? You went straight away and told him you'd stroked his horse?'

'It wasn't like that.'

'What was it like?'

Helen sighed. 'Oh, Charles! Must we go on with this? I've done as you asked and stroked—er—Lacey. Can we go back to the house now, please? I'm feeling cold.'

'Why? It's warm in here.'

'Charles!'

'In a minute, in a minute.' He clamped his jaw together, moving further down the gangway, speaking to some of the animals he passed, with little of the antagonism he had used towards his fiancée. He seemed determined to get his pound of flesh, and Helen wrapped her arms defensively around herself, wishing she had taken her own advice and not driven to Ketchley this evening.

'Come here, Helen.'

Charles's voice broke into her musings, and she looked up rather anxiously to find he was nowhere in sight. 'I—where are you?' she faltered, but when he called again, she guessed he had gone through the door at the end into the adjoining block.

'Must I?' she appealed, wishing she had never started this, but when he didn't reply she had no choice but to do as he wished.

It was only when she reached the end of the row of stalls

that she realised Charles had not gone into the next building. The door to the end cubicle was open, and Charles was inside, crouched at the feet of a huge black beast that seemed to loom over Helen like some malevolent monster.

Somehow, she didn't know how, she prevented herself from crying out, and as if disappointed at her lack of reaction, Charles rose to his feet again and nodded towards the animal.

'This is Poseidon,' he said, and Helen's heart lurched in recognition of the name. 'Look, I wanted to show you what that fool brother of mine caused to happen. Here—on the fetlock. Can you see? Come nearer. Luckily the tuft prevented a more serious cut, but it was pretty nasty all the same.'

Helen hung back. Poseidon was quiet enough now, but she did not trust its beady black eyes, or the way its ears lay back against its head. What was Charles trying to do? Cure her of her fears—or magnify them?

'I—I'd really rather not,' she got out, licking her dry lips. 'Oughtn't we to be going back to the house? I really am—very cold.'

'Coward!' Charles's tone was derisive, and she thrust her hands into the pockets of her jacket.

'Perhaps I am,' she agreed, refusing to be baited in that way. 'But at least I know what I am!'

'What's that supposed to mean?'

Helen sighed. 'Let's go back, Charles,' she suggested. 'I'm cold, and I see no point in provoking an argument with you. If you want the truth, that creature scares me. But you knew that before you even opened the door.'

'Poseidon?' Charles moved closer to the stallion, running his hand over the creature's smooth black coat. 'Poseidon wouldn't hurt you. Not while I'm here. He's beautiful, isn't he? So sleek, so streamlined. He's going to sire some magnificent foals.'

Helen was not impressed. A cold chill had invaded her spine when she looked into its wicked little eyes, and she doubted it felt any more sympathy towards Charles than it did to anyone else.

'Are you coming?' she asked now, looking longingly back down the gangway. 'Let's go down to the pub and have a drink. I—I could do with one.'

Charles gave her a pitying look. 'Been too much for you, has it? I thought it would. You're no equestrian, Helen. You never will be. And you can tell Manning I said so.'

Helen had had enough. Without waiting for Charles's permission, she marched away along the planked catwalk, not really caring what he thought of her. His attitude both shocked and disturbed her, and she was beginning to realise there were more traits to her fiancé's nature than she had ever dreamed. Unpleasant traits, too, traits she would rather not know about, and that made her overwhelmingly aware that Charles was insensitive when his wishes were in jeopardy.

The sudden flash of lightning followed closely by a heavy crack of thunder was startling, and she was glad she was near the door. All the animals were shifting a little restively in their stalls, and she guessed they were as nervous of the storm as she was of them. When she heard Charles cry out it was all one with the rumbling menace around them, and for a moment she thought he was trying to trick her again. But as the echoes of the thunder died away she could still hear Poseidon's excited clamour, and the unmistakable sound of his restless hooves.

'Charles ...' She stopped and called his name, but he made no response. 'Charles,' she cried again, 'Charles, answer me! Stop fooling around. You're frightening me!'

'Helen!' Charles's voice was faint. 'Helen, for God's sake, help me! I've—I've twisted my leg, and I can't get out.'

Helen stood stock still. She didn't know whether to believe him or not. Charles was in such a funny mood, and she was terrified that this was some new test he was devising.

'Where are you?' she called, her voice tremulous and uneasy, and she heard his curse of impatience.

'Where do you think?' he demanded hoarsely. 'In Poseidon's stall. He kicked me, the brute! For heaven's sake, give me a hand.'

Helen went back along the gangway on leaden feet. She was sick to her stomach, but nothing could have prevented her from going to his aid. No matter how frightened she was, he was her fiancé, and she could not abandon him.

The storm continued to rage about them, and every time

the lightning struck she expected the lights to be extinguished. But to her relief, although they flickered in protest, they remained constant, and at last she reached the end of the line.

She didn't know what she had expected to find. She supposed her worst fear was that Poseidon might be waiting to spring out at her, but as soon as she saw the situation she realised how foolish that was. The black horse was secured by a leading rein to the wall of the stall, and it was Charles who demanded her attention, crouched in an awkward huddle on the floor.

'Bloody fool,' he muttered, as Helen halted wide-eyed in the doorway. 'Come and help me up. The damn thing could have killed me.'

'Why? How?' Helen hurried forward, too concerned about her fiancé to be really scared of the horse. 'What happened? I thought you could handle him.'

'Oh, don't make a fool of me, Helen,' Charles snapped angrily, groaning as he struggled to his feet, his whole weight bearing down on her shoulder. 'How was I to know the thunder would spook him like that? If his hooves had encountered my head instead of my knee ...'

Helen thought that Charles should have anticipated such an occurrence, but she knew better than to say so, and leaning painfully on her, they managed to get out of the stall and close the half door.

'Is it very painful—your leg, I mean?' she asked, as they limped along between the stalls to the door, and Charles ground his teeth together.

'What do you think?' he retorted, offering no thanks for her assistance, and Helen kept her mouth shut until they reached the house.

In the sitting room, the full extent of Charles's injury became apparent. Poseidon had obviously kicked him violently, and the skin around the knee was black and blue already.

'Do you think it's broken?' Helen asked, kneeling down beside him, but Charles only brushed her concern aside.

'It's bruised, that's all,' he insisted, bending it with evident difficulty. 'Go and get me a double Scotch and soda.

That's all I need. No damned animal's going to get the better of me!'

'At least let me call the doctor,' she suggested gently. 'After all, it's going to be very painful for some time. He could probably prescribe some pain-killers——'

'Don't patronise me, Helen.' Charles snatched the Scotch and soda from her hand without ceremony. 'I know what you're thinking. You're thinking, it serves him right for forcing me to go into the stables, aren't you——'

'No!'

'—and if he had to call the doctor, everyone's going to know that Connaught can't control his own blasted animals!'

'No, Charles!'

Helen was appalled at his bitterness, but Charles only swallowed the Scotch at a gulp and demanded another. He downed it at the same pace, then viewed Helen with malevolent eyes.

'Come here,' he muttered, patting the couch beside him. 'Come and smooth my brow with your cool fingers. You're always saying I never make advances towards you when we're alone. Come and let me alter that opinion.'

'Oh, Charles ...' Helen shook her head helplessly. 'What is the matter with you? Please, let me call Doctor Bluthner. He only lives a few hundred yards away. I know he'd be only too glad——'

'I said come here, Helen.'

Charles stretched out his hand towards her, and with a feeling of intense unwillingness she joined him on the couch. When he turned towards her, she saw his eyes were bloodshot and slightly glazed from the amount of alcohol he had consumed, but what disturbed her most was the familiar brush of his hands across her thighs.

'Little Helen,' he said thickly, burying his face in the hollow of her neck. 'My sweet saviour! Well, you deserve something for what you did tonight.'

His hand moved to the zip of her pants and a feeling of cold rejection gripped her. What did Charles think he was doing? He had not kissed her or aroused her in any way. He seemed to have only one object in mind, and that with the sole intention of his own gratification.

She tried to push his hand away, but he was very strong and very determined. The zip was propelled downward, and his eager fingers sought to invade the secret warmth within.

'*No*, Charles!'

She fought him like a wild thing, struggling and heaving and kicking her legs, and as her efforts made contact with him, he was forced to release her.

'You bitch!' he muttered, both hands seeking his injured knee and cradling it protectively, and belatedly she felt a pang of remorse.

'I'm sorry, but——' she was beginning, when the sound of the outer door opening and voices entering the house suddenly silenced her. They also made her overwhelmingly aware of her state of undress, and she hastily dragged her zip into place and smoothed her ruffled hair as footsteps crossed the hall.

She did not know who she had expected to see, certainly not Vincent, Charles's brother, and with him, Jarret Manning. The two men halted in the doorway assessing the scene they had interrupted, and then Vincent broke the awkward stillness by saying: 'It's a filthy night, isn't it?' in wry amused tones.

Helen could not have felt worse. She could almost see what Jarret was thinking and Vincent was no doubt of the same opinion. Only Charles seemed unembarrassed by their presence, his reaction to their arrival taking on an entirely different aspect.

'What the hell are you doing here, Manning?' he snapped, making no attempt to get up and greet his brother, and Vincent swiftly intervened.

'He didn't want to come in, Chas, but I insisted. I rang him from the station in Malverley. There were no cabs to be had, and I needed a lift. The least you can do is offer him a drink.'

'We—er—we didn't hear the car,' Helen ventured, addressing herself to Vincent, and he grinned.

'I can believe it,' he teased, but when she didn't respond he added: 'I guess the rain drowns most things.' He turned to Jarret. 'Do you want a drink, mate?'

'No, thanks.' Jarret spoke for the first time, his gaze

flickering over Helen and then moving to her fiancé on the couch. 'I'd better be getting back. Can I give you a lift, Helen?'

'Me?' she gasped, and Charles said harshly: 'She's got her own car, Manning. She doesn't need any lifts from you!'

'The roads are pretty bad, though,' put in Vincent, touching Helen's sleeve. 'Quite honestly, I'd advise you to go with Jarret. You can always pick up your car in the morning.'

'You keep out of this, Vincent.' Charles glared up at him with angry eyes, and his brother viewed his position with some curiosity.

'You going to stop me, Chas?' he enquired unpleasantly, and as Helen tried to intervene, he went on: 'What happened to you? Why are you sitting there like a wounded cockerel? Helen kick you where it hurts, did she?'

'It was the horse—it was Poseidon,' Helen exclaimed, gazing appealingly at the younger man. 'Charles has damaged his knee——'

'Don't tell me Poseidon did the kicking!' Vincent evidently found it quite hysterical, and Charles turned angry eyes on his fiancée.

'Why the hell don't you learn to keep your mouth shut?' he demanded, hands clenching and unclenching round his drawn-up knee, but before Helen could answer him Jarret grasped the other man's collar.

'Just who do you think you're speaking to?' he grated, putting his face close to Charles, and Helen felt a rising sense of hysteria herself.

'For heaven's sake!' she exclaimed. 'This is ridiculous! Oh, I'm going home. I'm not going to listen to any more of this. You can fight it out among yourselves!'

Ignoring all of them, she crossed the hall and let herself out of the house. Vincent had been right, it was a filthy night, but she preferred the storm outside to the one going on in the house. She glimpsed Jim Stanford's Mercedes as she raced to her own car, and wrenching open the door she coiled herself thankfully behind the wheel. She didn't want to think any more, she just wanted to drive, and she set the car in motion without a backward glance.

The thunder had abated, but the rain had not, and the roads were minor floods as she turned towards Thrushfold. The blackness of the tarmac absorbed the reflection of her headlights, and it was impossible to see further than a few yards ahead of her. But she wasn't alarmed. Her desire to escape from the remembrance of the scene at Charles's home banished all fear, and she just wanted to reach her own home and her own room.

She supposed she had been driving perhaps ten minutes when she became aware of the headlights behind her. A car was following her, and she could guess whose car it was. Jarret had to come home, and this was the only likely route. The awareness of his encroachment on both her life and her emotions made her quicken her pace, as if by physically adjusting the space between them she could adjust her life accordingly. It didn't work, of course, he was just as disruptive to her peace of mind, and with a sob rising in her throat she pressed her foot down hard on the accelerator.

It was a risky thing to do in the circumstances. The tyres spun wildly on the slippery road, and the lack of traction sent her skidding sideways. She struggled to hold on to the wheel, but it seemed to be wrenched from her fingers, and she thanked God for her seat-belt, as the Alfa swung helplessly across the road and into the ditch.

She was not hurt, only shocked, but she was still sitting there, slumped in her seat, when the door was wrenched open and Jarret's anxious face appeared.

'Helen, for God's sake——' he was muttering, only to break off abruptly as she turned shamefaced eyes in his direction. He stared at her half angrily for a moment and then, gathering himself, he grated: 'Are you all right?'

She nodded, not trusting herself to speak, and he straightened, pushing balled fists into the pockets of his dark pants. Unlike her, he was not wearing a jacket, only the silk shirt he had worn for dinner that evening, and in the courtesy light from her open door she could see the rain soaking his thinly-covered shoulders.

'I—I'll be all right,' she got out jerkily, making a helpless gesture. 'You—you go. You're getting soaked——'

'And how do you propose to get out of the ditch?' he

demanded harshly. 'Can you lift it? Or do you expect to drive out of there?'

Helen knew his anger was justified, but she was at the end of her emotional tether. 'I've said I'll manage,' she retorted lightly. 'Go away, Mr Manning. I don't need your assistance. Go back to your writing. Playing Sir Galahad is not your scene!'

Jarret stared down at her with cold angry eyes. 'I could choke you, do you know that?' he demanded. 'Scaring me half to death, and then turning on me for trying to help you! I'm not to blame for your unsatisfactory love-life! You should have known better.'

Helen gasped. 'I don't know what you mean——'

'Oh, come on. You don't imagine I'm blind to that little discourse we interrupted, do you?'

'How dare you——'

'Forget it!' He turned aside, kicking viciously at the tyre that spun uselessly above the ditch. 'How the hell am I going to get you out of there?'

'I've told you, I don't need your assistance——'

'Okay. Okay!' With a savage oath he bowed his head. 'Stay there!' and he strode violently back to where he had left the Mercedes. His door slammed with a definite sound, and seconds later she heard the engine fire. He was leaving her, and Helen, lodged between the seat and the steering wheel, felt like putting her head down and howling. It was all very well facing him with bravado, but it was a hollow victory when she considered the prospect of the night ahead. She couldn't get the Alfa out of the ditch and she could hardly walk the three or four miles to the nearest garage in this downpour. Besides, it was dark now, and no doubt the garage would be closed. She was going to have to spend the night here, and she simply couldn't bear it.

It was a struggle to scramble out of her seat and up the ditch, and she guessed her cotton pants would be badly soiled with mud and grass stains. But she didn't care. She had to stop Jarret before he drove away, and she almost crawled into the road.

The Mercedes hadn't moved, and she faltered. Jarret's profile was a shadowy thing in the darkness, and she didn't know what his reaction might be after her behaviour. With a sense of humiliation she stood looking at the car, and as if aware of her feelings he opened his door and got out once more.

'Helen...' he muttered, and then, as if he couldn't help himself, he came towards her, jerking her into his arms and finding her damp lips with his own.

It was crazy to stand there in the pouring rain, but Helen had no strength to resist him. Nor did she want to. This was where she belonged, she thought with a sense of despair, this was the man she loved, and she gave herself up to the urgency of his lovemaking like a drowning man losing his last hold on survival. Jarret's body felt cold, but his mouth was warm, and his kisses deepened and intensified as she began to kiss him back. His lips forced hers apart, and the hunger of his mouth roughened as his passion increased. His kisses sent rivers of fire along her veins and weakened the muscles of her legs, spreading throughout her body in a mounting wave of desire. She was aware of him, of the hard muscles between his thighs, and of the fact that the wetness of their clothes made their embrace that much more revealing, but she longed for a closer intimacy, and she could think of nothing more satisfying than spending the night in his arms.

'We have to get back,' he groaned at last, lifting his head to stare down at her. 'Your mother will be concerned if she rings Ketchley and finds you're not there. And she might in this storm.'

Helen nodded. 'I—I know——'

'Okay.' With another hard pressure against her lips he released her, tugging open the passenger door with a distinctly unsteady hand, and Helen slid obediently inside. Then he circled the bonnet and got in beside her, turning on the interior light and surveying her with a disturbingly intent appraisal. It made her overwhelmingly aware that the rain had flattened her shirt against her breasts, and their pointed hardness was moulded against the cloth.

Jarret was obviously aware of them, too, and his eyes moved sensually to her mouth. 'Helen,' he said, exhaling a shaken breath, 'do you have any idea how I feel right now?'

'I—I think so,' she ventured huskily, moving nearer to

him, and with a gesture of impotence he hauled her up against him, covering her face with urgent kisses.

'This is madness,' he muttered against her mouth, his breath mingling with hers. 'I want you, Helen, but not here—not like this. I love you, and I want to love you, really love you, not seduce you in the back seat of a car.'

Helen's breathing felt suspended. 'You—you love me?' she choked against his throat, and his affirming nod was both eager and impatient.

'Of course I do,' he groaned, parting the lapels of her shirt to kiss her throat with heart-stopping tenderness. 'Don't you know that? God, it's been hell trying to keep my hands off you, knowing you're going to marry that stuffed shirt Connaught! I wanted to kill him every time he touched you, and that night he—well, the night you came home with that mark on your neck, I felt like taking a shotgun to him.'

'Oh, Jarret——'

'You love me, don't you? You don't feel this way with Connaught, do you? He doesn't do this to you?' and he bent his head lower to coax the burgeoning curve of her nipple with his tongue.

'No—oh, no,' she moved her head helplessly from side to side. 'No—no one but you has—has ever touched me as—as you touch me.'

'Good.' His voice was lazily satisfied. Then, with a regretful sigh, he drew away from her to rest his head against the misty window behind him, surveying her with possessive eyes. 'Come on, we have to get back. We've plenty of time. All night, in fact.' His mouth took on a sensual twist. 'What we both need is a hot bath, preferably together, but if not ...'

'If not?' she breathed.

'If not—you can come to my room afterwards,' he told her huskily. 'And I promise I won't lock my door. At least, not until you're inside.'

'Jarret!' Her eyes were wide and vulnerable. 'I—I can't——'

'Don't stop me,' he ordered softly. 'I need you, Helen. I want you with me, and I don't want anything to stand in our way. The reason Stanford came down here today was to tell me they want me to go to the States as soon as this book is finished—to sign the contracts for the film, among other things. I want you to come with me. Will you?'

'Stanford?' Helen clung on to that name, feeling a little dizzy now. 'But—but Margot——'

'Margot means nothing to me,' he averred gently.

'Nothing?'

'Nothing,' he agreed. 'Oh, I admit, she may have had some idea of making me husband number four, but she was wasting her time, and she knew it.'

Helen felt everything was moving too fast for her. 'Did—did you sleep with her?' she ventured, appalled at her own audacity, but he only shook his head.

'No.'

'And—and Vivien Sinclair?'

'God!' He stared at her, half in amusement, half in anger. 'What do you want from me, Helen? A dossier on the women I've known, and the extent of that knowledge? What does it matter? I never told Vivien I loved her, and that's the important thing. I've never said that to any girl except you.'

'You—you mean that?'

Helen gazed at him anxiously, and his eyes closed in mock resignation. 'I mean it,' he asserted roughly. 'I love you, Helen. I'm not fooling. But if you imagine I could have remained a celibate all these years, then you're impossibly naïve.'

Helen took an unsteady breath. 'I didn't say I expected that.'

'No——' Jarret raked back his hair with impatient fingers. 'Well, I'm sorry if I've hurt you, but hell, would you want me to come to you as virgin as yourself? Believe me, you wouldn't like that.' Helen's face burned with colour, and with a muffled imprecation, he pulled her close to him again. 'Helen, until I met you I didn't know what it was like to care for someone—really care for them, I mean. And believe me, I've gone through purgatory believing you hated my guts!'

'I—I never hated you, Jarret——'

'Didn't you?' He cupped her face in his hands. 'I think you did. But we won't talk about that now. There's your fiancé to be taken care of. And your mother. Do you think she'll let you come with me?'

Helen drew back from him suddenly, as the whole weight of the problems that faced them loomed before her. Until now it had been enough to know that Jarret loved her, but as the demands of their future cooled her blood, she wondered exactly how her mother would react to this incredible piece of news.

As if sensing her indecision, Jarret turned in his seat and started the engine once more. The rain was easing slightly, but the roads were still treacherous, and he pulled away slowly, passing the disabled Alfa with a wry grimace that Helen echoed as she realised how easily she could have been badly injured.

It didn't take long to reach King's Green, and Jarret stopped by the porch to enable her to dash inside without getting any wetter. With the engine running, and Jarret obviously waiting for her to get out, Helen almost lost her nerve.

'Wh-what will you say—what will *we* say?' she demanded jerkily, and saw the mask of impatience slide down over his lean features.

'What do you want me to say?' he asked, flexing and unflexing his fingers against the wheel. 'Let's see—I love your daughter, Mrs Chase, and I want her to break her engagement and come with me to New York. How does that sound?'

Helen licked her lips. 'Is that all?'

Jarret frowned. 'What more do you want?'

Helen gazed at him incredulously. 'How—how about marriage?'

'*Marriage?*' he repeated blankly.

'Y-yes, marriage.' Helen's tremulous voice gathered a little conviction. 'You do—want to marry me, don't you?'

Jarret rested his forehead against the cool steering wheel, and his delay before replying gave her all the answer she needed. With a feeling of sick rejection she groped blindly for the door handle, but before she could press it he reached past and prevented her escape. With the hard muscles of his forearm against her breasts, it was terribly difficult to remain motionless, but somehow she did it, pressing herself back against the leather upholstery in a chilled state of mortification.

'Before you go locking your door against me again, let me tell you something,' he muttered, his grim face only inches from hers. 'Okay, I didn't plan to buy a marriage licence before taking you to the States. Such conventionality has not been my style——'

'Obviously,' she choked bitterly. 'All those women! I should have known. They probably believed the same thing I did——'

'Which is what?' he grated.

'That—that you loved them——'

Jarret shook his head. 'I've told you, you're the only girl I've ever——'

'Oh, spare me the details!' she gulped. 'How can I believe you when——'

'I've never lied to you, Helen. You know that.'

'Do I?'

'Damn you, you should!' Jarret's anger simmered. 'If I'd wanted to lie to you, I would never have told you the truth about my life, would I?'

Helen pressed her head back, lifting her chin. 'That doesn't alter the fact——'

'*God!*' His teeth ground together. 'I love you, Helen, and if it's a marriage licence you want, then you shall have one. But don't imagine that little scrap of paper is going to make the slightest difference to my feelings for you!'

Helen shook her head. 'No—no! No, thank you. I—I can do without your—your patronage! Per-perhaps you're wrong. Perhaps I will be happier with Charles. At least he had the decency to offer me a ring before trying to get into my bed!'

'All right! All right!' With a savage oath Jarret flung himself back in his seat. 'I've had it. Get out, or I won't be responsible for my actions. Go back to your fumbling fiancé! He deserves you. I don't.'

'Jarret——'

For a moment the enormity of what she was rejecting filled her with despair, but his set face encouraged no appeals, and with trembling fingers she pushed open her door. But standing in the shelter of the porch, a real sense of disaster gripped her. Instead of driving the car into the stable yard as she had expected, Jarret took off down the drive, disappearing into the night, gears grinding and tyres screaming in protest.

Helen hardly slept at all.

Fortunately, Mrs Chase assumed Charles had driven her home, and as she was engrossed in the television as usual, Helen was able to slip away to her room without too many awkward questions. She felt sick and her stomach felt queasy, and although she climbed between the sheets her mind was too active to allow her to rest. Where had Jarret gone? Back to Ketchley? It didn't seen likely, but where else? He was soaked to the skin. Surely he would find somewhere to get out of those wet clothes, but where?

As the night drew on, other images came to plague her. In his state of mind, where was he likely to go? To some other woman, perhaps? To Margot? To Vivien Sinclair? It would necessitate him driving to London, but as the hours passed she became convinced that that was what he must have done. Lying there in the darkness, she tormented herself with thoughts of him with another woman, and his words about them sharing a bath took on a new and agonising meaning.

She must have dozed before dawn, but she was awake again at seven o'clock, and in the kitchen, making herself a cup of tea, when Mrs Hetherington came yawning into the room. She raised her eyebrows at Helen's cotton negligee and then said brusquely:

'I hope you haven't been helping yourself to my apple pie. I saved that for Mr Manning, and if you've eaten it——'

'I haven't,' cut in Helen shortly, indicating the kettle. 'I—I was just making some tea, that's all.'

'Hmm.' Mrs Hetherington viewed her thoughtfully. 'It's not like you to be wanting tea this early in the morning. I thought you preferred coffee. Would you like some coffee? I can easily grind——'

'No, thanks.' Once again Helen interrupted her. 'Tea is fine, honestly. The kettle has boiled. Do you want a cup?'

'When have I ever been known to refuse a cup of tea?' demanded the housekeeper dryly, and then her brows drew together in some concern as she watched the girl. 'Is something the matter?' she ventured, setting two cups in their saucers, as Helen brought the milk from the fridge. 'You look mighty pasty to me. Are you sickening for something?'

'I don't think so.' Helen added sugar to the cups. 'Two spoons, is that right?'

'If you don't know by now, you never will,' responded the housekeeper goodhumouredly, and then returned to her earlier enquiry. 'Didn't you sleep well?'

'Not very.' Helen poured the tea and handed Mrs Hetherington her cup. 'Mmm,' she sipped hers gratefully. 'This is just what I needed.'

The housekeeper frowned. 'There's nothing wrong, is there?' she persisted. 'I mean, you haven't been—sick or anything?'

Helen's half smile was rueful. 'I'm not pregnant, if that's what you're implying,' she assured her.

Mrs Hetherington looked a little flustered at her plain speaking. 'I wasn't suggesting that you were,' she protested, but Helen only shook her head.

'It doesn't matter.' She carried her cup across to the table and sat down on one of the wooden chairs beside it. 'Perhaps it would be simpler if that was what was wrong with me,' she mused, and then grimaced at the housekeeper's shocked face. 'Well!' she justified herself. 'At least then I'd know what I had to do.'

Mrs Hetherington frowned. 'And don't you now?'

Helen bent her head. 'No.'

'But you're going to marry Mr Connaught.' She made a sound of understanding. 'Oh, I see. You're worried because the wedding's getting nearer, and you're having second thoughts. Well, that's common enough, my dear——'

'It's not that, Mrs Hetherington.' Helen lifted her head as if it was too heavy for the slenderness of her neck. 'I—Charles and I—it's just the same as it ever was. Only more so.'

'Whatever do you mean?'

Helen hesitated. 'Tell me, Mrs Hetherington, did—did you and your husband ever—well, anticipate your wedding night?'

The housekeeper looked shocked. 'Well, I never!' she exclaimed. 'What a thing to ask!'

'I'm sorry.' Helen moved her shoulders in an offhand gesture. 'I didn't mean to—offend you, but—well, I just wondered.'

'Ah,' the housekeeper nodded, 'that's what's troubling you. You getting married in white, and all.'

'No!' Helen sighed. 'I—*we* haven't.'

The housekeeper shook her head. 'And you want to know if you should?'

'No. That is—oh, Mrs Hetherington, what am I going to do?' Helen folded her arms upon the table and burying her face upon them, burst into tears.

The housekeeper hesitated only a moment before coming round to her, encircling her shaking shoulders with a reassuring arm, cuddling her close in an effort to comfort her. 'There, there,' she whispered, smoothing Helen's silky swathe of hair with a gentle hand. 'It's Mr Manning, isn't it? He can charm the birds off the trees with that blather of his, and I knew your mother should have never let him into the house!'

Helen lifted her tear-stained face in amazement. 'How—how do you know?'

Mrs Hetherington shook her head. 'It's obvious, isn't it? If it's not Mr Connaught, it has to be Mr Manning.'

'But—but you like him——' Helen protested.

'Of course I do. I'm no different from anyone else. But I can see he could be a whale of trouble where you're concerned.'

Helen nodded. 'I love him,' she confessed, feeling almost relieved to be admitting it to someone else. 'I love him. So what am I going to do?'

Mrs Hetherington eased herself into the chair beside her. 'What about him?' she said gently. 'How does he feel? Does Mr Connaught know?'

'Heaven's, no! No one does,' exclaimed Helen, horrified.

'Except your two selves?' murmured the housekeeper thoughtfully. 'And does he care about you?'

'He says he does,' Helen yielded doubtfully. 'But it's not that easy.'

'Why not?' Mrs Hetherington frowned, and then her face took on a dawning recognition. 'Ah, I think I'm beginning to understand.' Her mouth tightened. 'The young devil! I'd like to give him a piece of my mind!'

Helen blinked. 'What are you talking about, Mrs Hetherington?'

The housekeeper tilted her head. 'He wants to have his cake and eat it, doesn't he?' she declared. 'He's quite prepared to cuckold Mr Connaught, so long as he has no responsibilities——'

'Oh, no. No!' Helen shook her head. 'It's not like that, Mrs Hetherington. He—he wants me to break off my engagement to Charles. But he doesn't want to marry me. Only—only to live with me.'

'Tch!' Mrs Hetherington was shocked. 'That's disgusting!'

'Is it? Is it?' Helen gazed at her dubiously, and then gasped in dismay when her mother's voice exclaimed: 'I should just think it is!' in shaken, disbelieving tones.

'Mummy!'

Helen jerked up from her chair as Mrs Chase came into the room, warmly attired in a candlewick dressing gown, her skin still shiny with the cream she had applied the night before. But Helen scarcely noticed her mother's appearance. Her attention was focussed on her mother's face and the horrified expression it wore.

'What is all this, Helen?' she exclaimed, and Mrs Hetherington spread a helpless hand as she left the table to wash their dirty cups. 'Did I hear aright? You're saying that Jarret has asked you to *live* with him?'

Helen sighed. 'That's what it amounts to, yes.'

'Are you mad?' Her mother came towards her briskly, laying a cool hand against Helen's hot forehead. 'Why, you're burning up! You must be having hallucinations. Why on earth would Jarret ask you to live with *him*?'

Helen shook her head. 'He says he loves me. Or—or he did.'

Mrs Chase looked absolutely staggered, and as if realising how she was feeling, the housekeeper came round the table and helped her into a chair. 'The kettle's on again,' she said reassuringly. 'I expect you'd like some tea, too.'

'Please.' Helen's mother nodded weakly. Then she looked up at her daughter again. 'You'd better tell me what's been going on? Are you pregnant?'

Helen gasped. 'Honestly, do I look as if I'm pregnant? No, no, of course I'm not pregnant.'

'No, no, of course not.' Mrs Chase spoke half to herself. 'Jarret would have more sense than to allow that to happen.'

'I haven't slept with him, Mummy!' Helen exclaimed helplessly. 'That's what all this is about.'

Mrs Chase sighed. 'Does this have anything to do with the fact that Jarret didn't come home last night?'

Helen nodded.

'Were you with him last night?'

'Part of the time, yes. He—he drove me home from the Connaughts'.'

'But you said Charles had driven you home.'

'No, you just assumed that,' Helen corrected her quietly. 'And I didn't contradict you.'

'And you had a row, I presume.'

'Something like that.'

Mrs Chase looked incredulously towards the housekeeper. 'I can't believe any of this.'

'There was no need for you to know, Mummy,' Helen put in unsteadily. 'I—I just needed to talk to someone, that's all.'

'And you couldn't talk to me?'

Helen bent her head. 'You were always so—so convinced that I was biased towards Jarret.'

'You were.' Her mother shook her head. 'You still are. Only now you're not aware of it.'

Helen shrugged. 'In any case, it's all hypothetical. Jarret's leaving for the States soon. They're going to film his first book, and they've invited him out there to sign the contracts.'

Mrs Chase showed little enthusiasm. 'And you? What about you? Are you going with him?'

'He invited me to,' Helen conceded.

'Oh, God!' Her mother gazed at her. 'What about the wedding?'

Helen felt slightly hysterical. 'That's my cue to say—what wedding, isn't it? Oh, Mummy, how can I marry

Charles when I don't love him?'

'It seems to me you're in no state to make any decision at the moment,' her mother retorted recovering slightly. 'When Jarret gets back, we'll have this out——'

'Oh, no!' Helen backed away from her. 'I—Jarret and I have said all there is to say on the matter. He—I—I won't live with him, and he doesn't want marriage. That's all there is to it.'

'And what about Charles?'

'Yes, what about Charles?' echoed Helen dully. 'Don't you see? I can't go through with the wedding feeling like this. I can't.'

'But it's still several weeks to the wedding,' protested Mrs Chase severely. 'Why, your dress is made and hanging in the wardrobe. The bridesmaids have all been chosen. Why, even the flowers——'

'Please ...' Helen couldn't bear for her to go on. 'I don't want to talk about it any more. I—I have to get dressed. Karen's expecting me at a quarter to nine.'

It was only as she was dressing that Helen realised her car was out of commission. It meant she would have to ask her mother if she could borrow the Triumph and the implications of that did not appeal to her. However, Mrs Chase had gone back to bed, with a headache according to Mrs Hetherington, and Helen only put her head round her mother's bedroom door and asked for the favour.

'Do what you like,' declared her mother tearfully, but Helen refused to be drawn. Closing the door again, she went quietly down the stairs and let herself out of the house.

As luck would have it, the shop had a busy day, and Helen succeeded in avoiding Karen's usually vigilant eyes. John Fleming's arrival as the shop was about to close was another stroke of luck, and Helen willingly agreed to close up alone so that Karen could leave at once.

'We're going on the river,' she confessed in the privacy of the back room, outlining her lips with a crimson lacquer. 'This business associate of John's has lent him his launch for the weekend, and we're going to have a look at it tonight.'

'Well, take care,' said Helen dryly, wishing she was as

uninhibited as her friend, and Karen chuckled as she sauntered out.

With Karen's departure, Helen picked up the phone. She had called at the garage on her way to work that morning, asking them to tow her car in for a thorough checkover, and they had suggested she rang that afternoon. To her relief she learned there was nothing seriously wrong with it, and she was agreeing to pick it up later when the shop bell rang.

Replacing the receiver, Helen went to serve the late customer, and then stopped aghast when she saw it was Charles. He was standing in the outer showroom, his usually pleasant features drawn into a tight scowl, and his expression did not alter when he saw her.

'Why, Charles,' she exclaimed, wishing she had been more prepared for this. 'What a surprise!'

'I've come to take you home,' he declared, limping as he crossed the floor. 'It is closing time, isn't it? I saw that Medley-Smythe woman leaving with Fleming. I see no reason why you should have to carry on if she's finished for the day.'

Helen sighed. 'I offered to stay on,' she explained. Then; 'How are you? How's your leg?'

Charles thrust his hands into the pockets of his sports coat. 'My knee is sprained, thank you,' he asserted. 'Had Bluthner look at it this morning, but I knew it was nothing serious. No thanks to you.'

'To me?'

Helen thought he was joking, but Charles was deadly serious. 'If it hadn't been for you, I'd not have been out there, frightening the animals and bruising my leg.'

Helen stared at him. She could have said that she had certainly *not* wanted to enter the stables, but there was no point in arguing. He would never listen to her, and besides, it wasn't worth the effort.

Instead she said: 'Well, I'm glad your leg's all right, Charles, but I don't need you to take me home.'

'Why not?' Charles's scowl deepened. 'I know you don't have your car. I saw it in Bethnel's garage this morning, and I guessed Manning picked you up. He did, didn't he? And brought you to work, no doubt. Well, I'm damned if he's going to take you home!'

'He's not,' retorted Helen, locking the till and the office door. 'I borrowed Mummy's car, actually. So I'm independent.'

'Hmm.' Charles snorted illhumouredly. 'All right then, I'll follow you back to King's Green. I want to have a few words with Manning myself, and now is as good a time as any.'

'You can't. That is——' Helen felt an intense weariness. 'What do you want to say to Jarret, Charles? He's not to blame for our problems.'

'Our problems! What problems?' Charles glared at her. 'We don't have any problems. Only interference.'

'That's not true.' Helen shook her head. 'I don't know if I can go through with our marriage, Charles. I—I don't love you. I don't think I ever did.'

Charles was obviously staggered now, and he gazed at her with disbelieving eyes. 'You don't know what you're saying——'

'I do.'

'—you're distraught. That business with Poseidon last night—well, I guess I was to blame, but you shouldn't have pretended you'd got over your fears.'

'It's not just that,' said Helen unhappily. 'We—we don't think alike——'

'What do you mean? We read the same books. We watch the same television programmes!'

'Oh, Charles, life is more than books and television programmes! There are other things ...'

'Sex, I suppose you mean.'

'That, too, of course.'

'It's the fault of that Smythe woman, isn't it? She's been filling your head with stories of her experiences, I suppose. Well, let me tell you most women would be glad—yes, glad I hadn't made any unnecessary demands on them——'

'*Unnecessary demands!*' Helen felt that recurring bubble of hysteria. 'Charles, sex is not an unnecessary demand! It's something wonderful—something beautiful! Something two people share—in love——'

'How do you know?' Charles pushed his face close to hers.

Helen hesitated. Then she knew she had to go on. 'I—I know because—because Jarret showed me,' she said, quietly and succinctly, then staggered backward as Charles's hand struck her savagely across the mouth.

'You little——' he snarled. 'How dare you stand there and tell me that Manning—that you and Manning——'

'Please go, Charles!' Somehow Helen was amazingly calm. Removing his ring from her finger, she placed it on the showcase beside him, before wrapping her arms closely about herself. 'I—I was uncertain. I did have—doubts. But—but not any longer.'

Charles stared down at the ring as if he'd never seen it before, and then he looked at her with disbelieving eyes. 'You—you can't do this,' he blustered. 'I mean, having an affair with Manning is one thing, breaking our engagement is another. Look——' He put out his hand appealingly, but she evaded it. 'Look, don't be hasty. I mean, I'm prepared to overlook what you've just said. I was overwrought, and so were you. It would be foolish to destroy our future over such a—such a paltry thing.'

'You hit me, Charles,' said Helen steadily. 'I can't overlook that. You were provoked, I know, but—striking a woman—I can't forgive that.'

'For goodness' sake,' Charles was cajoling her now, reaching out and shaking her in evident desperation. 'Helen—well, all right, I'm sorry. Yes, I am, I'm sorry. It won't happen again——'

'No, it won't,' said Helen flatly. 'Because I don't want to see you again.'

Charles's eyes mirrored his astonishment, but his hands fell to his sides. Then, as if realising he only had one more card to play, he added: 'You don't imagine Manning is serious about you, do you? You're just a little diversion he's provided himself with for the time he's here——'

'Go away, Charles!' Helen didn't want to listen to him, but he was relentless.

'I know his type,' he went on, 'I've met them before. Very successful with the ladies, oh, yes, very successful, but no staying power, if you know what I mean.'

Helen couldn't bear to listen to any more. Brushing past

him, she opened the shop door, saying tremulously: 'Are you going to leave, or do I lock you in for the night?'

Charles stared at her, his face contorting furiously. 'You little tramp,' he muttered. 'My God, to think I wanted to marry you!' He snatched up his ring. 'I must have been out of my mind!'

'One of us was,' agreed Helen tightly, bending her head as he charged past her.

## CHAPTER NINE

IT was the telephone that had awakened her, Helen realised, with a sense of disorientation. The telephone ringing shrilly at six o'clock in the morning, when she had only been asleep since four. Wearily she dragged herself out of bed and down the stairs, wondering why her mother never answered calls at unsociable hours. Perhaps she had taken another sleeping pill, she reflected. She had tried to get her daughter to take one, after all, and although Helen had resisted her efforts, she probably had not.

Helen hardly knew. She felt she hardly knew anything any more. It was four nights since Jarret's departure, and neither of them had slept well since. Mrs Chase's disappointment at her daughter's broken engagement had added to her emotional upheaval, but the fact that there had been no word from Jarret, no call to say how he was or where he was staying, had gradually superseded all other considerations. Neither of them had felt able to make the enquiries necessary to find out where he was, and in consequence Mrs Chase had acquired some sleeping tablets from the doctor, and Helen continued to have sleepless nights.

Now she padded barefoot across the hall, her toes curling against the polished wood. She had not bothered to stop and put on her dressing gown, and the tail of her nightshirt flapped coolly against her thighs, but she was hardly aware of it. She was only intent on lifting the telephone receiver and stopping the awful din.

'Hello?'

Her voice was husky, still drowsy from the deep slumber she had been dragged out of, but unmistakably feminine.

'Helen?' The response was energetic and masculine. 'Is that you, Helen? Thank God! I thought for a minute it was your mother.'

Helen blinked, rubbing one eye with the tips of her fingers. 'Vincent?' she exclaimed, hardly believing it. 'Vincent, what are you doing ringing at this hour of the morning? Do you know what time it is?'

'Yes. It's a little after six,' he retorted, sounding impatient. 'I had to ring at this time. I wanted to catch you before big brother catches me!'

Helen sank down wearily on to the chest beside the telephone. 'Big brother?' she echoed. 'Charles? What has Charles got to do with it?'

Vincent made an expressive sound. 'What has he not?' he exclaimed. 'Helen, stop asking questions and listen to me. Will you go and see Jarret?'

Helen was glad she was sitting down. If she hadn't been, she most likely would have collapsed in a heap on the floor. 'Jarret?' she said faintly, trying to gather her composure, and Vincent confirmed what he had just said.

'That's right. I know it's not an easy decision, but honestly, Helen, if you don't—well, I won't answer for what happens.'

Helen was disturbed now. There was an anxious note in Vincent's voice that bore little resemblance to his normally casual way of speaking, and his words were strange and unnatural. Helen, striving for command of her own feelings, had little left to spare for his, but she sensed he was concerned and that filled her with alarm.

'He hasn't—he isn't—I mean, he didn't have an accident, did he? Jarret, I mean,' she hastened anxiously, and Vincent broke in to deny this.

'You mean when he left the other night, don't you?' he demanded heavily. 'No, he didn't have an accident.'

'Then what?' Helen was growing impatient now. 'Vincent, for goodness' sake, what is all this about?'

Vincent hesitated. 'Helen, I'm worried about him——'
'Worried about him?'

'Yes.' He paused. 'Look, I don't know how you feel about him, but I guess you feel something, despite what Chas says.'

'Charles?' Helen drew an uneven breath. 'What does Charles say?'

'Oh, you know what Chas is like. He's so tied up with those horses of his, he hardly knows what's going on around him. So far as he's concerned, you're engaged, and that naturally precludes——'

'But we're not!' Helen interrupted him. 'Engaged, I

mean. I—I broke it off three days ago.'

'You did?' Vincent sounded at once astonished and relieved. 'But he's never said a damn thing. And neither have you.'

'Oh, Vincent!' Helen shook her head. 'Since—since Jarret left, we've been—I don't know—in a state of upheaval. Mummy's refused to see anyone, and seems to think if she doesn't discuss the matter, it will all go away. I thought Charles——'

'Well, he hasn't. Not a goddamn word. That's why I'm ringing you at this unearthly hour. I got back from London last night and——'

'Jarret's in London?'

'Yes.'

'At his apartment?'

'No.'

'Oh,' Helen's voice was flat, 'I see.'

'Do you?' Vincent didn't sound convinced. 'He's in Kennington, actually. At his stepfather's house in Lambeth Terrace.'

Helen gulped. 'But I thought——'

'I know what you thought. Some female, right? You don't know him very well, do you? It's you he's crazy about.' He paused. 'And I was all ready to blow you up for making a fool of him!'

Helen trembled. 'But you're worried about him, aren't you? Why?' Her brow furrowed. 'He didn't catch pneumonia the other night, did he? He was soaked to the skin when he left here.'

Vincent gave a grunt. 'He's been in rougher states than that, Helen. We were in Vietnam together, and believe me, getting soaked to the skin was the least of our worries.' He sighed. 'It's not that.'

'Then what is it?' Helen was getting desperate. 'Vince——'

'Drink,' he said flatly, heaving a breath. 'Like alcoholic?'

'Oh, *God*!' Helen felt sick. 'But how do you know——'

'—it's you?' he finished for her, and she nodded her head, even though he couldn't see her. 'Well now, let's see—would you believe, he told me?'

'No.'

Helen was very definite about that and he sighed again. 'Okay, so he didn't tell me. But I know, Helen, believe me, *I know*!'

Helen bit painfully on her lower lip. 'How can you be sure?'

'Can't you accept that I just am?'

'Vincent——'

'Aw hell!' He sounded desperate. 'He'll never forgive me if I tell you!'

'Need he know?' she exclaimed.

'Perhaps not.' Vincent sounded uncertain now.

'Vincent, please ...'

Her voice was breaking, and as if he couldn't stand any more, he said harshly: 'Okay, okay. His father called me. He'd found my address and telephone number in Jarret's wallet. I guess it was the first name he found. Anyway, he—well, he told me he was worried about Jarret, and did I know anyone by the name of Helen.'

'My name,' she breathed bewilderdly, and Vincent agreed.

'He asked me if I'd go up and see him, and of course I went.' He paused. 'Jarret was there, and we talked, but—oh God! Helen, he looks bloody awful.'

'Did—did he mention me?'

'Only once.' Vincent was reluctant to go on. 'He—well, he asked if you were okay.'

'And you told him.'

'Yes.'

'So—so far as Jarret is concerned, Charles and I are still engaged.'

'Yes.'

Helen's shoulders sagged. 'What, then?'

'Not a lot.'

'But my name——'

'When I was leaving,' declared Vincent heavily. 'The old man—you know, Jarret's stepfather, he accompanied me out to the car. He—well, Jarret wasn't dressed, and I guess he was glad of the opportunity to speak to me alone. That was when he told me.'

'Told you what?' Helen was getting desperate.

'That Jarret has been saying your name, over and over

again. During the night—you know, keeping the old man awake.'

'Oh, Vincent!'

'I know. And if Jarret ever finds out I've told you——'

'What—what's his address?' Helen's fingers were too cold suddenly to hold the phone, but she fumbled for a pencil and took down directions in an unsteady hand.

'Got it?' asked Vincent at last, and she agreed.

'Twenty-seven,' she repeated, and then after a moment's hesitation, she added: 'Thanks, Vince. I—I don't know what to say.'

'Just don't mess things up again,' muttered Vincent gruffly, and rang off before she could say any more.

Her mother was not up when she left, but she left a message for her with Mrs Hetherington. 'Just tell her I've gone to see Jarret. She'll understand,' she said carefully, and the housekeeper shook her head rather ruefully.

'So long as you know what you're doing,' she murmured, and Helen paused a moment to hug her.

'I love him,' she said simply. 'And if I can't have him my way, I'll have him his.'

It was a little after eleven when she crossed Vauxhall Bridge and began to follow the directions Vincent had given her. They were quite explicit, and in no time at all it seemed she was turning into Lambeth Terrace.

It was a row of Victorian houses, tall and narrow, each with its own narrow strip of garden and neatly painted front gate. Number twenty-seven was slightly less neat than the others, and she wondered why Jarret allowed his stepfather to live here when he obviously could afford so much better.

Parking the Alfasud, she looked up apprehensively at the curtained windows. There was no sign of life, and she wondered what she would do if no one answered the door. Somehow the journey had seemed less arduous with this goal in mind, but now she was here she was uncertain and not a little dismayed. What if Vincent was wrong? What if this was some cruel game he and Jarret were playing? That thought had never occurred to her, but now it did, and she knew the cowardly impulse to turn and drive away again.

The front door opening, however, gave her pause. An old man was emerging, closing the door behind him, and coming down the steep steps with a cautious surety that indicated a rheumatic condition. He looked suspiciously at the car and at Helen, and then, as if coming to a decision, he approached her.

'Can I help you?'

Surprisingly his voice was strong and pleasant, and Helen responded instinctively, pushing open the car door and getting out without a second thought.

'You must be—Jarret's stepfather,' she said, realising suddenly that she didn't even know his name. 'Er—I'm Helen.'

She knew at once that Vincent had not been lying to her. The old man's gnarled features took on an expression of such relief that she guessed he had not really expected her to come.

'Helen!' he exclaimed, putting out his hand, and automatically she took it, exchanging the greeting with real warmth, as relieved as he was that she had not been mistaken. 'Young Connaught spoke to you, then? He said he would.'

'Yes,' Helen nodded. 'I spoke to Vince this morning. I—where is Jarret? Can I see him?'

'That's what you're here for, isn't it?' the old man asked dryly. 'But I'm afraid he's not up yet. I—er—I was just going along to the shop to get something for lunch. Will you stay and eat with us?'

Helen hesitated, glancing up at the house once more. 'I—I don't know,' she ventured. 'After I've seen Jarret . . .'

'You may not see him until after lunch,' his stepfather essayed. 'You see, he doesn't like me to waken him, and——' He broke off apologetically, and Helen felt a sudden stirring of something akin to indignation.

'You mean he stays in bed all morning?' she exclaimed deploringly, and the old man sighed.

'I think he—doesn't see anything to get up for,' he offered. 'But when I get back——'

'Don't bother, I'll deal with this myself,' declared Helen, with a tight smile. 'Is the door unlocked. Can I get in?'

'Well, yes, but——'

'Thank you.'

With another reassuring smile, Helen marched across the pavement and up the path to the house. The door was not locked as the old man had indicated, and she let herself inside before her nerve gave out on her.

She found herself in a narrow, gloomy hall, with doors opening on the right and stairs mounting to the first floor on the left. She guessed Jarret would be upstairs. The doors she could see would give access to a front room and a dining room and a kitchen, and upstairs she would find the bedrooms and the bathroom, if there was one.

Her knees shook a little as she climbed the stairs. It was all very well telling herself that Jarret needed her, but nothing could alter the fact that he hadn't asked her to come. What if he refused to speak to her? How far was she prepared to go to persuade him that she no longer cared about anything but being with him?

There were two bedrooms, she discovered. The first, overlooking the street, was unoccupied. The other, at the back of the house, was Jarret's. Pushing open the door, her nostrils were at once assailed by the unpleasant odour of sour alcohol, and her appalled gaze took in the overturned bottles on the table beside the bed. Vincent had not been joking. No wonder he slept until lunchtime—he was probably unconscious.

The curtains were drawn, but it was a sunny morning, and the room was filled with a golden light that exposed the disordered bed and its occupant. Crossing the room to the windows to let in some fresh air, Helen could not prevent herself from halting beside the bed, and she looked down at the hunched figure with a helpless tightening of her stomach. It didn't matter how debauched Jarret looked, he was still the man she loved, and the sight of his lean muscular body, only lightly covered by a cotton sheet, stirred her senses. He was slumped against the pillows, at least two days' growth of beard on his chin, his hair a tangled silvery mess, but her heart went out to him, and almost irresistibly, her fingers touched the corded column of his throat.

He stirred. Perhaps he was slowly coming round from the drinking session he had indulged in the night before. Whatever the reason, his eyes flickered and an expression of pain crossed his face as the crippling results of the alcohol penetrated even his half-conscious brain.

'I told you not to wake me, Paddy,' he muttered, covering his eyes with one arm, and groaning as he rolled over on to his back. 'What time is it? I can't see the clock.'

'It's half past eleven,' said Helen quietly, and instantly the concealing arm was withdrawn and Jarret's pain-darkened pupils gazed disbelievingly up at her. Then, almost defensively, he rolled over on to his stomach, burying his face in the pillow and saying in a savage tone: 'Who the hell let you in?'

Helen stood her ground. 'I—I met your stepfather outside. He told me where you were.'

'Then he had no right to do so,' snapped Jarret angrily. 'Get out of here, Helen. At least give me the chance to get some clothes on.'

Helen's tongue appeared, to moisten her lips. 'I'm not stopping you, am I?' she ventured huskily, and with a stifled oath he rolled over to stare up at her once again.

Then, as if unwilling to believe what he could see, he clutched the sheet more closely around him. 'Go home, little girl,' he advised her harshly. 'I don't know what game it is you're playing, but you're crazy if you think you can come here and say things like that to me without provoking any retaliation.'

Helen shrugged, and adopting a casual manner she was far from feeling, she walked slowly across to the windows and drew back the curtains, leaning forward to thrust the windows wide. Jarret's moan of protest drew her eyes back to the bed, however, and she realised the brilliance was even more painful to him, and with a grimace she drew the curtains once again, leaving them to billow in the breeze that surged into the stuffy room. Then she walked back to the bed, resting her fingers on the rail at the end, and watching him with provocative intentness.

'Who told you where I was?' he demanded, rolling on to his side and propping himself up on one elbow. 'Lord, I need a drink!'

'No, you don't.' Helen's reaction was automatic, and moving swiftly round the bed, she removed the only bottle that had any liquor left in it out of his reach. But as she swung away again, he caught a handful of her skirt between his fingers and yanked her back to the bed. She stood for a moment looking down at him, and then the bottle dropped heedlessly from her hand as he bent his head and raised the silky georgette to his lips.

'Hell, why did you have to come and see me like this?' he exclaimed roughly, and with a little cry she sank down on to the bed beside him.

'I came because I wanted to. I—I love you,' she breathed, staring at him with wide adoring eyes, and he came upright in a second, brows drawn together in a disbelieving scowl.

'You don't know what you're saying,' he muttered. 'You're going to marry Connaught. Vince told me——'

'Vince doesn't know anything about it,' she whispered. 'I broke my engagement to Charles three days ago!'

Jarret's tongue moistened his dry lips. 'The day after—after I left?' he probed, and she nodded vigorously. 'Then why in God's name didn't you let me know?'

Helen bent her head. 'I didn't know where you were. I didn't know what your reaction would be!'

'You didn't know?' he echoed incredulously, then, as if he couldn't bear to go on talking to her in his present state, he raked back his hair with unsteady fingers. 'I need a bath,' he announced, glancing about him almost blankly. 'Look, if you'll get out of here, I'll shave and get some clothes on. Then we can talk.'

Helen gazed at him anxiously. 'Can't we talk now?' she persisted, half afraid she had come too late to convince him, and he looked at her almost angrily.

'Not like this,' he insisted, pushing her skirt away from him. 'Paddy should have had more sense than to let you come up here!'

'Paddy? That's your stepfather?'

'Patrick Horton, yes.' Jarret nodded, and then winced as his head throbbed painfully.

'He went to the shops,' Helen offered, making no move to go. 'He's invited me for lunch.'

'Has he?' Jarret, who had been avoiding looking at her, was forced to an unwilling appraisal. 'You're honoured. He doesn't usually approve of my girl-friends.'

Helen pressed her lips together. 'Girl-*friends*?' she

echoed pointedly. 'Do you usually bring them here?'

Jarret sat cross-legged looking at her, one elbow propped on his knee, his knuckles supporting his head. 'What do you think?'

Helen shook her head. 'I wouldn't know, would I?' she ventured, and Jarret uttered a heavy sigh.

'Will you let me get dressed?' he demanded, indicating the sheet which was all that covered his lower limbs. 'I promise we'll talk when I feel less disreputable.'

'Can you wait?' she asked in a tense voice, but she got up from the bed as she spoke, and he was forced to tilt his head to look up at her. 'You're very cool, I must say,' she added, and then, rather recklessly: 'I'm not so naïve, you know. I do have a pretty good idea what a man looks like!' and with this parting shot she marched towards the door.

She didn't make it. Jarret caught her before she had covered half a dozen feet, hauling her back against him and making her ecstatically aware that he was not cool at all.

'Helen,' he groaned against her neck, his hands sliding up over her ribcage to the swelling fullness of her breasts. 'I'm going to do this properly, however you taunt me. I'm going to take a bath, and shave, and put on some clean clothes, and then I'm going to make love to you ...'

'Isn't that the wrong way about?' she breathed, resting her head back against the smooth column of his throat, and his arms tightened. 'Don't we take our clothes off to make love?'

'Honey, if I didn't know Paddy was due back any minute now, I'd take you in the bath with me,' he told her huskily. 'As it is ...'

With a determined effort he put her away from him, and she turned half wonderingly as he rummaged about in the dressing table drawers for some clean clothes. He knew her eyes were on him, but he didn't respond to the invitation in hers. Instead he gathered shirt and pants and brushed past her, and presently she heard the sound of water running.

Wrapping her arms about herself, Helen wandered half dazedly about the room. Catching sight of her reflection in the dressing table mirror, she hardly recognised the hollow-eyed girl who had put on her clothes so anxiously that morning. Her lips were parted in expectation, and her eyes were shining, and as she drew her arms away she felt the curious aching feeling that thinking of Jarret always gave her. It was like a gnawing feeling inside, a need to feel him close to her, and the innocent awareness that only he could fill the emptiness that the aching void created.

She started half guiltily when the door was suddenly pushed wide and Jarret's stepfather stood in the aperture. She sensed he had seen her involuntary awakening, but his smile was gentle as he said:

'He's up, then?'

Helen nodded, her cheeks a little pink as she walked away from the mirror. 'He's having a bath.'

'Praise be!' remarked Patrick Horton wryly. 'You must have had a good effect on him. Jarret and water have not been bosom allies for days. Why don't you come downstairs and wait for him? I'm sure he won't evaporate in the steam.'

Helen hesitated. Then she agreed. 'All right.' She paused. 'You didn't mind my coming here, did you? I mean, Vincent said you wouldn't.'

Patrick Horton shook his head as they descended the stairs, and then led the way into a sunlit kitchen at the back of the house. 'I was only too relieved when Vince said he knew you. Until then I'd been at my wits' end. I didn't know any Helen, you see.'

Helen nodded. 'I'm glad Vince phoned me. I've been so worried.'

Patrick arched his brows. 'You have? But I understood Vince to say that—well, that you're going to marry his brother. Is that true?'

'It was,' said Helen, rather shakily. 'Until I met Jarret, and then I wasn't sure any more.'

Patrick nodded, and she perched on the edge of the table as he filled the kettle and put it on the gas stove. He seemed quite domesticated, moving about, setting out cups and saucers, turning butter into a dish, and she wondered whether he missed his stepson when he stayed at his own apartment.

'Do you live here alone, Mr Horton?' she asked, when he turned to look at her again, and he nodded.

'Ever since Jarret's mother died, yes.'

Helen hesitated. 'Haven't you ever thought of moving?'

'Moving?' He frowned. 'Moving where?'

'Oh, well——' Helen was embarrassed. 'I only meant hadn't you ever thought of—of getting a flat——'

'—in an old people's home, you mean?' he exclaimed, and she was alarmed at his hostility. 'I don't need any warden to look after me. I have the phone, and good neighbours. That's all I need.'

'Oh, of course, I only meant——' Helen broke off, and he seemed to realise he had been overly aggressive.

'I know, I know,' he grumbled, taking out the caddy and spooning the tea into the pot. 'You mean well. Jarret means well. He's always telling me I should let him get me a smaller place, with a bigger garden, but I'm quite happy here. This is my home, and this is where I'll stay.'

'Stubborn old cuss, isn't he?'

Jarret's amused voice came from the doorway, interrupting their exchange, and Helen looked eagerly towards him. In clean denim jeans and a matching shirt, half open down the tanned expanse of his chest, he looked young and disturbingly attractive, only the pouches beneath his eyes, evidence of the nights he had spent. Helen's heart hammered wildly at the realisation that he wanted her. She wanted him, too, but his stepfather's presence precluded any overtures on her part, and she was obliged to look away.

'Helen and I have just been getting to know one another,' Patrick retorted, surveying his stepson with mildly approving eyes. 'I must say you look a little more human, if still somewhat dissipated.'

'He's always so honest,' Jarret remarked dryly, coming across to where Helen was sitting and forcing her to acknowledge him. 'It's a strong case of familiarity, and like you, he knows my weaknesses.'

Helen blushed, she couldn't help it, but when his fingers slid between hers, she let him pull her down off the table and into his arms.

'I've been waiting for this,' he said, against her mouth, and the intimacy of that probing caress took her breath away.

She didn't want to let him go and it was certain that he

didn't want to release her, but somehow he managed to school his features and turn back to face his stepfather when Patrick said:

'Do you two want anything to eat? Or have you got enough there?'

Jarret grinned, albeit a little twistedly, and with his fingers tight about Helen's wrist, he said: 'I'm going to take Helen out for lunch, Dad. We—er—we need a little time alone together, but we'll come back later, if that's all right with you.'

Patrick grimaced, his eyes knowing. 'I thought my baked beans wouldn't be good enough for you,' he declared, but when Helen started to protest, he only laughed. 'I'm teasing, lassie,' he exclaimed, and seeing Jarret's amused eyes upon her, Helen realised she had been caught again.

They took the Alfa, with Jarret's lean length folded behind the wheel, and drove to the nearest delicatessen. Jarret bade her wait for him, and emerged fifteen minutes later with a long roll of french bread, some peaches and cheese, and a bottle of rich red wine.

'"And thou beside me ... in the wilderness",' he quoted softly, as he got back into the car, and Helen's heart flipped a beat as she met his caressing gaze.

He took her out of London, into the Berkshire countryside, where it was still possible to find a quiet country lane, with a lush green pasture and a tumbling stream at the bottom of it. The field was already occupied by a herd of brown and white cows and Jarret laughingly advised her to tread warily. But the docile creatures paid them no heed, and they found a shady corner beneath the branches of a spreading oak.

'Heaven!' sighed Helen, sinking down on to the grass and spreading her arms to the vista of rolling countryside and blue, blue sky, but when Jarret repeated the word he was looking at her.

'Dear God, I love you,' he muttered, taking her face between his hands, and then he lowered her back against the soft turf to cover her mouth with his own.

Helen had no will to resist him, even had she wanted to. Her bare arms were around his neck and the imprisoning weight of his body was all the stimulant she needed. She wanted him, all of him, and her lips parted under his. Her blood seemed to be rushing through her veins, making her acutely aware of the intimacy of their embrace, inflaming her emotions and firing her hunger. She no longer thought about what she was doing. She was all feeling, all woman, and instinctively intuitive of exactly how to please him.

'Helen ...' he groaned, as her fingers slid beneath his shirt to spread against the smooth flesh of his back. 'This isn't fair. I'm trying to keep my head, but you don't make it easy!'

'Don't,' she murmured simply, caressing his hips, and his unmistakable response made her arch her back towards him.

But even as Jarret's hand slid possessively along her thigh, he drew back, dragging himself up and away from her, thrusting strong but unsteady fingers into his hair at his temples.

'Jarret ...'

Chilled by his withdrawal, Helen struggled on to her knees to sit staring at him with anxious eyes. What was wrong? Why had he rejected her? Was it something she'd done? She was overcome with frustration at her own ignorance, and desperate that he should not walk out on her again.

'Jarret,' she persisted, touching his sleeve. 'Jarret, don't you want me any more? I—I don't expect any commitment from you. If—if you want me——'

'If I want you?' he muttered, turning anguished eyes in her direction. 'You're all I do want, Helen. Now. Always.'

'Then——'

Jarret shook his head. 'I—I made a promise to myself. That if ever I got the chance again, I wouldn't louse things up. And I don't intend to.'

Helen gazed at him in bewilderment. 'I don't understand ...'

'Helen, listen to me!' Almost against his will, it seemed, he turned and took her hands, one in each of his. Then, compulsively, he raised her hands to his lips, saying nothing for several seconds, just burying his face in her palms. When he had himself in command once more he went on: 'That night—the night all hell broke loose, I—oh God! I wanted you, Helen. I was desperate, and when—when you started talking about marriage, I guess I lost control. It seemed such a paltry thing compared to the way I felt about you, and I wanted you to want me that way, too.'

'I did! I *do*!' exclaimed Helen impulsively, but he silenced her with his hand across her lips.

'I guess I've lived so long with people who don't care to make any commitment to one another, who live for the day and let tomorrow take care of itself. I thought I could live that way, too, but from the minute I laid eyes on you I knew that sooner or later I'd have to make the choice.'

'You don't have to say this, Jarret,' Helen exclaimed imploringly. 'Honestly. I—I don't care. I love you, and I want to be with you. However long you want me.'

'And if that happens to be life?' he suggested softly.

'That's okay.'

'Well, it's not okay for me,' said Jarret huskily. 'You see, these last days I've realised what it's like not having any hold on you, not knowing from one minute to the next who you're with or who's making passes at you. I don't think I can stand that for much longer. Strange as it may seem, I want my ring on your finger, and all the protection that brings with it. Besides,' his lips twitched, 'I want children—*your* children and mine. And I don't want them growing up not knowing who their father is.'

'Oh, Jarret!' Helen pressed her lips tightly together. 'Are—are you sure?'

'Sure I'm sure,' he groaned, releasing her hands to seek the scented flesh of her upper arms. 'You ask Paddy. He's never seen me like this before. Pray God he never will again!'

Helen shook her head. 'I can't believe this ...'

'You'd better believe it. As soon as this book is finished, we're going to the States, and then how does Hawaii sound to you? For our honeymoon, I mean?'

'It sounds like paradise,' she confessed helplessly, and he permitted himself to touch her shoulder with his tongue.

'Good.' With an obvious effort, he released her and turned to the carrier of food he had dropped beside him. 'Now, are you hungry?'

'Only for you,' she breathed, taking the bread out of his hands and winding herself closely against him. 'Jarret, I have an ache—just here. Is there nothing you can do about it?'

'Helen ...' His voice was thick with protest, but her mouth parting his was more than he could resist. He bore her back against the lush blades of grass, crushing her beneath him and letting her feel the thrusting urgency of his body. Her limbs yielded to his, inviting his invasion, and Jarret's senses swam.

'Are you sure?' he said once, as her hands slid the shirt from his shoulders, and she nodded eagerly.

'Please,' she whispered, and with a hunger even he could not disguise, he took what was undeniably his.

She had not really known what she was inviting. Karen's descriptive narratives had still left chapters unexplored, and her own limited knowledge had prepared her to be disappointed, at least the first time. But it wasn't like that at all. The pain she had anticipated was swiftly absorbed by the intense physical pleasure of his possession, and soon only sweetness remained and an urgent wild abandonment. With his mouth exploring her ears and neck, returning again and again to the moist parting of hers, she felt on fire with emotions she had not even known existed, twisting sensuously beneath him, loving every movement of his powerful body.

When the release came, it was like a huge explosion of feeling, that ran down through her legs and arms, to every extremity of her body, leaving only weakness and satisfaction, and a warm, sweet lethargy. Her arms were around his neck, her limbs moulded to his, and his tender caress was like the calm after the storm.

'Did I hurt you?' he whispered, reluctant to move away, and her lips parted in a soft smile.

'You—you pleased me,' she said shyly. 'And I don't ache any more.'

'You will,' he told her huskily, and his mouth found hers again before he rolled away from her.

They lay in the soft grass, sharing the bread and wine, Helen breaking off juicy slices of peach to drop into his mouth.

'We must do this again,' she teased, hovering above him, and he crushed her down to him once more.

'And what if someone should come?' he breathed, between her breasts, but she only sighed.

'No one will,' she declared with surety. 'This is our own private place, and——'

'And?'

'—and I love you, Jarret. So very much.'

It was hours before they eventually returned to the car, both sleepy and satiated with lovemaking, all the hollows ironed out from Helen's face, and even tired, Jarret managed to look devastatingly attractive.

'What happened to your car?' Helen asked, snuggling up to him as he reversed the Alfa, and Jarret smiled.

'Margot returned it,' he conceded. 'Yesterday, actually. Once she realised I wasn't about to go looking for it. She had her chauffeur return it to the garage below the apartments where I live.' He shook his head. 'I saw the commissionaire when I went back to get some clothes. He told me.'

'Thank goodness!' Helen was relieved. 'Why did she destroy your typewriter anyway?'

'Can't you guess?' Jarret glanced at her. 'She guessed how I felt about you, and when I told her I hoped to take you to New York with me ...'

Helen shook her head, running a probing finger along his thigh. 'And what can you do about the machine?'

'Get it fixed, I guess. Fortunately, I've got a couple of others,' he replied, stopping her teasing finger from reaching its objective. 'Honey, give me a chance! I've got to drive this thing.'

'But you're coming back to King's Green, aren't you?'

'I'm going to buy King's Green,' he told her gently, and she lifted her head to gaze at him in amazement.

'You are?'

'Of course. I've worked so much better since I left London, and besides, I like the idea of keeping it in the family.'

'Oh, Jarret ...'

Helen pressed a moist kiss against his cheek, and he turned his head to find her mouth with his. 'Now, behave,' he muttered, forcing his concentration back to the road. 'I wonder how soon I can get a special licence. I have no intention of sleeping alone when we go to tell your mother the news. And somehow I don't think she'd approve of anything else, do you?'

Helen frowned. 'I wonder what I'll do about the shop?'

Jarret shrugged. 'Let Karen handle it. You can retain your interest, if you want to. Just so long as I have first call on your time.'

Helen smiled. 'You'll always have that,' she whispered, and his eyes softened dramatically.

'I'm sorry . . .'

'For what?' She was puzzled.

'For—well, for wasting so much time,' he muttered.

'Three days?'

'It's seemed like three years,' he protested feelingly. Then, as the atmosphere became more intense, he deliberately lightened it. 'Do you think you could bear to eat fish and chips for supper? They're Paddy's favourite, and we did promise to go back.'

'Can I stay?' she asked anxiously, half alarmed that he might send her to an hotel, but his low growl was humorous.

'Did you think I was going to let you out of my sight?' he demanded. 'Mind you, it is only a single bed . . .'

'Too big, you mean?' murmured Helen huskily, and his profile relaxed into a smile of intense satisfaction.

## The Mills & Boon Rose is the Rose of Romance

Every month there are ten new titles to choose from — ten new stories about people falling in love, people you want to read about, people in exciting, far away places. Choose Mills & Boon. It's your way of relaxing.

### January's titles are:

**BED OF GRASS** by *Janet Dailey*
Judd Prescott had been the reason for Valerie leaving home. Now she was back, but Judd still didn't know what that reason had been ...

**WINTER WEDDING** by *Betty Neels*
Professor Renier Jurres-Romeijn regarded Emily as a 'prim miss'. So it wasn't surprising that he so obviously preferred her lively sister Louise.

**DANGEROUS DECEPTION** by *Lilian Peake*
Anona Willis was engaged to the forceful Shane Brodie — but he had admitted that he had no staying power where women were concerned ...

**FEVER** by *Charlotte Lamb*
The attraction between Sara Nichols and Nick Rawdon was immediate — but somehow Sara could never clear up the misunderstanding about her stepbrother Greg.

**SWEET HARVEST** by *Kerry Allyne*
Any thought of a reconciliation between herself and her husband soon vanished when Alix realised that Kirby had chosen her successor ...

**STAY THROUGH THE NIGHT** by *Flora Kidd*
Virtually kidnapped aboard Burt Sharaton's yacht, Charlotte was told that if she didn't co-operate with him, he would ruin her father ...

**HELL OR HIGH WATER** by *Anne Mather*
Jarret Manning was attractive, successful, experienced — and Helen Chase felt mingled antagonism and fear every time she met this disturbing man.

**CANDLE IN THE WIND** by *Sally Wentworth*
Shipwrecked, her memory lost, Sam had to believe her companion Mike Scott when he told her she was his wife ...

**WHITE FIRE** by *Jan MacLean*
Rana had fallen wildly in love with Heath Markland, to the fury of her domineering mother. But perhaps she knew something about Heath that Rana didn't ...

**A STREAK OF GOLD** by *Daphne Clair*
Eight years ago, Ric Burnett had cruelly told Glenna to get out of his life — but now they had met again ...

If you have difficulty in obtaining any of these books from your local paperback retailer, write to:

**Mills and Boon Reader Service**
P.O. Box No 236, Thornton Road, Croydon, Surrey CR9 3RU

# The Mills & Boon Rose is the Rose of Romance

## Look for the Mills & Boon Rose next month

**SUMMER OF THE WEEPING RAIN** *by Yvonne Whittal*
Lisa had gone to the African veld for peace and quiet, but that seemed impossible with the tough and ruthless Adam Vandeleur around!

**EDGE OF SPRING** *by Helen Bianchin*
How could Karen convince Matt Lucas that she didn't want to have anything to do with him, when he refused to take no for an answer?

**THE DEVIL DRIVES** *by Jane Arbor*
Una was in despair when she learned that Zante Diomed had married her for one reason: revenge. How could she prove to him how wrong he was?

**THE GIRL FROM THE SEA** *by Anne Weale*
Armorel's trustee, the millionaire Sholto Ransome, was hardly a knight on a white horse — in fact as time went on she realised he was a cynical, cold-hearted rake...

**SOMETHING LESS THAN LOVE** *by Daphne Clair*
Vanessa's husband Thad had been badly injured in a car smash. But he was recovering now, so why was he so bitter and cruel in his attitude towards her?

**THE DIVIDING LINE** *by Kay Thorpe*
When the family business was left equally between Kerry and her stepbrother Ross, the answer seemed to be for them to marry — but how could they, when they didn't even like each other?

**AUTUMN SONG** *by Margaret Pargeter*
To help her journalist brother, Tara had gone to a tiny Greek island to get a story. But there she fell foul of the owner of the island — the millionaire Damon Voulgaris...

**SNOW BRIDE** *by Margery Hilton*
It appeared that Jarret Earle had had reasons of his own for wanting Lissa as his wife — but alas, love was the very least of them...

**SENSATION** *by Charlotte Lamb*
Helen's husband Drew had kept studiously out of her way for six years, but suddenly he was always there, disturbing, overbearing, and — what?

**WEST OF THE WAMINDA** *by Kerry Allyne*
Ashley Beaumont was resigned to selling the family sheep station — but if only it hadn't had to be sold to that infuriating, bullying Dane Carmichael!

### Available February 1980

If you have difficulty in obtaining any of these books from your local paperback retailer, write to:
Mills & Boon Reader Service
P.O. Box 236, Thornton Road, Croydon, Surrey, CR9 3RU

# Masquerade
## Historical Romances

## Intrigue excitement romance

### MOON OF LAUGHING FLAME
*by Belinda Grey*

Could Deborah forget her old, strict life in Victorian England and become the obedient squaw of Adam-Leap-The-Mountain — the arrogant half-breed brave who was willing to kill to gain her?

### THE ICE KING
*by Dinah Dean*

A season in St. Petersburg at the court of Czar Alexander was Tanya's one chance of gaiety. Yet she fell in love with Prince Nikolai — the Ice King — a man of whom she knew nothing . . .

Look out for these titles in your local paperback shop from
**11th January 1980**

# SAVE TIME, TROUBLE & MONEY!
## *By joining the exciting NEW...*

## Mills & Boon Romance CLUB

**WITH all these EXCLUSIVE BENEFITS for every member**

## NOTHING TO PAY! MEMBERSHIP IS FREE TO REGULAR READERS!

IMAGINE the *pleasure* and *security* of having ALL your favourite *Mills & Boon* romantic fiction delivered right to *your* home, absolutely POST FREE... straight off the press! No waiting! No more disappointments! All this PLUS all the latest news of *new books* and *top-selling authors* in your own monthly MAGAZINE... PLUS *regular* big CASH SAVINGS... PLUS lots of wonderful strictly-limited, *members-only* SPECIAL OFFERS! All these exclusive benefits can be *yours* – right NOW – simply by joining the exciting NEW *Mills & Boon* ROMANCE CLUB. Complete and post the coupon below for FREE full-colour leaflet. It costs nothing. HURRY!

*No obligation to join unless you wish!*

**FREE CLUB MAGAZINE** Packed with *advance* news of latest titles and authors

**Exciting offers of FREE BOOKS** For club members ONLY

**Lots of fabulous BARGAIN OFFERS** – many at **BIG CASH SAVINGS**

## FREE FULL-COLOUR LEAFLET!
**CUT OUT** *CUT-OUT COUPON BELOW AND POST IT TODAY!*

---

To: MILLS & BOON READER SERVICE, P.O. Box No 236, Thornton Road, Croydon, Surrey CR9 3RU, England. WITHOUT OBLIGATION to join, please send me FREE details of the exciting NEW Mills & Boon ROMANCE CLUB and of all the exclusive benefits of membership.

Please write in BLOCK LETTERS below

NAME (Mrs/Miss) ...................................................

ADDRESS .................................................................

CITY/TOWN ............................................................

COUNTY/COUNTRY............................ POST/ZIP CODE............

*S. African & Rhodesian readers write to:*
P.O. BOX 11190, JOHANNESBURG, 2000, S. AFRICA